M000304017

INGRID THE VIKING MAIDEN

KELLY N JANE

18th Avenue Press

Ingrid, The Viking Maiden

Copyright © 2018 by Kelly N Jane

Published by 18th Avenue Press

Cover design by Alfred Obare Designs

All rights reserved.

No part of this book may be reproduced in any form or by any electronic or mechanical means, including information storage and retrieval systems, without written permission from the author, except for the use of brief quotations in a book review.

All characters, places, and incidents are either the product of the author's imagination or are used fictitiously. Any resemblance to actual persons, living or dead, events, or locales is entirely coincidental.

Library of Congress Cataloging-in-Publication data available

ISBN (Paperback) 978-1-947695-05-4

ISBN (eBook) 978-1-947695-04-7

To find out more about Kelly visit www.kellynjane.com to sign up for updates and special offers through her newsletter. You can also find her on Twitter, Instagram, and Facebook at @kellynjanebooks

To Sydney and Audrey for following your dreams

To Craig for giving me the opportunity to follow mine

CONTENTS

"I am the warrior maiden, Ingrid, the great and strong."

The open grasslands carried her voice along the hillside. She twirled in circles as a cool breeze blew her long, blonde hair and tugged at her apron. Bringing the sheep up to the spring pastures was a lonely job, but at least it was outdoors and away from the weaving loom. Spring flowers bloomed in vibrant yellows and purples against the lush green. They floated their sweet messages to the bees and butterflies as Ingrid danced among them.

The usual shepherds, Lukas and his little brother Nels, had gone hunting with several others the week before, but the group hadn't returned as it should have. Ingrid was asked to make the trip with the sheep in their place.

I'm a shieldmaiden, not a shepherdess. I should be protecting the village from raiders, and going on voyages to find new lands.

She would have preferred to go along on the mission to find the lost hunters, but she wasn't allowed—her father had made sure of it. Most of the girls her age had several years of combat training, so even if they never left the village, they could protect themselves. Yet Ingrid was coddled and treated like a breakable doll. No one believed her when she talked about her plans.

They'll be surprised one day. Not everything is about brute strength. Let them underestimate me; I'll show them their mistake.

Her petite form and lack of strength were no excuse to treat her like she was too fragile to fight, in her opinion, and it shouldn't make a difference that her cold hands dropped things several times a day—that's why she kept them covered, after all.

It's not like I would drop a spear or a shield. Who cares about a stupid broken cup now and then?

Thoughts swirled through her head as she guided the flock along the path to the high meadow that would be their home for the summer. Softly bleating, the gentle creatures plodded along and nibbled grasses, unfazed by their animated guide.

A strand of beads looped between the brooches on her tunic, and clicked together while she danced around. Her scissors, knife, and comb hung from the string like a beautiful utility belt rather than a necklace. Stopping for a moment, she put her hand on them.

Beads were gifted for various reasons: to note a particular skill, commemorate an occasion, mark a friendship. Ingrid's were carved from stone, wood and bone, but a special one, made of amber, hung in the center, larger than the others.

It had been the first she received, when she was only five or six years old. A woman passing through their village had smiled at Ingrid and told her she was meant for something special. It was one of the rare memories she had from her early childhood. Most of them were lost to her, like a fog she couldn't see through.

She gripped the amber bead and began singing again, making up grand adventures in which she was the heroine. Her grandmother had been a shieldmaiden. She'd gone to Valhalla when Ingrid was a baby, and everyone in the village honored her; stories were told around the evening fires about her many victories.

Ingrid pictured herself in these tales instead—going to battle at sea to fight off warriors trying to steal their ship, or standing firm in battle to defend their farms and homes. In her favorite saga, she outwitted a group of raiders, leading them into a trap, and securing the safety of her warriors.

Picking up a long stick from the ground, she twisted it around in the air, pretending it was a spear. "I'm light, but I'm fast," she told the sheep closest to her, spinning her makeshift spear around and crouching in a mock fighting stance. "I am the granddaughter of Thorhild, the great shieldmaiden. She was quick and used her wits to win every battle she fought, and I will do the same someday. "Take that! And that!" she yelled. "You are no match for me!"

The stick whooshed through the air as she swung it, and its bark dug into the palms of her hands, even through the woolen, fingerless gauntlets she wore. Ignoring the irritation, she thrust her spear forward into an unsuspecting hazel bush, infusing the air with the smell of smoky wood and dirt, while letting out a high-pitched battle shriek.

The sheep continued to munch peacefully on the grass while Ingrid battled on.

In the middle of an intense altercation with a small birch sapling, the little hairs on the back of her neck tingled. She stopped moving and tried to calm the pounding blood in her ears. Her chest heaved from the exertion of her warrior moves.

No birds chirped, and even the breeze seemed to have stilled, creating an eerie quiet. She noted several clusters of boulders and dips in the hillside that could provide cover from danger, as she scanned the field. The rush of her efforts still clouded her hearing, but she gripped the stick more strongly, feeling the bark against the scrapes that had formed on her hands.

Instinctively, she spun around and dropped to the ground, just in time to dodge a pair of hands grabbing at her. Rolling over her shoulder and coming up in a crouching position, she heard laughter before her eyes registered the sight of her brother, Hagen, and his three friends. Two more rose from behind the nearest sheep and joined the others, who were doubled over in hysterics.

"A grand shieldmaiden you'll make for sure, Ingrid," bellowed Hagen. "You have saved the sheep from a vicious raiding party."

"Get out of here, Hagen, and let me be," Ingrid flared back at him. Rising to her full height, she still had to crane her neck to see his square, stubbled jaw—perfect for slapping, if she could reach it with any impact.

Ruffling her hair as if she were a small child instead of only a couple years his junior, he looked down at her with his gray-blue eyes, crinkled by a smile. He pushed her down onto her backside with a thud, then led the boys past her to hunt birds over the ridge. "Keep singing and dancing, and maybe next time the bushes will yield," Hagen called over his shoulder as he trotted away.

One of the boys, Jorg, stopped and smiled at her. "I thought you looked quite impressive," he said with a wink and a grin, then hurried after the others.

Ingrid pressed her lips tightly together. Too frustrated for words but a growl escaped, ending in a little screech.

The quivers bounced against the boys' backs as they jogged away, the arrows within making melodic clacking sounds as they rattled. Ingrid would have found the effect enjoyable if she weren't so angry.

After they were far enough away, she willed herself to choke down the lump in her throat.

"I will not cry," she declared out loud to the cottony flock.

When the silhouettes of the boys had disappeared over the hill, she pulled her knees to her chest, and let the slight breeze caress her cheeks. Closing her eyes, she smelled the sweet aroma of the fresh grasses, as well as the musty odor of lanolin coming from the sheep. It soothed her chafed nerves, allowing her to give thought to the earlier events.

Hagen had been able to sneak up on her because she'd let herself become distracted, assuming there could be no danger in doing a job so mundane as standing in a meadow with a bunch of sheep. Of course, there were dangers like wolves and shadow cats and such, but not likely during the day.

"Carelessness—that's what it was. No denying it, that's my

fault," she said out loud, restarting her conversation with the sheep. "I have to be on alert always. Nowhere is safe enough to forget your surroundings." She sucked in her bottom lip and rolled it between her teeth. "You should all take note of that mistake, understand." She narrowed her eyes, and pointed her finger at the group. "You will need to be careful when I leave."

She walked up to one of the lambs and wiggled her fingers on its fuzzy head. Smiling at the peaceful creature, she felt a bit more settled.

Ingrid stitched her needlework in between daydreams and frolics around the pastures. She was obligated to stay with the sheep until Old Einar relieved her, whenever he deigned to show up. Depending on necessity, he worked many different types of jobs for the village, and he would be the one to stay in the little cabin that was wedged into the hillside until the shepherds returned.

Ingrid didn't know why he couldn't have taken the sheep to the pastures himself, but she planned to ask him.

"I wish Selby could've come with me today," she said to no sheep in particular, plucking a blade of grass, and shaking her head.

Her best friend was loud and obnoxious most of the time, keeping Ingrid and anyone else near them entertained. She'd let her sassy mouth get her into trouble again, though, and was spending the day mucking out the empty sheep pens.

Ingrid couldn't help but smile as she pictured Selby standing in the middle of the wet dung with a scowl on her face. *I bet she's coming up with all kinds of new phrases. I'll hear every one of them tonight at the evening meal.*

Late afternoon shadows were crossing over the grasses when she heard the crack of branches just below the clearing. Stashing the soft wool she held into her apron, she lowered herself behind the boulder she'd been using as a seat.

Ah, it's only Einar. She was hoping she would get another chance to prove herself to Hagen. *If he's brave enough to pass this way again.* She smirked.

Ingrid hadn't even bothered to open up the cabin; she'd enjoyed the fresh air too much to care about it. Years ago, so the stories said, strange, dangerous beasts had attacked the sheep, but no one had seen anything unusual within Ingrid's lifetime. She released an extended breath, stood, stretched her back, and rolled her neck in anticipation of her walk home.

Einar didn't wash often, and he spoke only when necessary. His large, bushy mustache and beard hid most of his face, that held a permanent scowl—like a cornered animal ready to strike —which meant no one dared talk to him, either. Ingrid thought there was something about him that seemed sad, almost haunted. She wished she could do something to ease whatever pain he carried.

"Hello, Einar."

A grunt was all the response she got as he strode past her, across the meadow and to the cabin.

Why yes, I've had a beautiful day out here, how nice of you to ask. It was as dull as expected, but enough about me, how was your day? Ingrid rolled her eyes and skipped to the trail, on her way home at last.

Her eagerness to watch the shieldmaiden practice hurried

her. The hour-long trek to the village took Ingrid through briar bushes and muddy bogs. The latter could be chest deep for the average villager, but for a girl of Ingrid's small stature, the risk of being completely covered was a real threat.

The farmlands surrounding the village were fertile, and produced abundant crops. Twice a year, several of the long-boats would sail down the river to Jorvik, filled with produce and supplies to trade or sell. Hagen and his friends had gone on their first voyage five years ago, but when she'd reached the same age, Ingrid had not. The spring trip would sail soon, and she was planning a convincing argument for her inclusion. What she would say to persuade her parents occupied her thoughts as she navigated the trail.

The vinegar smell of pickled herring stung Ingrid's nose, signaling to her that she was close to home. Wood cracked against wood, and high-pitched shrieks rang out as she rounded the corner toward the center of the village.

She pumped her legs faster through the muddy streets until she reached the edge of the practice area, then climbed on top of a barrel, out of the way, to watch. After only a few minutes, Selby hopped onto a barrel next to her. Her coppery brown hair held a couple straggling pieces of straw from her efforts in the pens.

"Are you not going to join in?" Ingrid asked.

"I'll watch with you for a while, and see if I feel like it later."

Both girls grinned at each other, knowing that Selby had bested most of the girls at one time or another. However, no one had yet won a match against Selby's sister, Helka, or her friend Anka. There was also the little problem that part of her punishment for the day was restriction from practice.

"How are you supposed to get experience if you can't be a part of stuff?"

"That's what I said. Now I have extra chores for using my witty mind. Again. Whatever. I was right."

Judging by the small cut on Selby's lip, Ingrid could tell that extra chores weren't the only punishment she'd received. Her father was not a patient man. She gave Selby's hand a quick squeeze, and let the topic drop, turning her attention back to the practice.

The shieldmaidens used wooden-tipped spears and wood-carved axes, but the knives were sharp iron. The fighters paired up to work on holding the spear, spinning it to use both the blunt end and the tip to defend themselves, and to block an attacker. It was serious business, and the blows were hard. Every girl had to be willing to take a hit and continue; a lot of pride went along with every bruise and cut lip. Ingrid watched the camaraderie between the girls increase with their skills, knowing they could defend each other when or if the time came.

I should be in there.

Toward the end of the drills, the shieldmaidens formed a circle. In the center, a few selected girls prepared for mock battle. Today there were five—Selby's older sister and her friend against three others.

"Nice try, but three isn't going to be enough." Selby's pride in her sister bubbled over.

"Shhh, just watch," Ingrid chastised. Selby was always a little too loud.

The battle was fierce. The first girl went down right away; Anka dropped low and swept her opponent's leg, giving Helka the chance to spear her in the chest. But partnerships only lasted while they were needed; they would continue until only one girl remained.

Ingrid's heart raced like a rabbit running from a hound as she watched them, until she felt the sharp sting of something slap against her side. She turned in time to duck another swing. Selby had found a long, thin stick and was using it as a mock-spear.

Selby grinned, her hazelnut-colored eyes glittering, and tossed another stick to Ingrid. "Come on, let's practice!"

Without a word, Ingrid grabbed the stick and swung it at Selby's knees. Both girls jabbed, ducked, lunged, and twirled until they were panting and dripping with sweat. In the end, they both fell to their knees in the mud, laughing. When they had rested for a few minutes, a zing of fear struck Ingrid's heart like lightning.

Throwing her stick to the ground, she jumped to her feet. Few people now walked about, and the hollers and cheers of the mock battle had silenced.

"Practice is over! We're late! I'm going to be in so much trouble!" she cried out.

"Hurry, and maybe we can sneak in unnoticed!" yelled Selby as they both ran toward the longhouse.

As soon as the girls pushed through the doors, Ingrid met the raised eyebrow from her mother that confirmed her fears. She would be in trouble, but at least not until after supper. Rushing to help serve the food, she didn't look up again until everyone was eating. Then she went to her mother for reprimand.

"Eat first, Ingrid," her mother told her. "We'll speak outside when you're finished."

"Yes, Mama," she answered, casting her eyes to the floor.

This incident would be used as one more piece of evidence that she was not mature enough to handle the duties of a shieldmaiden.

2 #

Ingrid filled her wooden trencher, and went to sit out of the way while she ate. The hot, brown stew filled her nose with the earthy smell of carrots, potatoes, and venison. The guilt of neglecting her responsibilities should have put her stomach in knots, making her unable to eat, but all she could think about was the fun she'd had sparring with Selby, and how hungry she was from the activity.

Prickly furs scratched at her as she settled crossed-legged into her favorite spot in the corner, leaning back against the smooth, wooden wall so that she had a view of the entire room. Tall, arched ceilings bounced the sounds of voices and laughter around the expansive space. Candle sconces hung every few feet, but even with the long, central fire, it was darker where she sat. Shadows played against pillars that towered like guardians over long dining tables, down each side of the room.

After a few minutes, Selby plopped down next to her to eat.

"So, how bad will it be, do you think?" she asked.

"I don't know. I get to eat first, so that's a good sign."
Ingrid smiled.

"No one in my family noticed me come in," Selby said.
"There's too much excitement over Helka's win today." There
was pride in her voice, but also envy.

Helka was the oldest in Selby's family of eight, and she
carried herself with a noble grace, even though she could fight
better than anyone. Much of the time, Selby felt lost in her
sister's shadow.

Ingrid decided to distract her friend with a game of fox and
geese while they ate.

As she ran to get the game board and pieces, she failed to
notice the leather-clad foot that slipped out in front of her to
trip her. She fell to the ground, landing on her elbows and the
side of her head before rolling and ending on her back.

A tremendous roar of laughter made the ringing in her ears
that much more pronounced. Peering up from her posture of
submission, she saw the faces of Hagen and his prigs, writhing
with pleasure.

Hagen offered her a hand up, but she slapped him away,
doing it on her own.

"You need to watch your surroundings, Meyla," he teased,
calling her the pet name her father sometimes used.

"I hope you broke your foot!" She brushed herself off and
headed to the shelf, retrieving the game.

"How could I break even a toe from such a small bird?" He
smiled and went back to laughing with his friends.

"You should be kinder to your sister," Jorg said in a low
voice, but loud enough for her to hear.

Ingrid shot a glare toward him, but noticed he was the only one of the boys without a smile. *What was that about?*

She turned to walk back to the corner, only to find herself face to face with her mother. She always seemed to appear at just the right moments.

"You need to go and check on the horses for the night," Agnethe said to Hagen.

"I already did," he replied.

The expression on his mother's face made him decide to check again.

"Leave the game and come with me, Ingrid," Mother said as she turned toward the door, not waiting.

Obediently, Ingrid followed, giving a shrug of disappointment to Selby as she passed. It was time to face her punishment.

Agnethe walked to the well outside of the longhouse, and, to Ingrid's surprise, invited her daughter to sit down on the edge, facing her—eye to eye, like equals. They'd never sat like this together, in the quiet of the evening, with only the brightness of the thousand stars overhead, and the far away clanking of the boats in the bay.

Agnethe took hold of Ingrid's hand, and Ingrid looked into her mother's face. Instead of seeing a cross scowl, she saw a warm smile.

"I was like you once, Ingrid," Agnethe admitted. "I wanted to have the adventures of the shieldmaidens. Go on voyages across the sea, defend our homes, be wild and free."

"You did?"

"Oh, yes, very much. But I learned I had other gifts that

had been bestowed on me, and the life of a shieldmaiden wasn't one of them. You and I are alike in the way we look—have you noticed?" her mother asked.

"Yes." *That doesn't mean we want the same things, though.*

They shared the same light, golden hair, as well as a paler complexion than most of the others in the village. But she knew it was their eyes of bright turquoise that set them apart more than anything else.

They both sat quietly for a few minutes, listening to the muted conversations and laughter of those still enjoying the evening in the longhouse. The smell of meaty stew wafted through the door occasionally, whenever someone came or went.

"Hagen looks like your father. Tall and strong, he will make a great warrior and protector of our village, just as your father has all these years. But I'm not a very tall person, and neither are you. I've watched you carry buckets of water to the sheep, and they nearly knock you over." Mother smiled.

"I can do it, though. I'm stronger than I seem," Ingrid insisted.

"I know you are. But I'm afraid that the strength it takes to hold a shield, and the attitude necessary to throw a spear in the heat of battle might be more than you are capable of."

It was said gently, but Ingrid bristled with anger anyway. If she worked at it, she believed she could learn the necessary skills. Practice and determination, that's all she needed to fulfill her heart's desire.

"I know you don't believe me," said Agnethe, "but maybe you'll understand later. You do have a stubborn heart, and there is so much you don't understand yet. We can talk about it more another time. For now, please do your work the best that you can, and be on time to help with supper, alright?"

"Yes, I will," Ingrid promised. "But I'll not stop learning to fight."

"And you'll continue to be covered in bruises, but I'll not stop you. If you want to try, you are old enough to work this out for yourself. But promise me you will pay attention to how you feel, and stop before your injuries are too severe." Mother's eyes held a hint of sadness and something else. Something she wasn't sharing with Ingrid.

It made no difference in that moment. All Ingrid had heard was that it was for her to decide if she would be joining the practices, and that was what she had been waiting to hear her entire life.

Selby was just about to leave the corner when Ingrid came bounding back into the longhouse. She rejoined her friend, picked up her trencher, and shoveled several bites into her mouth while trying to share her news.

Selby's eyes widened, and she laughed. "I can't understand a word you are trying to say. But it doesn't look like you got into too much trouble."

Ingrid swallowed a large mouthful. "I said I get to train."

"Your mother gave you permission?"

"Better. She told me I could decide for myself!" Ingrid kicked her feet and squealed as quietly as she could, but still turned a few nearby heads.

"Oh, this is the best news I've heard, ever. We are so going to be the best." Selby had a grin that practically split her face in two. Her eyes gleamed, and Ingrid could almost read her friend's thoughts as her eyes drifted toward her sister.

"I'm going to need a lot of practice before I can keep up with anyone," Ingrid warned. "Don't go off and make any threats to Helka. I want to train, not die."

"Why would you say that? You know I'm the perfect example of self-control. I'd never spout off anything I couldn't back up."

The two girls stared at each other for a minute. Ingrid wasn't sure if Selby really thought that about herself or if she was joking until she saw the little tug at the corner of Selby's mouth. Both girls erupted into uncontrollable laughter, and didn't stop until they had tears running down their cheeks and couldn't breathe.

A voice boomed above all the others in the longhouse, and it hushed the girls' laughter. Ingrid recognized the voice as her father's.

"We should never forget the heroes of our past. As long as we keep telling their stories, we never will," Klaus said proudly about honoring the deeds of their ancestors.

Ingrid's father was the village chieftain. He towered over most of the other men, and Ingrid thought he must be as tall as Odin himself. His hair color was a darker honeycomb shade than hers, and—according to her mother—the deep, dark blue color of his eyes was like the ocean.

She longed to see water that color. The river in front of the village was a murky, greenish-brown that smelled like dirty feet.

Ingrid sat up taller, a broad smile on her face, when Klaus looked in her direction and gave her a playful wink.

"Who should we honor tonight? Gisli the Outlaw?" His voice boomed to the entire house. He looked at Ingrid's bright, expectant eyes and said, "I know! We have not heard a maiden's story in a long while. How about the adventure of our own Thorhild in Gotaland?" he asked.

The crowded hall cheered, and Klaus began to wander among the crowd, readying the story in his mind. His face glowed from the hearth fire in the center of the open room, captivating everyone's attention. Bearded faces, glistening from spilled mead, followed his trajectory, and the light danced around each eager listener as they leaned forward to hear his words. A comforting heat from bodies wrapped in furs hugged the room.

As Klaus started into the story, the heavy, wooden doors of the longhouse burst open, bringing a gust of wind that made the flames of the fire bounce higher. Ingrid's heart jumped as her father glared toward the intrusion, and the flash of orange glowed against his face.

Several men stomped into the warmth. Steam rose like a fog off the newcomers, courtesy of the rains that had begun earlier in the evening.

After a tense silence, they were recognized as the search party and the lost hunters, and the room erupted into chaos. Everyone wanted to welcome the lost men, as well as hear the story of where they had been.

Ingrid and Selby ran to help fill trenchers with stew and biscuits, and passed them around as the men settled near the warm hearth. Sweat glistened on Ingrid's temple from the increased heat and humidity of the room. One man, in reaching for the wooden bowl, laid his hand over the top of

Ingrid's. The contact tingled on her skin and she paused, muscles and thoughts frozen in curiosity.

The touch only lasted a second or two, but it felt much longer as a strange sensation filled her body. Her hands heated like branding irons, an effect that even holding the hot stew could not accomplish.

The man was injured, and for the brief moment they shared a touch, Ingrid felt a pull from deep within her chest, as if something inside her was looking for the man's pain. She pulled her hands back and put them behind her a little too quickly, causing the man to nearly drop the bowl.

He peered at Ingrid with narrow eyes. "What kind of stew is this?"

"Just the regular skause," Ingrid said. She looked down and rushed off to bring the hot meal to others.

She avoided going near him again.

Maybe I should tell Selby about this?

Ingrid served more of the men, careful not to touch anyone. She stole a glance at the man who'd made her flinch earlier, and he was eating as if nothing had happened.

No, she'll think I'm crazy. I think I'm crazy, what else could it be?

She pushed the thoughts out of her mind, and moved nearer to her father.

"Olin, let's hear the tale of your journey," Klaus said, laying his hand on the older man's shoulder as he sat next to him.

The room silenced except for the occasional slurp of meat or mead.

Olin nodded and pushed his food away. He stared into the fire; the flames danced like sprites in his eyes. "On the second day of the hunt, we walked through some thick bog myrtle.

We gathered some as we went, to make ale later." He swallowed and rubbed his hands on his thighs.

"Go on," Klaus encouraged.

"There was a screeching sound. It was coming from everywhere and nowhere. We tried to pull together, but the bog was too thick. The soggy peat sucked at our feet and slowed us down as we tried to run. The screeching turned into roars, and they grew louder. I'm an old man, and I've never heard that sound before. It was like a dagger straight into my ear."

The loud thump of a fist hitting the table made everyone startle. Some men grabbed at the hilts of their blades, and started to stand, but the man who had slammed down his fist just shoved his way through the people crowded around to listen, and headed outside.

Ingrid's gloved hand had twisted into her father's tunic in the tension. She unwound her fingers and wiped them on her apron, but stayed close to her father's shoulder as he sat in front of her.

"What was it? The thing that made a noise," Ingrid asked once the man was gone.

"Ingrid!" Hagen glared at her from across the table, and shook his head for her to stay silent.

She huffed and turned back to Olin, but glanced back at the way Hagen's arm folded around Helka. And the way Helka's hand clutched his tunic the same way Ingrid's had her father's.

"We didn't know what it was, but we ran. There was a small strand of trees not far ahead where we could take cover, so we headed there. The skies turned dark as the beast flew overhead; we felt a gust of wind and heard a boom as its wings lifted it higher. I was the last to make it to the trees."

Down the row of tables, someone tried to muffle the sounds of their crying.

Ingrid looked around. Everyone was either focused on Olin or staring off into the dark. All the bodies huddled so closely together accentuated the pungent odor of sweat and fear.

Flinching when a hand slipped into hers, Ingrid met the wide eyes of Selby, knowing they mirrored her own. They squeezed each other's palms, and turned back to the storyteller.

"The leaves of the trees flapped like a storm each time the beast flew low. It circled us, keeping up its blasted noise. There wasn't a plan—none of us knew what to do other than hide. Each time that thing came around, it was closer." He paused a moment. "I've only heard stories, but I'd stake my life that it was a dragon."

Noise broke out around the tables at the disclosure of a beast not seen in generations. Some scoffed that it was untrue while others gasped, but when Klaus demanded silence everyone leaned forward to listen to the rest of the story. Ingrid squeezed closer to her father.

"It's true, I assure you. All six of us could stand in its shadow with room for more. Its wings spread out nearly as long as this hall. When they were stretched, you could see light coming through them like a bloody haze. The whole thing was the color of fresh, dark blood. Scales at least as big as a man's hand, and claws on each foot that'd rip anything apart. But the way it swung its head from side to side, its gaze scanning everywhere, told us that nowhere was safe."

Movement across the table caught Ingrid's attention. She watched as her mother stepped closer, clutching her middle as if she were in pain, and staring at her husband. Then Agnethe turned her stricken gaze on Ingrid, unshed tears glistening in her eyes.

Ingrid's own stomach flipped in on itself. *Nothing scares her; she's always so steady. Reliable.* She felt tremors roll through her body, but she forced herself to listen again to the story.

"Little Nels panicked. There's no shame in it," Olin said, bringing Ingrid's attention back to him. "I don't know how much longer I could have stayed hidden, either. His little body slipped right past all of us, and he took off running."

His shoulders heaved as he breathed in and out. He reached out and picked up his cup, spilling most of the mead as his hands shook their way to his lips.

After he managed a couple swallows, he continued. "We shouted at him to get back under cover, and Lukas started to run after him, but then there was a blast of heat, and the ground shook and knocked us all down." Olin tried to check his emotions but his voice wavered. "When we could look up again, the beast was gone, and so was Nels."

Bile rose in the back of Ingrid's throat. She dropped to her knees, and forced herself to breathe. Selby sat down and leaned into her side.

"Did you try to track the beast?" Klaus asked.

"The ground was blackened like there had been a pyre, and we didn't know which way to start searching. It seemed best to head toward high ground, so that's what we did. A few days later, we came across a cave in the hillside. It was empty, but there was a huge nest toward the back. Bones were scattered all around—some old, others so fresh, they were practically still warm. None that seemed like a boy's, though. We hid outside the mouth of the cave for two days, but nothing showed up. That's when we decided to start back."

Nels' mother moaned and let out a sorrowful cry. Ingrid was shocked to see her standing in the crowd, but she had listened to the story along with the rest of them. Agnethe ran to her, and she and several other women carried away the inconsolable mother.

Olin's voice was thick as he proceeded. "For three days, we walked in silence; the smallest sounds made us jump. We had settled down to sleep one night, when there were sounds in the dark at the edge of our camp. Next thing we knew, a group of men came crashing through the underbrush. Emotions were running so high it almost came to blows, but it was settled in a couple minutes. They were a hunting party, too, looking for a couple men they lost. The thing was, the beast they described was black as tar, not like the one that came on us."

The longhouse was still; only a few sniffles and cleared throats could be heard as everyone sat stunned. There was more than one dragon hunting the skies.

Olin rubbed his face with both hands, then shook his head and stood up. Without another word, he shuffled outside, his arms hanging limply from his slumped shoulders.

"There have not been dragons since before our fathers or our forefathers before them," Klaus said once Olin had gone.

He was tense. Ingrid could see the muscles in his face moving as he clenched his jaw in time with the fists he was making by his side.

"We saw it. It is out there," one of the hunters, Nels' uncle, countered.

Lukas and his father were among the returned group as well, but neither looked up. Sitting with untouched trenchers between their hands, they remained silent.

"I'm not doubting your word, brother." Klaus stood to set a hand on the man's shoulder, and gave it a slight squeeze. "They have just been gone for so long, I'm wondering what has drawn them back. Did the others you came across have any ideas about that?"

"No, but . . ." He swallowed hard and closed his eyes for a moment before speaking again. "They did say that they'd seen more than one. There's no telling how many there are out there."

Klaus nodded and looked around at the men. "We are glad that you have returned safely. We will mourn for young Nels before we decide what to do next."

He walked over to Nels' father, and laid a hand on his and Lukas' shoulders, offering a prayer to the gods for their grief. Ingrid watched as several tears fell to the dusty floorboards by the men's feet. While the mist of steam had lifted as the men dried, a new fog fell over everyone in the longhouse—one of sorrow, dread, and anger.

Without any more discussion, Ingrid's father dismissed everyone for the night, and a meeting was scheduled for the next day. Selby gave Ingrid a quick hug as she left with her family. As Ingrid was getting ready to head to her room, she felt a prickle at the base of her neck.

She turned and caught the eyes of Jorg, who had apparently

been staring at her. He appeared as if he wanted to approach her, but then he turned and stomped out through the doors.

Blowing a sigh out of her nose, Ingrid shook her head. She didn't have the energy to figure out what she might have done to make Hagen's friends mad at her right then. She walked to her room at the back of the longhouse, and changed into her nightclothes, certain she would not be able to sleep that night. Maybe ever again.

3

The next day, Ingrid plopped down on the bench outside the front doors of the longhouse, and waited for the men to gather in the open meeting area. Shielded from a wet drizzle by the roof's overhang, she busied her hands straightening a basket of wool with a set of combs, preparing it to be spun later. The village well sat near the center of the meeting space and was always busy with people. It made for a good distraction.

About twenty boats, tied to the wooden docks or simply anchored, rocked in the gentle waters of the bay beyond the well; all of them unique, built based on the family that owned them. The biggest one, her father's, sat tall and majestic, ready at a moment's request to head down the river and out to sea. It had a giant dragon head carved into both ends, looking as if it could devour anything in its path.

Ingrid shuddered at such a creature existing in real life.

She grabbed a big piece of raw wool from her basket, and used the paddle-like combs, spiked on one side, to pull the tangled fibers in the same direction. When one section was finished, she set the straightened wool down into a waiting basket on her left, and picked up another handful of lumpy wool from her right. Over and over and over. It was a good job to occupy her while she waited for the men to gather. She also knew Selby would be showing up, so she watched the people milling around.

Hagen's group walked around the corner across from her. His three closest friends—the 'Stink Brothers', as Ingrid called them, and Jorg—never seemed far from his side.

Sten and Ove were older and younger than Hagen, respectively, but neither could plan an intelligent idea on their own. Sometimes, if they worked together, they could come up with one that might make sense, but that was a rare occasion. They were tall and well-muscled, and that's all they counted on, constantly rushing into fights without hesitation.

You two are so lucky that Hagen let you follow him around when we were all too young to know better.

Their hulking size and long, unkempt, dirt-brown hair, which included full, bushy beards, made them look more like shaggy pets than boys. Ingrid giggled, imagining what animals they might be. As she exchanged another chunk of wool, she peered again at the group of boys, and continued her musings.

Jorg was different. His family had moved to the village only four years before. Shy and quiet, Jorg was welcomed by Hagen as if by a brother, and they became inseparable. Both boys used to be around Selby's height, but over the winter, they had grown two heads taller than her.

Hagen was now about the same height as their father and, while not as filled in, his broad shoulders and muscled arms and legs would equal that of their imposing patriarch soon.

Jorg was a couple inches taller than Hagen; though he was not as thick through the shoulders, he still wore an equal amount of muscle on his body.

At this observation, Ingrid almost dropped the combs from her hands, and she took a deep breath to clear her head a little. Then she peeked at Jorg again, casually.

He wore his dark brown hair shorter than most of the other men, to just below his chin, and left it unbound to show the waves it carried. Among so many hairy men in the village, his smooth, creamy skin, revealing the one dimple on his left cheek, stood out like a glowing beacon. His eyebrows had an arch to them that, with his dark lashes, framed his hazel eyes nicely over his perfectly straight, unbroken nose.

Ingrid let out a huff of air. Lost deep in her thoughts, she hadn't realized that Selby had joined her on the bench.

"What was that sigh for?" Selby asked with a wicked little grin, making Ingrid jump. "And I believe that wool is a lost cause."

The fibers Ingrid had been working on were now a tangled mess. She looked at her best friend, and shrugged her shoulders the tiniest bit. "Oops." They both laughed as she tucked that piece down along the side of her finished basket. She'd deal with it later. "And I did not sigh."

"Oh, yes you did. I'll bet it had something to do with a certain handsome friend of your brother's over there."

"Jorg? He's not handsome," she lied.

"Yes he is! He's beautiful—in a manly sort of way, of course." Selby grabbed a piece of wool, and used her own set of combs to help Ingrid whittle down the pile.

"He is one of Hagen's friends; I don't pay much attention

to him." The need to defend herself prickled her nerves. "What's more, he has picked on me as much as Hagen over the years, and I don't see him as anything other than a pest."

"Yeah, right. Whatever you say, my lying-to-herself friend. It doesn't matter—Hagen's still cuter."

Selby had had a crush on Ingrid's brother since they were about seven, and it still held her captive though they'd reached their teens.

Her friend pulled in a deep breath and let it out with a little whine.

"Now *that* was a sigh," Ingrid laughed. "You need to stop hurting yourself about him."

Hagen had never known about, or at least acknowledged, Selby's crush on him; he was all eyes for her tall, slender, beautiful sister, Helka. She returned the attention, too, which thrilled both sets of parents. Hagen would take over for his father one day, and Helka had also been raised to be a leader.

"I know. I will, someday, if anyone better comes along," she smirked.

"You think about boys too much." Ingrid teased her friend, even though she found it happening to herself more and more lately.

She glanced back over at the boys, and swallowed hard when she noticed Jorg's gaze on her. He grinned and looked away. Her heartbeat raced, and the paddles nearly slipped from her slick palms.

"Uh-huh. *I* think about boys too much. Yep, just me." Selby jabbed her elbow into Ingrid's side, making her yelp and scoot down the bench a little.

They both broke into giggles as more and more men milled around the center.

"Did you get any sleep last night?" Ingrid changed the subject.

"Not much."

"Me either."

An involuntary shudder shook both girls.

"Do you think dragons have really returned after all these years?" Ingrid asked.

"It sure sounded like it. Poor Nels. Can you imagine being eaten?" Selby stared off into space, her full eyebrows squished together and her mouth turned down into a frown.

"Don't say that. Maybe he didn't. Maybe it dropped him somewhere."

"It's nice that you have hope, but I don't think you're right."

Ingrid's father walked up to the gathered group of men, and the girls put their combs aside to get closer to the crowd. A wave of nausea hit Ingrid as the smell of sweaty bodies and wet furs flooded her senses. She squished her way through the crowd, and stepped into the open air, next to Klaus. Selby arrived a half-second later and stuck her tongue out in an imitation of gagging.

Bath day was not for two more days.

Ingrid smiled at her friend's play, and nodded, then turned her full attention to what her father had to say.

"The information we have been brought is too important and dire to ignore. If the dragons are returning, there is more at play here than we may know. I think it would be best to send word to all the leaders . . . This must be addressed by every clan, for no one is safe. We will call for an emergency meeting in Jorvik."

Cheers and conversations erupted throughout the crowd. People were excited to take action, rather than wait for more disaster to strike.

Raising his hands, the chieftain quieted them again. "I will send messengers today, but we shouldn't delay our departure. Only three boats will make the journey; there is no need to pull all of our men and leave the village vulnerable."

He selected two other boat owners from the crowd.

"Settle your families, load your supplies, and meet back here in the morning. We leave at first light," he concluded.

Roars of approval rose into the clouded sky. Ingrid felt the bloom of a thought spread throughout her mind and warm her body. Years of being held back and left out exploded into a crazy idea. She grabbed Selby's hand, and pulled her away from the group, dragging her behind a pile of wooden crates and briny smelling fish nets. A quick check of the area proved they were alone.

"We're going to Jorvik." The words rushed out, and Ingrid could feel the flush of excitement in her cheeks, and the tingles that buzzed her skin while she paced in front of Selby, her hands on her hips.

Selby let her jaw drop open. "What?" She looked back over her shoulder to be sure the rebelliousness hadn't been overheard.

"I'm tired of no one believing that I can be a warrior. If we go to Jorvik with the men, they will *have* to treat us as adults. Then we can help find the dragons!" Ingrid bounced on the balls of her feet.

"Our fathers will never let us go. Mine wouldn't even let me join the search party when I asked. How do you expect to persuade them to let us go on a trip like this?" Selby demanded.

"We're not going to ask." Ingrid stared into Selby's rich brown eyes, which had gone wide to match the open hole of her mouth. "Don't you want the adventure?" Ingrid pressed. "You are as strong a warrior as Helka, but no one in your family notices. This way, we have a chance for glory, to have our stories told around the fire."

"How would we do that?" She looked around, trying to process Ingrid's idea, and fidgeted with her necklace, rolling a bead between her fingers. "We'd have to sneak onto the boats, and we'd get caught in seconds. They would only throw us back on the docks, if we're lucky. You would be fine, but you know how my father is; I'd be left with stripes on my backside."

"We won't get caught. We'll sneak on board when they're loading—act like we are helping—then, when no one is watching, we'll hide. When the boats are too far down the river to turn back, we'll come out, and they'll have to let us stay." Ingrid paced and rubbed her hands on her thighs, rolling her lip between her teeth as she thought through her plan. "It'll work. We'd just have to be really quiet and find a place that no one will check for a while."

"You're mad—and that's coming from me."

"Maybe, but we're doing this. I'm not getting left behind. Besides . . . *Jorvik*. How can you not want to see it?"

"I want to. It's just . . . where would we hide? What would

my family think? My father isn't going, so they wouldn't know where I am or what happened to me."

"They would figure it out, I'm sure. My mother will talk to them, and they will be fine."

"I don't think I should go." Selby crossed her arms over her stomach, and the middle finger of her right hand picked at her thumb.

"It will work out. I know it. Don't fuss over it so much." *She'll thank me when everyone cheers for us later.*

Ingrid's smile stretched across her face, and she bit down hard on her bottom lip. They were going on the boats with the men. No one would treat them like weak, little girls after they returned. They were going to see the Capitol and would have stories to tell.

We'll be heroes.

They resumed combing their wool, as if they were not planning the adventure of a lifetime. For at least half an hour neither said anything—an unheard of circumstance since they'd become friends as toddlers.

Hagen and the Stinks started to pass the girls to go into the house, when Hagen stepped back and stared at them.

"Why are you two so quiet?"

"We're busy," Ingrid said.

"No, you're not. You could both do that in your sleep. What's up?" He narrowed his eyes at each girl in turn, but settled his stare on Selby, knowing she'd be the easier one to crack.

"Don't knock it. It's about time they shut up anyway," the older Stink taunted.

At least, Ingrid thought it was the older; she didn't bother to look. She rolled her eyes and kept to her work.

Selby couldn't help but take the bait. "You should try it. Then maybe you wouldn't have so many people wanting to kick your arse all the time." Ingrid nudged her, worried she'd get going and forget to keep their plans secret, but Selby ignored her. "You're missing one of your followers, aren't you? Didn't think any of you went anywhere alone."

Oh man, I'd rather she talk about sneaking on the boats. Don't ask about Jorg!

"Why? You worried you won't see him before he leaves in the morning? Maybe you should offer him a kiss goodbye." Brother number two laughed at his own comment.

"Shut up," Hagen scolded his friend, but bit the inside of his lip to keep from smiling. He looked back at the girls. "You two are never quiet, but I'll let you keep your secrets. We have work to do before we leave in the morning. Oh, and if you *are* worried where Jorg is, he went home to get his stuff ready. He's staying with us tonight." He smirked at Ingrid, who had snapped her head up at the information. Then all three boys walked into the house.

She slapped Selby on the arm, and growled at her. "Why did you have to ask about Jorg?

"I was changing the subject so that Hagen wouldn't ask any more questions. I was afraid I might say something to those idiots and ruin our plans. They always know how to push my buttons. Besides, why do you care? They thought I wanted to know about him."

"Hagen didn't. Just don't do it again. Good job keeping your mouth shut about our plans, though." *Thank the gods for small miracles.* "Maybe you should stay here with me tonight," Ingrid suggested. "It would be easier for us to get on the boats together that way."

"I was thinking that, too. Since my father isn't going, I'd rather not be at home." Selby fiddled with her thumbs.

"Do you think he's angry about staying?"

"Yeah, I'm sure he expected to go."

"So you'll stay here. Then as soon as they start loading the boats, we go and help. I've never been on one before, have you?"

"No. I'm not allowed. 'It's for the men'." Selby used a husky voice in a mocking, male tone.

"We'll have to guess at where to hide, then. Behind kegs or under something."

The girls continued planning, trying to figure out what they would take with them and how they would get it on board. They were so deep in their conversation that they didn't notice the extra activity building up around the docks until someone shouted, and a small argument broke out.

"They're loading already." Ingrid jumped up and tossed her combs into her basket. "They'll have the boats ready tonight to sail out at dawn. What are we going to do?"

"Think. We can figure out something. Maybe we just have to sneak on early?"

Ingrid started pacing and biting her lip. *This has to work. I am not staying behind. This is the perfect chance to prove myself.* "You're right. We need to get on early, but not in the morning. We should do it tonight so we don't risk being late." She stopped in front of Selby and smiled. "I've got it. I'll say I'm staying with you tonight, and you say you're staying with me. Then we'll get on the boat after dark."

"And no one will miss us in the morning, because they'll think we're just still at each other's house. Perfect."

"We need to go home and gather our stuff. When you come back for dinner; we'll eat, and then leave after that."

Selby put both hands over her mouth, but it didn't hide the wide smile on her face. "We are really doing this," she said behind her fingers.

Ingrid nodded and gave her a quick hug before gathering up her baskets and heading inside to pack.

Her stomach started to wobble, but her heart soared.

The village was a blur of activity all afternoon. Like busy ants storing food for the winter, those who were going on the voyage bustled about, packing their boats. Small, wooden planks bounced up and down as large bodies hurried supplies onto the ships. Taut ropes creaked as they rubbed against the hulls. Those who would be staying behind helped to make sure they were prepared to function with fewer men.

Ingrid and Selby made themselves useful so they could watch how the boats were loaded. The smooth, wooden sides of the boats rose high out of the water in a crescent shape. Ingrid craned her neck to see inside, but even at the lowest point the boats rocked with the bustle of motion, the sides were still too high for a peek.

"Papa, can I take this onto the boat for you? It's a crate of extra linens that mother packed," Ingrid called to her father, who was standing in the ship near the main mast.

"Leave it there on the docks, and I'll have it brought onboard."

"Oh. Okay." She put the crate on the dock, and turned to walk back toward the village.

"Ingrid."

Turning, she looked up at her father. "Yes, Papa?"

"Would you like to come and see what the boat looks like?" He smiled at her.

"Oh, yes! Thank you."

Running to the plank laid from the docks to the ship's edge, she stood at the bottom, gained her balance, and walked slowly up the small, unsteady board. As she made it to the top, her father reached out his hand and pulled her over the rail.

"It's so much bigger than I thought it was," she admitted as she looked around.

"It has to hold forty men plus supplies."

Each crewman brought his own trunk of personal items and they ran down each side of the hull. They doubled as benches where the men sat to work the oars to propel the boat through the calm river waters. Ingrid looked back toward the dock, but her head only poked above the side rail when she stretched high on her toes. The mast held the one large sail that was the boat's main power. At both ends, there were raised platforms where supplies were stored below and men could sit above.

Ingrid took special notice of those areas.

"Whoa," she huffed as she lost her balance, stretching out a leg to widen her stance.

Her father smiled at her and wrapped his arm around her shoulders. "It's a feeling that feeds the soul, once you get it in your blood. I actually miss it if I've been on land too long. Someday I'll take you for a small trip, and you can see how it feels with the sail up."

"Could I go this time?" *Might as well ask, since he brought it up.*

"No. This is not a time for fun. There is too much at stake, too much danger on this trip."

"You are letting Hagen go."

"Hagen is a man now, and it's time for him to join me. Mind your place, Ingrid."

"He's only a little older than I am; I could help. And I can take care of myself."

Klaus rubbed a hand over his face. "Meyla. I believe you, but not this time. Show some respect, and let this go. Stay with your mother, work hard on your training—I expect to see how much better you are when I return."

A sly grin etched her face. "You know that I'll be training? And you're okay with it?"

"Of course I know. Your mother and I don't keep secrets from each other. I am fine with my strong-willed daughter fighting for what she wants. It makes me proud of you." He leaned over and smiled like he had a secret. "You remind me of your stubborn Papa. Just be careful, and rest when you tire." He pulled her into a hug. "Now, go back and help get things ready for the boats."

Ingrid hugged him tight once more. "Okay, Papa."

She took one more look around the boat to make mental notes. She hoped her father would feel the same about her fighting spirit in the morning, when she and Selby came out of hiding.

The docks still buzzed with activity. Ingrid strolled toward the village center, and came upon Hagen and Jorg. They carried packs on their backs, and were rolling kegs toward the longboat. Ingrid took a deep breath and stood a little taller as she approached them. Expecting to be teased for staying home, she wanted to be ready for them. There was no way she'd let them rile her up.

Won't they be surprised tomorrow . . .

Movement caught her attention over Hagen's shoulder. A small child, a girl maybe, toddled around on the shoreline. Ingrid stopped in her tracks. Her mouth went dry, and her vision spun like she was standing on a high ledge. The scene in front of her changed, just for an instant. A child stood near some tall grasses, and something shiny was on the ground all around her.

Panic crashed over Ingrid like a wave, and she blinked several times.

The child was gone, and light flickered in and out of Ingrid's perception. Her bones turned to water, and she felt her knees crack against the wooden dock at the same time that a strong pair of arms pulled her away from the edge.

Jorg's wide, hazel-green eyes stared into hers as her focus returned.

Shouting rang out in the distance, and she could feel the vibrations of the dock bouncing beneath her. The cold wood cut into her fingers as she pushed herself to stand, succeeding only when Jorg wrapped his arm around her waist to steady her.

Shouts and commotion finally broke through her daze, and she turned to see where it was coming from.

A young boy lay on the dock in the middle of a pool of liquid, pieces of splintered wood scattered around him.

Without hesitation or knowing why she felt so compelled, Ingrid ignored her wobbly legs and rushed to the boy, pushing past the gathered crowd to kneel down next to his supine figure. The smell of ale stung her nose, and the coppery tang of blood hung in the air. The boy's chest barely moved up and down; a quick glance told her why. A splinter of wood, longer than Ingrid's hand and a third as wide, protruded from his leg.

With a deep breath, she latched onto the splinter and pulled as hard as she could. It slipped out easier than expected, and her arm flung out wide from the force she'd used. Dropping the bloodied piece, she slapped her hand over the hole in the boy's leg and closed her eyes. She concentrated her thoughts, willing the injury to close so he could wake. She ignored everything and everyone else.

In a heartbeat, she felt a jolt through her chest. A strange, warm, nearly hot sensation ran down her arm and into her hand. Ingrid knew she was holding her breath, but she dared not release it. Her hands pulled away from the boy's leg and dropped into her lap.

With a small flutter, the boy's eyelids lifted.

He coughed, and Ingrid barely had time to scoot back before he vomited all over himself. Every muscle in her body felt as heavy as iron, and she sagged back onto her heels. A couple of men helped the child to sit up as he sputtered some more, and the color started to ease back into his pale face.

Ingrid stole a glance down at his leg, and gasped; he wasn't bleeding anymore.

Her head drooped toward her chest.

"What did you do?" one of the men asked, his eyes as wide and unblinking as an owl's.

"Nothing. I . . . don't know . . . I just wanted to help him, that's all."

A hand reached out and pulled Ingrid back, away from the crowd, and she stared up into the worried faces of Hagen and Jorg. Over their shoulders, she saw her father coming from his boat.

"This way." Hagen put his hand on her shoulder and turned her toward their father. "You need to get out of here."

"Why?" Disoriented and wobbly, she felt as though she might fall down.

"Why are your hands so hot?"

"What happened?" Klaus asked as he reached them, deep lines carved across his brow.

"I don't know. Ingrid started to fall down, and Jorg caught her before she fell off the dock, but the keg he was rolling got away and crashed. It broke, and hit that boy; he was bleeding, but now he's better," Hagen explained. Then he turned to Ingrid. "How did you do that?"

"I didn't do anything. I don't know," her voice trailed off as she shook her head. Air caught in her dry throat as she tried to breathe. *What did I do?*

"Why are your hands warm?"

"They aren't." Jorg was clutching one of Ingrid's hands.

When did that happen? She looked up into his strained face.

Grabbing the hand Jorg held, then the other one, Hagen

felt them again. "They *were*. Not just warm, but hot. I swear it, Father."

"Ingrid, what caused your fall that started all of this?" Her father narrowed his eyes at her and waited for an answer.

"I saw a child, Papa. I don't know. It's like I was here, and then, for a second, I was seeing something else. I can't explain it."

She could feel the sting in her eyes, and tried to keep the tears from falling, digging her nails into her palms, but it was no use—they slid down her cheeks anyway. Dropping her face to stare at her toes, she tried to hide behind a curtain of hair.

A finger under her chin raised her eyes to meet her father's. He was not smiling as he stared at her with an intensity that made her want to turn and run as fast as she could. "Go home," he urged. "Stay inside with your mother until I get there."

Nodding her head, she turned to walk away. When she did, many in the crowd surrounding the boy watched her. Willing herself to walk as if no one else existed, she ignored the stares and headed for home. Whispers and mumbles reached her ears; tones ranged from confusion to awe, and even some fear. The hair on Ingrid's neck stood on end, and her insides caved in on themselves. As soon as her feet touched the soft earth of the shore, she ran as fast as she could, not stopping until she flung herself down onto her bed.

4

Ingrid rolled over on her bed and blinked her eyes several times in the darkness. They felt like they were filled with sand, and were tender when she rubbed them. Apparently, she'd cried herself to sleep.

Voices drifted to her ears from the main room; it had to be meal time. Light flashed briefly when the door flap was moved to admit someone. It closed as the visitor tiptoed toward her.

"Oh, good. You're awake," Selby said when Ingrid sat up.

"Yeah. Did you hear what happened?"

"There are different stories floating around. I wanted to come to you earlier, but I had to help my mother. She insisted on helping supply food and extra linens for the trip, even though my father is staying home."

"What are people saying?"

"Well, it varies, but most versions have something to do with you causing a keg of ale to smash into a boy, and his injuries range from a broken leg to a wooden spike through his leg to death." Selby used her fingers to keep track of the different options as she spoke. "But they all end with you doing some kind of seiðr magic to heal him."

Ingrid shook her head and rubbed her face, taking slow, deep breaths to force down the bile rising to her throat. "They think I used Freya's magic, like the witch in the woods? I didn't even know what I was doing, I just did it."

Selby smiled and sat down on the bed next to her friend. "Most people around here farm or fight, where thinking isn't necessary. Besides, they'll forget about it and move on to their next problem soon enough." Lowering her voice, she leaned closer to Ingrid. "Especially when we won't be here for them to see."

"You still want to come with me?" Ingrid's shoulders softened.

"What you did is odd, I won't lie, but I'm not worried. I do want to know what really happened, though. Not because I'm afraid, but because I'm nosy." She bumped Ingrid's shoulder, and gave her friend a wide grin.

Ingrid smiled back, took a deep breath, and told the truth of what happened.

"So Jorg saved your life. You could have fallen off the dock and been crushed by a boat, or drowned."

"*That's* what you take from what I just said? I had a vision, or something, and somehow healed an injury, a bad one. Those are the bigger issues, here."

"Yeah, yeah. Those we need to deal with, too. What do you think the vision meant?"

"I don't know."

They sat in silence for a couple minutes.

"I felt different when I touched the boy." Ingrid said it so quietly that Selby almost didn't hear her.

"How?"

"I don't know how to explain it. It's like my body moved, but I couldn't see it because I was wrapped in a big, warm blanket. When I stood up, Hagen grabbed my hands, and said they felt hot, but when Papa took hold of them, they were cold again."

"Maybe you have some kind of awesome healer skills." Selby smiled, but was staring at Ingrid's hands.

"How would I have anything like that? I'm just regular. Not even shieldmaiden-worthy, so everyone likes to tell me."

"I don't know. Don't let it bother you, I'm sure there's some kind of explanation we aren't seeing right now. One problem at a time. The first thing we need to do is eat—I'm starving. Then, we figure a way onto your father's boat, and hide until morning when we will be far down the river. See? We have much bigger things to worry about right now." She smiled again and grabbed Ingrid's hand to pull her toward the door.

Ingrid thought Selby's face looked a little pinched, but she excused it as hunger, and followed her out of the room.

The place was packed. It was tradition for the departing men to bring their families to the longhouse for a feast the night before they left. In their usual corner, the girls tried to ignore the occasional stares and whispers directed their way.

Selby crossed her eyes and stuck out her tongue at a mean, older woman who kept sneering. Ingrid held back her chuckle as the woman huffed and walked away.

"Idiots," Selby muttered.

Songs of brave warriors and tales of old battles began after most of the meal was finished. Ingrid and Selby used the distraction to talk with their parents and put their plan into action. They wasted no time in packing Ingrid's things; in her earlier panic, she hadn't done anything. Selby already had her pack stashed outside, ready to grab as soon as they could leave.

"We should go now while everyone is singing, that way no one will notice us on the docks," she suggested from her spot on Ingrid's bed, as she watched her friend tie a piece of leather around her clothes bundle.

"I think so, too. Let's say a quick goodbye to my parents and get going."

"Maybe we should just leave. What if they start asking too many questions?"

"I need to say something. You know my mother; she'll probably walk to your house later if I don't tell her goodnight before I go."

"Probably right." Selby sighed and looked at Ingrid. "You have a good family, you know that, right?"

"Yeah, I do. Let's go before I talk myself into acting like the obedient girl everyone expects me to be."

"This was your idea, remember? Don't even think of backing out."

They smiled at each other and held hands as they walked into the other room.

Both of Ingrid's parents were sitting in their chairs on the dais at the back, where her dad presided over village business. They gave Ingrid concerned looks when they saw her, but didn't say anything about the day's earlier events, letting her leave after hugs. Her father promised to bring her a gift from Jorvik, which made her stomach clench. She hated lying to her parents, and might have surrendered at that moment if Selby hadn't grabbed her wrist and pulled her away.

As they passed Hagen, he stopped them. "Aren't you going to say goodbye?" He directed the comment to Ingrid, but shot Selby a small grin. He toyed with her sometimes, just to be a pest.

"Goodbye. Enjoy your journey; I hope you don't find too many surprises you don't know how to deal with," Selby replied. Her voice dripped with sweetness, and Ingrid wanted to slap her.

"There's nothing we can't handle." He motioned to all of his friends, sitting beside him at the table.

They laughed and patted each other on the back—except Jorg, who watched Ingrid with his brows together, deep in thought.

"Are you feeling better, Ingrid?" he asked.

"I'm fine, thank you."

"While we're gone, don't let anyone bother you about what happened today."

Ingrid narrowed her eyes and glared at him. "Why would they? The only people who give me a hard time are sitting at this table."

He gave her a half-grin that made his dimple peek out at her, and she swallowed a lump that formed in her throat, feeling the heat rush to her cheeks. "Then I guess you should be safe," he teased. The other boys laughed again.

Grabbing Selby's sleeve, Ingrid steered them both toward

the door. "'Bye." She called out, unwilling to risk any more conversation with him.

Selby retrieved her pack, and they strolled around the village center casually, checking the docks for anyone that might see them. They headed toward the end, where Ingrid's father's boat waited. It would be first in line to leave in the morning. The sparkling gleam of the moon reflected in the gentle ripples on the bay.

"Eep! I can't believe we are really doing this." Selby practically vibrated with excitement.

"It sounded a lot less scary before—now I think I might throw up."

"Do it now, before we hide. There's no way I want to go through all this trouble if we're not even going to make it to the untying of the ropes." Selby smiled, but her voice sounded shaky and lacked her usual bravado.

Ingrid took a deep breath and let it out slowly. "Let's do this."

Walking quickly up to the boat, she heaved her pack harder than necessary to be sure it would clear the railing. Selby followed with her own, and then they each took hold of a different rope that kept the boat in place.

"Together on three," Ingrid said. "One, two, three!"

They pulled themselves up and wrapped their legs around the rope to shimmy to the rail. Ingrid refused to need Selby's help, and pulled herself over the edge almost at the same time as her strong friend. Both girls fell with a thud, and groaned as they knocked against the wooden seats, then fell to the floor. When they had caught their breath, untangled their skirts, and checked for broken bones, they crouched onto their feet.

"Do you think anyone heard us?" Selby asked.

"No one is out here, and inside, it's too loud. I'm sure we're safe."

They hurriedly grabbed their packs, then headed toward the bow. The moon overhead provided some light, but in the near dark, shadows played tricks with their nerves. Both girls stumbled as they made their way, unsure on their feet as the boat rocked and bounced against the dock.

All of the supplies were packed in tight. The girls had to squeeze between two kegs to find enough space to hide, next to some crates along the hull. Ingrid stuffed her pack under her and leaned against the cool, rough wood, trying to slow Thor's hammer beating inside her chest.

Selby, just out of arm's reach, settled in much like Ingrid had, only a little more squished.

They looked at each other with huge grins across their faces, and whispered squeals of delight escaped their lips as they settled in for their long, cramped wait.

Sometime during the night, Ingrid's legs had gone numb. It could have been from being tucked up under her, or from the freezing cold coming through the planks of wood. She slept in small amounts, and knew that Selby had, too, from her occasional snores. Now, both were wide awake, as activity on the boat buzzed all around them, and Ingrid's jaw ached from clenching her teeth, unsure if her discomfort came from the cold, her nerves, or her screaming bladder.

Horns sounded, signaling the ships to leave the harbor, and

her father's boat drifted away from the docks. Butterflies took flight inside Ingrid's stomach as oars sloshed water against the side of the boat as they pulled out of the bay. Rowers held tempo with a rhythmic "ho" as each oar sliced into the water like a perfectly timed dance. Each time the boat moved forward, a little jolt made Ingrid's back bump against the boat's hull.

There was a lot of laughing and conversation above her, but she could still hear the quacks of ducks among the reeds on the shoreline. The smell of a pear tree in full spring bloom hinted at her nose. She inhaled, long and deep, but instead of smelling flowers, the scent of the fish stored in the barrels surrounding her flooded her senses.

The excited butterflies turned into honeybees, jostled from their nest and angry. Another jolt from the oars, another waft of smells, this time the sour milk barrels. She squeezed her eyes tight and clamped her hand over her mouth. The last thing she wanted to do was throw up in such tight quarters. The confinement closed in on her, sweat rolled down the side of her face, and her body trembled.

"Ingrid, stop holding your breath and blow out, slowly, through your mouth," Selby whisper-screamed.

She did, but that just made her stomach more restless, and the back corners of her mouth tingled with more saliva.

"Picture yourself floating on your back, letting the sun warm you, like we do when we go swimming."

Selby tried to help, but Ingrid couldn't listen. It took all of her effort to calm the storm raging in her middle. She opened her eyes, but slammed them closed again. With only enough warning to lean over as far as she could, out flew the bees in an angry horde.

Shaking and clammy all over, she felt like her insides had been wrung like a wet rag. One more heave, then she sat limp with her head hanging between her knees. Pangs of regret washed over her, and she wished she could lie down in her bed at home.

We shouldn't have done this. What was I thinking? Now we're stuck under here.

Ingrid battled her stomach and her conscience until her exhaustion won.

Disoriented, she woke with a start some time later.

It took a second to remember where she was, but then the gentle, rocking rhythm of the boat cradled her nerves. The thrust of the oars was gone, which meant they must be under sail. Selby grunted from her left.

"Are you ok?" Ingrid whispered to her hoarsely. Her throat was thick, like she'd swallowed a burning twig.

"I need to get out of here. Do you think it's been long enough?" Selby answered.

"I think we're under sail now."

Selby nodded her head in agreement. "Let's go, then."

Ingrid felt stuck; she couldn't feel her legs, and wasn't sure how to unfold herself. Pushing forward onto her hands and knees, she was thankful she had thrown up away from where she needed to crawl out.

Inch by inch, the girls squished between the crates and kegs until they could see filtered light. Seeing the terrified look on Selby's face, Ingrid guessed it matched her own, and she reached out, giving her friend's hand a squeeze of false reassurance.

Leaving their packs for the moment, they crawled out into the open air . . . right smack into a pair of leather boots, worn by one angry Norseman.

"What is this?" a voice bellowed.

Ingrid cringed at the tone, immediately recognizing her father's deep timbre. Strong hands grabbed her arms and pulled her to a standing position, but she struggled to feel her legs. Rather than crumple to the ground, however, she was lifted high. Eye to eye with her father, his stare was like lightning bolts into her brain. A vein at his temple pulsed at the same speed as Ingrid's racing heart.

"What are you doing here?" he growled between his teeth, his lip curled up on one side.

"I . . . we . . ." Ingrid's throat was so tight, she couldn't get the words out.

"We?" Klaus turned and saw Selby propped up by one of his men. He inhaled deeply and closed his eyes for a second before stepping toward the platform. Ingrid's legs dangled over the edge when he sat her down.

He turned and walked away, and the man holding Selby deposited her next to Ingrid.

"Don't move, if you know what's good for you," he said looking at each of them.

They both nodded, not saying a word. Every man on the boat glowered in their direction. Ingrid lowered her eyes into her lap. She heard footsteps coming toward her and closed her eyes.

"I specifically forbade you to come when we talked yesterday. Why would you disobey me and put yourself in this kind of danger? Look at me, Ingrid!"

Her body jerked as Klaus yelled.

"I wanted to prove I was brave enough to be a warrior," she said. Her voice was hoarse, but she looked up and met his eyes.

She couldn't remember hearing him raise his voice at her before. Tightness squeezed her chest, but she sat up straighter, and gathered every ounce of courage to hold his stare.

"Which one of you came up with this plan?" He turned his head to look at Selby. "Was it you?"

Selby's lips trembled, and her face turned ashen white as she stared wide-eyed at Klaus without answering.

"It was my idea, Papa," Ingrid said, her voice stronger than the last time. "I persuaded her to come along."

"And I'm sure that was hard to do. How long did it take before the two of you decided to have a grand adventure?" Ingrid knew better than to think he wanted an answer. "How long have you been under there?" This time he did expect an answer.

"We climbed in while everyone was still singing."

He rubbed his hand on his face and looked up to the sky. Walking away, he braced his arms on the rail, and stared out toward the shoreline. Ingrid's heart was racing so hard as she watched his back; the pounding in her ears covered any sound. Klaus motioned over his shoulder for her to join him. She rolled over, slid to her feet, and stumbled her way to his side at the rail.

"I should put you on Rolf's boat and make him take you home," he said without looking at her. Ingrid held her breath.

"We are going to a dangerous place to talk about dangerous things. You should not be here."

"Please let us stay. We won't get in the way, and we'll be helpful to you. I know it was wrong, and I'm sorry for disobeying you, but . . . please, Papa. Let me do this." Fixated on his face, she squared her feet and pushed her shoulders back, the muscles rigid in her arms as she held them tight to her sides.

"This ship is no place for a child," he yelled.

"I am *not* a child. It's time you stopped looking at me as one. I'm here now, and I won't go back." Swallowing hard, she struggled to keep her lips from wobbling and her knees from buckling trying to be as brave as she hoped she sounded.

Klaus rubbed the back of his neck. "Your mother is going to kill me when she finds out I let you stay."

Ingrid sucked in her lip and bit down on it to keep herself from smiling—not successfully. "She'll be fine when we're back home and sees that we're safe."

Klaus turned to face her. "So say you. It's not your hide that will be missing some parts." He smirked. "Go sit down by the bow and stay out of the way."

A broad grin spread across her face that time, and it took all her willpower not to jump up and down.

A snort from behind made her turn to the left, and she caught Jorg trying to stifle a smile of his own.

She raised her chin and walked with as much dignity as she could on a moving boat. *How do I get up to the platform without looking the fool?*

A wooden box half-protruded near the edge where Selby's

legs dangled. Ingrid stepped up as if it were a common daily occurrence, and settled next to her friend.

"We get to stay," she said with as calm a voice as possible, doing her best to keep her face neutral.

A few seconds later, Selby nudged Ingrid with a shoulder, and she nudged her back. They both looked down at their laps while little giggles escaped.

I'll work on being mature later.

5

Several hours passed while the boat glided through the waters of the river.

"I love this so much," Selby said. There was a softness to her voice that surprised Ingrid.

The river was wide enough that all three boats could sail even with each other, but they formed a V-shape, like migrating geese. Every now and then, water would spray over the bow as the current picked up and increased the rocking motion of the boat.

From their position high on the platform, the girls could see the expanse of countryside beyond the dense brush of the shoreline. Feathery, green bracken, and clusters of yellow star flowers colored the landscape and gave the breeze a fresher, sweeter scent than it had back home. Birds trilled and crickets chirped.

Ingrid spent most of her time distracted by the argument taking place in her stomach. A bustle of motion jostled her as Selby switched places and shoved her next to the rail.

"Lean over the side. You'll need to, if you stay that color of green much longer," Selby said.

"Thank you."

"If you look further away, toward the horizon, it will help your stomach to settle," she added.

"How do you know that?" Ingrid asked.

"I've heard my uncle say it. He gets teased sometimes for the same problem." Selby scanned the scenery again. "Look, over there. Two otters. Do you see them?"

"Aw, they're cute."

They were rolling and playing, sliding into the water and then back onto the shore, chasing each other.

"I don't think I'll be content to stay home anymore after this," Selby told her as they watched the creatures play. "I thought I wanted that before: a home, a family, a peaceful, quiet farm."

"Why haven't you told me that before?" *Since when did my warrior friend want to be a simple farmer?*

"I've never told anyone. My house is always loud and messy, so I have to be bold and fight for everything. I never have any time to myself. But out here . . . I didn't know this existed." She swept her arm in an arc to include the boat, the river, and the shore.

"I'm not sure boats are my thing." Ingrid breathed a laugh and then settled her gaze again on the horizon. "I'm so glad you came with me to see all of this."

"Me, too."

The rest of the afternoon drifted slowly by, with the occasional need for men to move the sail or shift some of the cargo. The girls talked or rested, learning that privacy would be a rare commodity on a ship full of men. As the sun started to stretch shadows across the water, Klaus gave an order to pull over to an expanse of shoreline where the brush was sparse.

The lazy pace shifted immediately. As soon as the boats were secured on the shore, everyone sprang into action. There were extra sails to unload and use as tents, all the supplies needed for the evening meal, and blankets, bedding, and other sleeping essentials to arrange for everyone. No one was idle.

Ingrid was given the task of helping prepare the fish. When she opened the lid to the large cask, a pungent smell of vinegar burned the small hairs in her nose. She had to ladle out enough for everyone and load the shimmering silver herring into two large pots. By the time she was finished, her sleeves and the front of her apron were soaked with the sour-smelling whey. Water leaked from her eyes, even though her nose had given up the battle for fresh air.

She hauled buckets of water to and from the river—the fish would need to be rinsed several times before getting warmed in buttermilk to eat—then she hung a cauldron of skause from a tripod over the fire.

The early evening air cooled down rapidly, and rosy-gold streaks of sunlight peeked out from the clouds. Ingrid had spotted a large patch of bilberry bushes not too far back along the river, so she grabbed a basket and went to collect some before darkness settled in. Her mouth watered at the prospect of a slab of bread covered in honey and berries. Selby had been recruited to help somewhere else, so Ingrid headed out to find them by herself.

She had filled the basket with a couple handfuls of berries

before she heard rustling among the grass in front of her, down by her feet. A small bird hurried over her toes. With a shriek, Ingrid jumped back, losing her grip on the basket, and before she could blink, a hand grabbed her arm, and she was hurled behind a dark figure.

Squealing, she was engulfed by tall grasses as she landed on her knees in the mud. Dazed, confused, and frightened, she could make out the shape of a person, male, standing with his back to her.

It was the lean body of Hagen, straightened up to his full height.

Tightening her lips, she huffed and tried to push herself up, but her hands sank into the mud. Hagen turned around, holding something that made her body freeze and her eyes grow wide. Whether it was the thick, dung-like odor of the mud, or the oozing insides of the headless snake still quivering in Hagen's hand that filled her nose, she didn't know, but it made her queasy either way.

The fragments of images came together, and she recalled the open mouth that lunged toward her foot a split-second before she flew backward. Hagen had thrown her to safety as he charged at whatever danger had scared her.

Anger subsided into a mixture of fear and gratitude.

"What is it?" she asked.

He smirked at her, but before he could remark, she added, "I know it's a snake. What kind, though?"

"Oh, it's just a grass snake," he said. "I was trying to decide if it was worth trying to eat it." A puzzled look crossed his face. It was big enough, for sure, considering the body filled

Hagen's large hand, where it hung like a slippery piece of thick rope.

"Wouldn't it make us sick?" Ingrid wrinkled her nose in disgust.

"No." He reached down and inserted his knife into the snake's cut-off head. He gave it a solid toss, and the chunk sailed off the blade, far out into the deep of the river. "On second thought, I don't think I want to eat anything that thought your scrawny foot looked like a tasty meal." He chuckled.

"A young plover scampered across my foot first." She shuddered at the memory.

Hagen snorted his understanding, and with a giant heave, flung the dead body far out into the lazy current. The momentum of the toss made the headless carcass twist into an "S" shape. For an instant, it looked as if it had come alive again before landing with a splat.

"What are you doing out here?" Ingrid asked as she managed to stand.

"I was following you. I thought we could talk, and I might have a little fun and knock you into the mud, but not like this. I'm sorry you were really afraid," he said gently as he looked at all the mud she wore.

"Hmm. Well, whatever, I guess you got your wish. It adds to the smell of herring." She brushed at her clothes, but it did no good. "Why did you want to talk to me?"

He looked down and kicked at the base of a clump of grass. Sighing, he said, "I'm angry that you're here."

She stared at him. His shoulders were slumped a little and he was biting the inside of his cheek. He hadn't shaved for a few days, and a small beard was growing along his jaw; it sparkled with red highlights in the waning sunlight. He did look handsome, if she was forced to admit it.

"Why?" she asked finally.

"Because this is my chance to show I'm a man. To prove myself. But now you're here, like it's some kind of shopping trip that we're all going on for the fun of it. Father will be so distracted making sure you stay safe that he won't even notice me."

"That's not true. Besides, he already knows you're a man. You're right by his side whenever he talks to the others, and he slaps you on the back like you're one of them. I'm his little baby girl, not capable of anything. I'm the one that needs to prove myself."

"You're capable," Hagen argued. He looked at her and shrugged. "Annoying, but able to take care of yourself." He gave her a half-grin, which she responded to with a glare. "Truthfully, I've followed all the rules and done what I should. You're my silly little sister who sings and dances around all the time, yet you had the guts to come out here, and to stand up for yourself." He pressed his lips flat and shook his head. "All of my training in weapons, hunting, fishing, working on the boats, even in business dealings—is all so that I can learn how to be the leader after Father. Now you're here, like it's some sort of game."

Ingrid felt her mouth go slack, but couldn't move to close it. *He's jealous of me?* "You can't be serious. You have nothing to prove." She narrowed her eyes and peered sideways at him. "Except that you can stop picking on me."

He chuckled under his breath and bothered the mud with

his foot. "You're my pest of a sister, and you make yourself an easy target." Ingrid bit her lip and forced the sting out of her eyes. "I'm sorry. I guess I haven't realized that you are getting older, either. I'll work on that."

"Humph." Ingrid looked away, took a couple steps, and picked up her basket. "Will you get your friends to stop, too?"

"Yeah. They'll leave you alone if I tell them to." Watching her for a moment, he sighed. "I haven't noticed Jorg teasing you in a while."

Ingrid rolled her eyes, but didn't know how she felt about that. "Tell him he should keep it that way, if he wants me to see him as a man I can respect someday." She didn't look at Hagen, surprised that she had said the words out loud.

Her brother shot a quick glimpse sideways, trying to keep the grin off his face. "I'll let him know."

A few seconds of silence followed, with neither of them looking at the other.

"You have a tender heart," Hagen said finally. "We will face dangers on this trip; promise me you'll try to stay safe."

Ingrid fiddled with the basket handle, and kept her eyes on the ground. "I will. I'm stronger than you think, you know. I can be a shieldmaiden."

"I know. But this isn't the village, where you can practice, and the dangers aren't pretend. This is real, and you aren't ready for it yet."

"I'm more ready than you think," she snapped.

"Don't get all crabby. Just be careful." He blew out a long sigh. "It's getting dark. Forget about the berries; let's go back."

The berries no longer sounded good to her anyway, so they started along the path toward camp.

"I won't give up on my dreams." She said it out loud, as much for herself as for Hagen. She lurched forward from a shove on the back of her shoulder. "Hey, what's that for? You're trying real hard to stop being a jerk, I see."

Hagen laughed. "You need to see the real talents that you have. You care for others, and try so hard at things. I would have given up a long time ago, if I had kept getting bruised and battered by my friend during 'practice'," he chuckled.

"I never thought you could sound so grown up. It's weird." She smiled.

"Don't tell anyone, or I'll toss you into the river with the snake!" he teased. After a moment, he asked, "What was all that about on the docks yesterday, by the way?"

"I don't know. I don't want to talk about that."

They walked the rest of the way in silence.

'Real talents'? Was that how I helped that boy? Her head ached, and she wondered again if staying home would have been better.

After dinner, everyone went straight to bed except Ingrid.

Ducking behind some bushes with a bucket of water, she took a quick bath, and scrubbed her clothes after the men went to sleep. They would be leaving at first light, and a good night's sleep was important, but so was getting rid of the fish smell and caked-on mud.

She eventually went to bed, but between worry of another snake, and mulling over what Hagen had said, Ingrid barely slept at all. Grumpy and tired, she roused the next morning to help with breakfast and get the ships reloaded.

"You need to fix your braids," Selby said without preamble as she settled next to her in their spot at the bow.

"What do you care?"

"Sor-ry." She looked past Ingrid with her lips tight together.

"I didn't mean that, sorry, I didn't sleep well. How are you so rested?"

"I don't know. I like being out here, I guess. And I didn't have a snake try to bite me, so I'm sure that helped," Selby said, and Ingrid shuddered again at the memory she'd shared over dinner. "Do you want me to help you with your braids?" she offered.

"I really don't care, but sure, if you think I need help."

"Well, you might be too grumpy to notice, but you have an admirer. I'll help you, and you can thank me later."

"What? No one admires me." Ingrid didn't have the patience to talk about boys right then.

"Mm-hmm. Then why does Jorg keep looking over at you and smiling?"

"Because he's a jerk and probably making fun of me. Why do you keep thinking it's something more?"

"You need to open your eyes. There." Selby finished tying the ends of the two plaits together. "You're welcome."

"Thanks." Ingrid stole a glance in Jorg's direction and straightened her clothes. Selby smiled. "What?"

"Nothing."

Ingrid turned her attention to the horizon, and ignored the

others. The crisp morning air brought hints of chamomile and sweet balm.

The rest of the journey down river was much the same as the first couple of days had been, with Ingrid fighting her nausea by day and camping by night. Finally, Jorvik came into sight, and the crew prepared to land.

Everyone jumped ashore and tied the boats along the wooden docks, leaving a few men with each to guard their property. People and boats lined the walkways, making it difficult for Ingrid to see the city.

"I know you are excited, but this is a dangerous place," Klaus warned her. "You have to watch your surroundings and stay close to me. Do you understand?"

"Yes, Papa."

They made their way to the main street and headed toward a small hill that rose above the ramshackle rows of huts about a quarter mile away. As a group, they made a formidable impression through the narrow streets. Ingrid watched as Hagen followed their father, and was amused by how hard he tried to mimic his movements. She heard Selby sigh, and followed her gaze for the source. Her friend's eyes were fixed on Hagen as well, but apparently for a different reason.

"You need to look around. Find another target for your affections," Ingrid told her, smiling.

"Why? Look at him. He's as tall as your father now, and so commanding. I'd follow him anywhere."

"Ew. You're pathetic. Get a hold of yourself, or I'll make you walk between the Stinks."

Selby snorted. "Yeah, like that's going to happen."

"This isn't what I thought the capitol would look like,"

Ingrid said, changing the subject and drawing Selby's eyes away from her brother.

"I know. I thought it would be nicer than our village, not the other way around."

There were a lot more houses than in their village, but they were not as well constructed or cared for. They were made the same, with stone or plank walls and thatched roofs, but there were gaps that hadn't been repaired. The grasses of the thatch were rotted in places, and many sagged dreadfully. More than one they passed had caught fire at some point, and the entire structure looked tired and weak. Yet families still inhabited the rickety hovels.

The view in front of them did not match the images Ingrid had formed in her mind before they arrived. Gray skies and drizzling rain made the streets a muddy mess. Streams of water flowed in deep ruts made by carts and wagons that lumbered along what passed for roads.

She'd expected something much more grand.

The smell of rotten midden heaps pushed in from every side, and there wasn't a market, but peasants either set up tables outside the door of their own ramshackle homes, or parked a wagon somewhere and sold wares from it.

Even so, the harbor was full of ships from faraway lands, and what was for sale was brilliant: glass from Italia, spices from the Indies, and embroidered silk from Frankia.

"Hagen thought I would think of this as a shopping trip; I told him I didn't, but I might have lied. I want to look around at all this stuff," she whispered to Selby, nodding toward a cart boasting fabric in the deepest shade of red she'd ever seen.

"I know. I was thinking the same thing."

Even though they didn't have to go far, getting anywhere in a hurry was difficult. Thick mud coated them in splatters to their knees, and Ingrid looked at herself in disgust.

In the middle of grumbling about the need for clean, dry clothes, a sound grabbed her attention, and she stopped walking.

"Where is that music coming from?" she asked.

"I think just ahead. I've never heard anything like it," Selby answered. Ingrid nodded in agreement while she started to walk again, intrigued.

Warm, fresh, bread smells wafted out of one door they passed, and Ingrid's stomach rumbled. *A slab of bread and a warm mug of spiced cider would be delicious right now.* Thoughts of warm food and dry clothes kept her occupied until they finally reached a stand at the end of the street, where dead geese hung from their feet.

Around the corner was a man dressed in a pair of stained and patched breeches, with an equally patched, loose shirt hanging over a protruding belly. A large, floppy hat kept the rain away from his face, and he played a bone flute made from the leg of a swan. A jolly little tune fluttered through the air. Under his feet lay a mat of woven reeds, and he tapped his toes to the beat.

Ingrid danced a little in time with his tune, and Selby clapped wildly with her when he finished. The crowd persisted, calling for another tune, and much to Ingrid's delight, her party stayed to listen. This song was different, however. It was beautiful and slow, melancholy.

Mesmerized, Ingrid closed her eyes and swayed her body to the music, picturing grasses on the moor back home rippling in the breeze, the purple heather flooding the hills with their earthy, floral smells, and the sad call of a heron looking for its mate.

Voices shouted in the back of Ingrid's awareness, interrupting the beautiful scenery. Suddenly, she realized the music had stopped. Opening her eyes in time to dodge a large body hurtling past her, she stood frozen like a deer in a meadow. Selby's hand grabbed her arm in a vice-like grip, and yanked her to a run.

Shouts and the hissing of swords being pulled from their scabbards sounded all around them. The coppery smell of blood filled the air as men clashed, driving their weapons into each other. The girls dove under a nearby wagon, as the clamor of metal meeting metal and shrieking battle cries rang out.

Shivering in the mud, they huddled together, struggling to distinguish one person from the next. Selby screamed and covered her face with her hands, as Ingrid lay silent, rooted to the ground while her entire body trembled.

Within a few harried moments that felt like hours, the fighting was over. The raiders had flashed upon Klaus's men and jumped away just as quickly.

Stunned, Ingrid and Selby emerged from hiding, and several injured men near them moaned. Without thinking, Ingrid ran to their side.

The first warrior she reached was bleeding so profusely that his shirt was soaked through. Ripping the sopping material away from the wound, she held her breath to keep from retching. He was splayed open from collarbone to navel. Touching the man's forehead, she said a quick prayer, then moved to the next man.

"Ingrid!" Selby ran after her. Not all of the men were convinced the fight was over, and weapons still clanged in her ears. "This isn't safe. You need to come with me."

"No."

The man in front of her also had a gash across his chest, but it was not as deep as the previous man's had been. Closing her eyes, she laid both hands on the sliced flesh. Warmth embraced her as she concentrated. In only a few seconds, she felt the cool air around her again and, without checking her impact, scrambled to the nearest body, continuing to move from one to the next.

There were no sounds in her ears except the thrum of her own heartbeat. Time didn't exist. Nothing mattered to her at that moment except the next injury. She didn't notice the person, only blood, broken bones, and ripped flesh until she pulled her hands from the last man she could help.

Then, cold air blasted around her as if her warm blanket had been snatched away, and everything went dark.

6

Ingrid blinked her eyes, and her vision adjusted to the darkened room in which she stood. The only sliver of light filtered in from between the curtain and the frame of the room's single window.

As a stranger in the corner, she viewed the scene: a family huddling together over a woman holding a small child on her lap. Soiled towels lay on the ground. The woman was crying, but Ingrid could not hear any sound as she watched. Silence encased her like a tomb.

Recognition squeezed her heart and burned through her chest; this was her home and her family.

Her mother held the child, her disheveled hair pulled loose and falling over her shoulders. Her father sat back on his knees, his head bowed, but tilted enough that Ingrid could see tears streaming down his face. Hagen was there too, only much younger. He screamed at her. Not the her standing there in silence, not the stranger who was witnessing their pain, but the small her, the her that squatted near the ground, several feet away from the others, her arms around her legs as she rocked back and forth. There was blood on her hands and arms.

Ingrid struggled to stay upright, and swirls floated through her vision. Unbalanced, she bumped into the wall behind her, feeling sweat break out at her temples.

Is this real? Is this one of my lost memories?

Walking toward her mother, she stepped past her younger self. No one else saw her; they had no idea she was there. The child, no more than two, was soaked in blood that flowed from its middle, thick crimson smears on its skin from obvious attempts at helping the poor thing. It was dead.

Ingrid let her tears fall down her cheeks without care. The sting in her eyes told her that she was connected to this scene, yet also separate. Darkness tried to swallow her into the pain, and she turned to find a way out of the room, stiffening when her own young face stared at her.

Young Ingrid bore glowing, turquoise eyes into the true Ingrid, acknowledging her presence among them. "I tried to save her, but I don't know how to use it."

Her younger self's voice was small, but it vibrated against the inside of Ingrid's head as if she'd shouted—an intensity that made Ingrid swallow the dry lump in her throat, and want to run.

Her younger self stood calm, eerie, detached, and said, "Learn."

The room spun, and blackness swallowed her again. It sucked all the air from her. She saw nothing, heard nothing, felt nothing.

Then sounds began to prick at Ingrid's mind. Voices. She

heard them in the distance, as if she was trapped in a dark pit, and they were far above. Her surroundings felt cold and damp, and she wanted to climb up to the people. They called her name.

I need to be with them.

Struggling, a blast of bright light blinded her, and sounds pounded into her skull. She tried to cover her ears against the clamor, but her arms were trapped by her sides. Crying out, she pulled her hands free and lifted them to her head. Hesitantly, she opened her eyes and saw her father staring down at her. His forehead furrowed in lines, he was saying her name over and over.

"Please. Don't. Shout," Ingrid whispered.

Squeezed close to her father's chest, he rocked her back and forth. She turned her head to the side so she could breathe, and the overwhelming racket and bright light dimmed. Pulling back, she blinked until her eyes focused; her heart stuttered as she saw the faces that surrounded her in all directions. She was laying on her father's lap in the mud, and everyone was staring. Selby, Hagen, and Jorg were closest, sitting on their knees next to her.

"What happened?" she asked.

"You need to tell us, baby girl," Klaus said as he brushed strands of hair away from her face. "But not now. Let's get you inside so you can get dry and warm."

Standing up with her still in his arms, he walked toward a large, open gate. The others followed close, creating a protective circle around the pair. Beyond the gate was a longhouse, and they walked directly through the door without stopping. A woman ran up and ushered them to follow her to a back room.

The room was large, and sconces holding lit candles flickered light against the shadowed walls. Several woven rugs in yellow, indigo, and red overlapped and covered the floor. A bowl filled with white and purple crocus petals sat on a small table, adding a sweet scent to the air.

"Can you stand up, Meyla?" Klaus asked. Ingrid nodded, and he lowered her from his arms until she was standing, but he didn't let go.

Swaying, she held onto his arms until she was sure she felt her legs under her. "I'm okay, Papa. I can stand by myself now."

"Go out, and I'll help get her clean and warm," the woman told Klaus, and pushed Hagen and Jorg out the door with him.

Selby brushed against Ingrid's side and wrapped her arm around her shoulders. Sagging into her friend, Ingrid gave her a slow smile, grateful not to be left alone.

"I'm Greta. My husband is the king. Well, one of them. You are safe here with us."

Behind them, someone knocked on the door and, without waiting for an answer, several people hurried in with a tub and buckets of steaming water. They filled the tub and then left a couple buckets to use to warm it up, if necessary; then they left.

"Now, let's get you out of these filthy clothes so you can warm yourself."

Selby and Greta helped Ingrid bathe and dress in some borrowed clothes, before tucking her into a bed filled with warm furs. The scent of heather wafted up from the bed. Ingrid's teeth chattered despite all of the coverings.

"You will warm up soon. Try to rest, and I will be back to

look in on you," Greta said, then she turned to Selby. "You should wash and change, too. There are more clothes in that trunk." Smiling at both girls, she hurried out.

"She is really nice," Selby said.

"Y-yes. Sh-sh-she is."

"Don't talk, just work on getting warm." Reaching into the trunk Greta had indicated, Selby chose some clean clothes and started her own bath.

"Wh-what happened?"

"Which part? Before or after you fell into the mud, and we all thought you died?"

Ingrid stared at the ceiling trying to remember. *Did I die? No, I couldn't have. Could I?* Finally, she said, "I remember the fight was over, and there were bodies on the ground. Something inside me pulled me toward the injured men. It's hard to explain—like needing to breathe, only I needed to touch." She stopped to take a couple deep breaths, as her stomach started to churn with the memories. "I don't know why I did it. There was blackness, and then I was in the middle of a room and saw . . . something. It's fuzzy." Shaking her head, she tried to bring it all back into focus.

The furs poked between her fingers as she clutched the blankets. She looked over at Selby, who had stopped washing and was silently staring at her from the tub.

"We tried to grab you. To pull you away from the mess, but it was like you were stuck to those men, covered in their blood and crawling through the filth. You were possessed or something." Selby resumed scrubbing away her own gore as she recalled the scene. "Your father, Hagen, me, even Jorg—we all tried to pull you away, but none of us could. And you didn't go to the men who were dying or already dead. It was like you knew exactly who to help. To heal." She looked directly at Ingrid for the first time.

"Did I? Heal them?"

"Yes."

"I don't know how."

"When you fell at the end, your hands were hot. Just for a minute, but Hagen said they'd felt that way on the docks, too. When you healed that boy."

Ingrid rubbed one hand over the other. It was a weird sensation, to feel her hands without her gauntlets, as she rarely took them off, but they were cold. Not just on the inside, but cold to the touch, as if they'd been stuck inside a snowdrift.

Selby got dressed and sat on the edge of the bed. She took one of Ingrid's hands into her own.

"They are so cold. Do they hurt?"

"My whole body feels cold inside, like I've been drained. It doesn't hurt, but I'm tired." Gooseflesh no longer covered her skin, but the heat of the blankets had yet to seep into her core.

"You're pale. You should rest before you have to talk with your father about all of this." She rubbed Ingrid's hand gently.

Greta pushed through the curtain door carrying a tray with steaming mugs that smelled like roasted meat. "I've brought you both some warm broth. Eat up, then rest so you can regain your strength." She smiled at Selby. "Both of you. I won't let anyone else disturb you, and what I say goes around here." She cocked an eyebrow at each of them.

Ingrid sat up, and Selby wrapped more blankets around her shoulders while she sipped the broth. She climbed under the mound of covers, too, when Ingrid insisted, and they snuggled next to each other when they'd finished their broth.

Late afternoon light filtered into the room despite the covered window and door. Ingrid was exhausted, but couldn't sleep. Every time she closed her eyes, she saw images of bodies covered in blood or worse.

"Are you awake?" Selby nudged Ingrid.

"Yes."

"I know what happened out there today was weird and hard to understand, but you need to know, no matter what happens—I'll always stay by your side. And, whether you like him or not, I'm not the only one. Jorg is all about you."

"What?" It took her a second to realize what her friend had said. *I don't want to think about this.*

"He went wild trying to get you away from all those men. He even fought a couple, standing guard over you like some sort of protector. He almost hit your father before he realized who he was," she said with a giggle.

"Why?" Wings fluttered inside Ingrid's chest as she thought about what Selby told her. An image of Jorg's dimple when he grinned made her bite her lip to keep from smiling. *What's happening to me?*

"You need to open your eyes, girlie. He's always staring at you like he wants to grab you and run off into the woods." She gave Ingrid a couple little jabs with her elbow, and snickered.

"He does not. You're terrible."

"Maybe, but if he looked at *me* like that, I wouldn't run away. You need to pay more attention."

Ingrid thought about that. *He likes me? Am I ready for that?* "I can't care about that right now. I've got to deal with whatever this hot-hands-that-heal thing is that's turned me into a freak show."

Selby snorted a chuckle through her nose.

"Besides, I've seen lots of girls flirt with him—including you, I believe."

"I flirt with all the cute boys, that's just fact. And not the point."

"You're impossible. Let me rest, I'm tired," Ingrid said dismissively, and closed her eyes.

Jorg's smile and drool-worthy dimple replaced the gruesome images behind her eyelids.

Queen Greta insisted that Ingrid and Selby continue to stay with her as the days passed. Ingrid's strength returned and she did not have any more visions, but she was happy to have the warmth and care of her kind benefactor. Selby, however, itched to get out and explore the city, follow the men, and have the adventure she'd been hoping for when they left.

When Ingrid's father arrived on the third morning to resume his meetings with the king, Ingrid asked him to allow them some time away.

"I can't spare any men to go with you, and it's too dangerous for you and Selby to go alone," Father said.

"We will be careful and stay together, Papa, please. We've been inside too long. Did we work so hard to get to Jorvik only to see the inside of a room the whole time?"

"That's not a very good argument. I could just say it's a fitting punishment for your disobedience." He rubbed the back of his neck. "But I will allow you some time to walk around today. You can go along with Hagen on his business."

Ingrid pressed her lips flat and sighed through her nose. The last thing she wanted was to give Hagen any more chances to lord over her and make her feel like she was too young to be there. "Can't you spare anyone else, Papa?"

"No. If you don't want to follow the leadership of your brother, you can stay here." He walked to the doorway and then turned back to her. "I have meetings to attend. Shall I tell Hagen of his duties today, or are you staying put?" He cocked his eyebrow, and she knew that he would not tolerate a plan to sneak away.

"We'll follow him. But does he have to bring his friends? I think Selby might try to kill one, if we spend too much time together."

Selby let out a choked snort from the other side of the room.

Chuckling, Klaus shook his head. "I will tell him to just choose one other to go with him. You do your part to keep your friend in line, and we'll see who makes it home at the end of the day." He pushed through the curtain door, and she could hear him laughing quietly as he walked away.

It's better than staying in, I guess.

"Finally. I'm so tired of being inside." Selby threw herself onto the bed.

"I'm so sick of being coddled, though. We don't need to be escorted."

Just then a knock came from the doorway. "Ingrid, we are leaving in five minutes. If you want to come, get your arse out here, or get left behind," Hagen growled from the hall.

Four minutes later, the girls stepped out of the front door and walked up to where Hagen and Jorg waited, a few feet away.

"Let's go. Stay close, understand?" Hagen commanded, looking from Ingrid to Selby.

Ingrid rolled her eyes, but Selby cocked her head sideways and gave a wicked little grin. Taking a step closer to Hagen, then another, she stood only a half-arm's length away from him. "This close?"

Exhaling through his nose, the muscles in his jaw twitched. "Just keep up." He turned and strode off toward the gates.

Selby looked back and gave Ingrid a muffled giggle, which made her bite her lip to keep from laughing.

From the corner of her eye, Ingrid noticed Jorg shaking his head, and turned in his direction. He smiled in a way that made his hazel-green eyes shine like sunshine on a meadow, and his one dimple was fully on display. Her heart jumped and made her forget everything else.

I need to stop listening to Selby's nonsense!

"After you, ladies. We'd better do as he says." Jorg stretched out his arm, gesturing for them to go ahead of him.

Selby slipped her hand through Ingrid's arm, and they walked off after Hagen. Ingrid shook her head, but knew the day would be eventful.

They wandered through the streets toward the pier where they had first arrived, and Ingrid was again struck by the stench of waste and the mucky grime that covered everything. Rows of small houses sat side by side, leaning on each other as if for support. Ingrid was starting to question her desire to explore the city when they turned a corner and came upon a market street.

It was lined with the same dilapidated houses, but each had tables set up out front with wares for sale. Packed with buyers and sellers, the corridor resembled a crowded, muddy stream filled with hungry fish.

They stopped to watch for a couple minutes before navigating through the narrow passage. Handcarts were pushed, and wagons pulled among the crowd. Some were even harnessed to goats, and the group learned to jump out of their way.

The girls stopped at a table featuring beautiful beads. Ingrid was drawn to the jade, teal, and cobalt-colored glass ones that sparkled in the light. As she ran her fingers over them, the amber bead of her own necklace illuminated, as if it had come to life.

Ingrid felt the air around her thicken. The little hairs on the back of her neck tingled, and her lungs tightened, making it hard to breathe. Turning slowly to her left, she saw a woman in the middle of the street. The flesh on Ingrid's arms rose in small bumps. The woman stood the length of two wagons away, yet even from that distance, a power radiated from her. Ingrid shivered as if it was mid-winter, but she felt drawn to the woman.

She moved to take a step toward her, and felt a hand on her elbow. Dazed, she broke her gaze from the woman to trace from the hand up the arm, and she found Jorg looking back at her. He had creases in his brow and a question in his eyes.

"Is everything alright?"

"Yes. I was just going to go see that woman over there. "

"What woman?" His eyes roamed back and forth, scanning the street.

Turning back to where she had seen her, Ingrid examined every face. "She was just there," she pointed, "watching me."

"What did she look like?"

"She was tall. She wore a beaded cloak with the hood pulled up, but I could clearly see her face. It was beautiful, and she had long, brown hair spilling over her shoulders."

Jorg furrowed his brows further. "If you see her again, don't go to her alone. Make sure I'm with you." He hesitated, then added, "Or Hagen. Promise it."

"What's with the overprotective act? You two boys need to give us a little space," Selby interjected.

"There are a lot of people here, and it would be easy to get separated and lost, that's all." Jorg still held Ingrid's elbow while he stared at her.

She nodded to him and looked down. Up ahead a few houses, Hagen was buying several skewers of some type of meat. They walked up to him.

"Here, try one of these. It's dried elk, and tastes delicious." He handed a skewer to Ingrid, and one to Selby. "Don't say I'm never nice to you."

As Ingrid took a bite of the snack, she felt the familiar tingle on her neck. She turned to find the woman watching her again.

This time, the woman nodded with her chin that Ingrid should follow her.

Ingrid nudged Jorg without taking her eyes off the woman, and he followed her gaze. Pushing Ingrid behind him, he glared at the woman, who raised an eyebrow as she looked back at him.

As if a question had been answered, she nodded her head and then smiled at Jorg before turning and disappearing into the crowd.

Hagen had noticed his friend's movement. "What's wrong?"

"There was a woman watching Ingrid, but she's gone now."

Hagen questioned Ingrid, and she repeated the woman's description.

"Let's keep walking," he decided. "We have business to take care of at the skeldergate, but speak up if you see her again."

"We don't know that she means any harm."

"You are too trusting," he arched an eyebrow at her. Lifting his chin to Jorg, he told him, "You stay on that side."

Jorg nodded, and they started to walk, with Ingrid in between them.

"Don't worry about me. I'll stay right here, behind all of you. Safely protecting myself," Selby whined in a mocking voice.

Ingrid smiled over her shoulder. The boys pushed through the crowded street, making room for them to keep three abreast, and ignoring the angry comments as they did. Selby shook her head and followed.

7

They walked among the scattered barrels and baskets, stopping to admire fine fabrics or braided leatherwork. Selby purchased a beautiful filigree box filled with kohl.

"Since when do you wear kohl?" Hagen asked.

"Mind your own business," Selby answered.

"He just wants to make sure you'll share with us," Jorg teased.

Ingrid chuckled as they enjoyed a moment of fun. Her mind was distracted, though, with the sticky mud and the clamor of the crowds that reminded her of the battle days before. The coppery smell of blood while she had tended the wounded, and the way her hands squished with gore plagued her memories.

Could I really swing a spear or an axe at a person? Would I? Maybe everyone is right; I'm not supposed to be a shieldmaiden.

She trudged along behind Selby. They left the tight corridor, and turned a corner toward the sounds of water. Up ahead were the river and a different set of docks, but the entire street was lined on both sides with shield-makers. Ingrid gasped and stopped walking.

Skeldergate. She couldn't believe her eyes.

Rows and rows of shields leaned against each other. There were large ones and small ones. Some had pounded iron elements, while others were made of all wood. All of them possessed a beauty that entranced Ingrid. The intricate carvings of dragons, snakes, wolves, and bears marked some. Vivid colors or none at all made no difference in their beauty. The craftsmanship was extraordinary.

Ingrid walked from artisan to artisan, admiring all the work. Some of the crafters also made weapons, and there were spears, hammers, axes, and maces.

Lost in the dazzle of sights, she startled when Selby spoke next to her.

"This is incredible."

Ingrid nodded as she continued to stare.

"We need to speak to a man farther down to have a few more shields made for father's men," Hagen said.

"They are all so wonderful." Her voice held a reverent quiet, as if she stood in a holy place.

"Come on, Ingrid." Selby walked quickly down the street, but Ingrid slowed her steps, mesmerized.

She came to a cluster of shields that were smaller than most. Ingrid put her hands on one, and a voice from just inside the hut's doorway said, "Go ahead. Pick it up and see how it feels."

She did, and was amazed. It was so lightweight; her arm didn't strain to keep it in position.

"How is this possible?" she asked. "It's so light. Wouldn't it splinter apart if it was used?"

"No, I use linden wood. It's coated in linen rather than leather so it stays light. Still just as hard, and works just as well. It's a good shield for tight places and quick action."

Ingrid looked down the street to where the others stood. Selby was turned toward her, and she gestured to tell her not to worry.

"Do you think you could make me one? Light like these, and to fit my size?" she asked, lowering her voice as she spoke.

He peered sideways at her, skeptical, before he answered. "Why are you asking me? Who does your family buy their shields from?"

"They have a maker, down the way," she pointed toward her group, "but theirs are not as light as yours. I have money and I will pay you myself."

This was true. Her skills at spinning thread and nålbinding rivaled someone twice her age, and the women of her village paid well for her help.

"There's no need to worry about what my family does," Ingrid assured him. She pulled her shoulders back and met his eyes with an unflinching stare. "When can you have it ready for me?"

"I can have it ready when you need it, but the faster I have to work, the more it will cost you," he warned with a smile.

Ingrid reached into the pouch hanging from her belt and pulled out a couple coins. "I will give you this now, and the rest when it is finished," she said. "I will be back to let you know when I need it."

"Fine, I'll get started with this, but if you don't come back today, I will not continue."

"I'll be back. And I'll expect your best work when it's finished."

The crafter gave a snort but smiled. Ingrid savored the independence she felt as she strolled toward the others.

An hour later, as the group made their way back down the street, Ingrid stopped to adjust her gauntlets.

"Is there something wrong? Are your hands feeling warm?" Selby asked.

"I'm fine. Really. Go ahead with the others, I'll catch up."

"I'll wait."

"It's okay. Keep walking and make sure the boys don't make a big deal about me stopping."

"You're up to something. What is it?" Selby squinted her eyes and chewed on her lip. Her eyes popped open when she looked beyond Ingrid. "You are going back to the shield-maker I saw you at earlier, aren't you?"

"Shhh." Ingrid glanced toward Hagen and Jorg, but they were still ambling up the street. "Yes, but be quiet."

"Will he make one for me, too?" Reaching into her own purse, Selby pulled out some coins. "This should be enough to start, shouldn't it?"

"Fine, but keep them busy so I can go over there. How do you want yours to look?"

"Surprise me!" Her friend's eyes gleamed, and she gave a little squeal.

"Hurry and catch up to them," Ingrid pointed toward the boys. "I'll be as fast as I can."

"They are a couple of mother hens when it comes to you."

She snickered and hurried off down the street while Ingrid rushed over to the shield-maker.

Not long after, Ingrid strutted up to Selby with a satisfied smile and gave a pump of her eyebrows.

When they returned to the shield-makers' street later that week, Ingrid was anxious. She wasn't sure how she would explain what she'd done, or even how she would be able to pick up her and Selby's shields unnoticed. To decrease the risk, she decided she'd pay for Selby's, but leave it for her to snatch up on her own when they rolled by with the wagon.

It had all been unwarranted worry, however. Everyone was so busy inspecting and loading the new shields onto the cart, that no one even noticed when Ingrid slipped away.

There was a surprise waiting for her when she arrived at the shield-maker's tent. He had understood her perfectly when she explained that she wanted something light for her size. He'd also gathered her desire to assert her independence, and had taken it upon himself to make another item for her: a wooden mallet.

Instead of being made of heavy fir or alder in the usual manner, he'd used the lighter linden wood, like the shield. A sturdy loop of leather was laced through a hole in the end of the handle to secure the instrument around Ingrid's wrist.

The hammer was perfect, and when the man saw how it fit Ingrid's hand perfectly, he offered to give it to her at no charge.

"This is quality work and you deserve your fee." Even if it were perfect for her, she wouldn't accept it for free. She'd forced her way onto this trip to prove herself and she would pay her way.

After a few moments of negotiations, they finally settled on a price that Ingrid suspected was still below value. But that might be helpful to show her resourcefulness to her father when she explained to him what she'd done.

The man had anticipated her acceptance and took her to the back of his shop, where he had nailed a straw-filled shirt to a post. Here, he had her hold the red and yellow painted shield in her left hand, and then slip her right hand through the leather loop of the hammer before gripping the handle.

Ecstatic, Ingrid beamed like a one-hundred-foot bonfire.

The weight of the mallet felt like an extension of her arm rather than a heavy burden. She thrust up and across, contacting the dummy with an ease she'd never known before. Her training had only ever involved sticks, but she mastered the movements in no time, jumping up in order to come down on an enemy with all of her weight.

The merchant guided her for more than a quarter of an hour. She paid him the remainder of the balance for all three items, and was grateful that she had earned enough to cover the extra cost of the mallet.

Without another thought about what she'd say to her father, she strutted out onto the street. Holding her possessions properly in each arm, she made her way over to the others.

Klaus noticed her first, and walked over to where she stood. "So, what have you got there?" he asked.

"A shield I commissioned for myself," she answered boldly, without a hint of remorse.

"Ah." He nodded and jutted his chin. "And what of the other?"

"This was a surprise, but it was made just for me, and I can wield it well."

"How did you make these purchases?" Klaus sounded stern, but there was a sparkle in his eyes.

"From the extra work I do around the village. I used my own coin."

"Then you have earned the right to keep them." He smiled.

Ingrid smiled back. Pride and satisfaction coursed through her veins, knowing she'd made a mature decision and he would honor it.

By afternoon, the shields were all loaded, and the slow journey to the boats began. While the skies now held their moisture, enough rain had fallen earlier to make the busy area sloppy and thick. Wagons slipped and sank into the mud at regular intervals, making progress agonizingly slow.

Ingrid, useless to help with either the large ox or the heavy cart, distracted herself at the market tables. She kept an eye toward the group while perusing beads, pottery, and jewelry. One vendor had hair combs made of gold, some inlaid with jewels or ivory. They were far too expensive for what coins she had left, though, so she wandered on. The next table had containers filled with various colors of body paint. Intricate carvings on the pots made them as beautiful as the contents promised on the inside. Ingrid had never decorated her face like most of the other girls her age did. Selby had urged her to try, but the effort didn't interest her.

Maybe it's time I tried this? I'd look more mature.

Running her fingers over a small, round pot carved from

wood and painted with red, yellow, and green swirls, she was reminded of the grassy fields back home, adorned with their floral jewelry.

"That would be a good choice for you," the woman next to the table said. She smiled at Ingrid. "A little kohl would make your turquoise eyes brighter."

Ingrid's chest tightened, and she flashed a glance toward the wagon. It was stuck in the mud again, and no one was looking in her direction.

I could borrow Selby's, . . . though it wouldn't hurt to have some of my own, for special times. "How much?" she asked the woman.

After wrapping the box in a section of linen, Ingrid secured it in her purse. Her two remaining coins jostled alongside her purchase. She looked over to the wagon, still anchored in the mud; everyone's focus was on getting it moving again. Satisfied with her choice, she tied the purse to her belt and ambled toward the next vendor, across the alley.

Without warning, a hand snaked out from behind and covered her mouth. Another wrapped around her waist and pulled her back into the alley behind the market huts. A girl and a boy stood in front of her. Both were taller and weighed more than her, but they were about her age, as far as she could tell. The warring smells of body odor, bad breath, and general stink came from a third captor, the boy behind her, causing her to gag behind his rough fingers.

Her legs quivered, and her heart pounded against her rib cage. She'd watched this scenario while the girls practiced at home, but it was intimidating rather than entertaining when it was for real.

The boy behind her released her and stepped back, but she

could still feel the heat of his too-close body. She stood her ground, hoping they couldn't see the tremble of her hands. The option of screaming flashed through her mind.

No, I will handle this myself. I need to handle this myself.

"Nice shield," the girl sneered, and black holes gaped between yellowed teeth. "If you drop it now, I'll let you run home to your mother." Dark eyes peered out of tiny slits below bushy eyebrows as their owner spat the words. The girl was as dirty as the boys, her hair matted into stiff ridges above a scar over her left eyebrow.

Ingrid remembered from one demonstration, how Helka had stood poised and ready before her attackers. Mimicking that attitude, she squared her shoulders.

"You can try," she said with forced indifference. Her gut churned, and a trickle of sweat slid between her shoulder blades. She willed her arms to relax as she tightened her grip on the shield.

"I was hoping you'd stay." The girl curled her lip into a crooked grin.

The boys stepped back, deferring the fight to their leader, and gave the girls an impromptu arena. The mallet hung by its cord on Ingrid's wrist, limp against her knee.

Quick as a cat, the girl lunged at Ingrid. On instinct, she raised her shield and pushed her weight into it. Stunned not by the impact, but at her ability to stop the girl, Ingrid's courage soared.

Smug with her skills, her arm dropped for a brief second—enough for the girl's hand to reach over and take hold of Ingrid's hair. Surprised, Ingrid stumbled over her feet as she flew forward.

A solid thud landed on her back from the girl's other fist.

Disoriented, Ingrid barely kept herself from falling face-first into the mud. Staying on her feet, she spun around in time to use her shield to deflect the next blow. Within a split-second, she leaned down to let the mallet touch the ground so she could wrap her fingers around the handle. Before she could stand up, a fist struck her hard across the face.

Blood filled her mouth, and she felt one of her teeth wiggle as she spat the coppery-tasting liquid. Ingrid jammed the shield's edge into the girl's stomach as she lunged for another strike. The girl's eyes widened, and she grunted as she lost her breath. Ingrid swung her mallet sideways as the girl doubled over; the crack reverberated through her arm with a shudder as the mallet landed on the back of the girl's shoulder.

The girl's body lurched forward, and her head slammed awkwardly against a barrel. The girl looked up for a moment before her eyes rolled up into her head and she crumpled to the ground.

Ingrid's chest heaved as she tried to catch her breath. Both of the boys stared at the girl in silence for a second until the boy nearest Ingrid reached for her shield. She pulled it back and faltered, but readied for a second attempt.

As if from a slingshot, a body hurtled into the boy from the direction of the main road. The second boy launched himself at the new attacker while Ingrid abandoned the melee and rushed back to the girl.

She dropped to the ground, her own injuries ignored, and huddled over the girl's wilted body. A light moan and raspy breath proved she was still alive. Ingrid's shoulders slumped forward, and she scrunched her eyes closed. Blood soaked the girl's hair and trickled into her ear. Ingrid reached out to touch her, but before she could, she swooshed through the air and was slung, undignified, over a shoulder. Her mallet hung from her wrist as her arms dangled toward the ground.

She had no energy to fight anymore, and bounced along, barely able to breathe, as her stomach was pressed tight. She was dropped behind a stack of wooden boxes around a corner, and strong arms held her down, a barked whisper ordering her to 'stay still'. A few silent moments passed before she was allowed to sit up.

When she was, she found Hagen crouched next to her. His lips were pressed into a tight line, and he huffed angrily from his nose.

"Ingrid!" he growled. "When you wound an enemy in battle, you leave them there to bleed, not rush to their side."

She turned away as tears welled up behind her eyes. *Crying like a baby isn't going to help.*

Hagen blew out a big sigh of air, then said in a soft voice, "You can't have it both ways, Meyla. Either you fight without hesitation, or you help the wounded." His voice had lost its anger, and he spoke with tenderness. "If you can't do that, you will get yourself killed."

He was right. She hated that he was, but hated herself more for not knowing what to do. It was her first fight; she'd done well and wanted to revel in it. The coppery taste of blood still swirled in her cheeks, and the bruise on her jaw ached. Her heart couldn't feel joy, though as the look on the girl's face before she fell crossed Ingrid's mind.

How could I do that? What if she'd died? "I was so proud of myself. Scared at first, but then . . . ." Her voice trailed off. "I thought I was lucky—it was a chance to prove myself." She put her hand over the side of her face, where the swelling made talking difficult. A warming sensation spread across her cheek, under her hand, and she pulled her hand away. *I deserve the pain*.

Hagen rubbed her arm. "You have to decide which way it's going to be," he said plainly. Concern for her sat thickly in his eyes.

Lowering her gaze to the ground, she answered in a small voice, "I know. I could do it, though. I'm stronger than everyone thinks; faster, too."

Hagen bumped her shoulder. "You did well. I was going to jump in right away, but there was no need."

"Humph." A pleased grunt came from her throat as she let her smile fade.

"Let's go catch up to everyone." He pointed to the red and swollen area on her jaw. "You'll have to explain that, though. Better think of how you'll tell the story."

She nodded, too sore for any more words.

They peeked cautiously around the crates before they stood, but the boys hadn't followed them. Ingrid pushed up from the ground, and winced as her back screamed with the movement. Light danced at the edge of her vision, but she trudged after Hagen. He handed her the shield he'd carried for her.

It was light compared to the weight of indecision riding heavily upon her shoulders.

8

When they reached camp, Ingrid walked to her tent and went inside without another word to Hagen. Images of the fight swamped her thoughts: the vibrations of the mallet as it landed on the girl, the look on her face.

Melting to the ground, she pulled her knees up to her chest, and buried her face in them. *What is happening to me? Hagen's right. I can't fight like a shieldmaiden if I stop to heal everyone afterward.* Frustrated, she let out a loud growl and pounded her fist into the hard earth.

"Troubles?" Selby asked as she crawled through the tent door in time to see Ingrid's outburst. "That shield-maker did a great job. I can't believe our shields are so light! Whoa, what's this?" She picked up the mallet, and noticed that all the mud wasn't very mud-like. "Is this blood? Did you fight someone for this? I don't remember you saying you were buying a mallet . . ." Selby rubbed her hand over the rust-colored, crimson and blackish splatters on the mallet, pulling at some of the stickier spots with her fingers. Grimacing, she wiped her hands in the dirt and then on the hem of her skirt.

"I didn't. The shield-maker made it for me." She watched as Selby turned the mallet over and inspected it, momentarily forgetting about the blood on it. "I got in a fight on the way back."

Selby's head snapped up, and she stared at Ingrid with wide eyes. "Are you hurt?" She fell down on her knees in front of her and pushed her hands into Ingrid's hair, searching for any signs of injury beyond the bruise on her jaw. Lowering her voice, she sat back on her heels, and mused, "Or . . . did you heal yourself already?"

"I didn't get hurt, not bad anyway, just a few bruises. The blood is from the girl I was fighting." Selby gaped at her with eyes so wide they seemed able to fall out. "What? You really can't believe that I might be able to defend myself and walk away with fewer injuries?" Ingrid pressed.

"It's not that," Selby said, biting her bottom lip. "It's. Well . . . you've never done it before. That's all. What happened?"

Ingrid relived it all over again as she retold the story. "If Hagen wouldn't have shown up, those boys would have beaten me. I'd be lying in the mud right now. Probably dying," She finished with a blank stare. "What does it mean? Should I have listened to everyone all along?" She wasn't really asking, and Selby didn't answer. "At first, Hagen was angry with me. But after he calmed down, he was kind—a little scared for me even, I think. I'd rather he'd stayed angry."

Selby reached over and took one of Ingrid's hands in her own. "He cares about you and is probably just scared. I'm scared for you, too." She sighed and looked down in her lap for a minute while they sat in silence. "Something is happening to you, and none of us know what it is. You're changing somehow. Until we know more, I think you should be more careful, and maybe . . ." She swallowed hard. "*Maybe*, put aside the shield for a while."

All the air seemed to leave Ingrid's lungs at once, like she'd been hit in the stomach. She'd lost Selby's trust and support. The one person who had always believed in her, and had stood by her side against everyone else. The one person who had promised to train with her, to fight with her. The one person she needed most.

"I need some air." She stood up and left the tent.

She had walked about ten steps when she came upon Hagen and Jorg, standing alone talking. Hagen's back was to her, but Jorg was standing with his legs apart and his hands balled into fists, as if he were ready to jump into a fight. A warrior's expression on his face, he wore tight lips, flared nostrils, and narrowed eyes.

As Ingrid tried to turn and go a different way around them, he called her name, loudly and full of anger.

"Ingrid! Stop walking."

She didn't turn or stop, but picked up her pace a little. Seconds later, she was grabbed by the arm and spun around to meet the angriest face she had ever seen directed at her.

Jorg's eyes almost glowed, as if they were made of molten iron.

Hagen caught up and stood just behind his shoulder. "Let's talk somewhere more private," he said. It wasn't a suggestion. The commotion had drawn the stares of several men who were gawking in their direction.

Jorg nodded, but kept a hold of Ingrid as he followed Hagen.

She tried to pull away as he dragged her along beside him.

"Let go of me, you're hurting my arm."

"No."

Glaring at him, she bit her teeth together so hard she thought one might crack, and yanked her arm to free it. She was rewarded with a tighter grip for her efforts, as well as almost tripping on a log she didn't see.

When they got to the edge of camp, Hagen walked into the trees until he was sure they were out of earshot. When he finally stopped, Jorg let go of Ingrid, and both boys stared at her.

"Why are you even here?" she yelled at Jorg. "Hagen always treats me like the frail little bird Papa thinks I am, but *you*. You have no right. This is none of your business."

Part of her instantly wanted to take it back. Deep down, she was happy that he cared and wanted to keep her safe. But he was wrong, and she wasn't going to show weakness to either of them right then.

"Hagen is my friend. My loyalty to him extends to you," he said through his teeth.

Some of the anger dissipated from his eyes, replaced by flashes of what looked like hurt, causing Ingrid to hesitate in her resolve. Hagen glanced at Jorg then back at Ingrid, but didn't say anything. She looked to the ground and took a deep breath.

Turning her focus to Hagen, she glared at him. "We took care of everything already. Why couldn't you leave this alone? There isn't anything else to talk about."

"You're my sister, whether either of us likes it or not some days; that means I protect you. Right now, the biggest danger to you seems to be you."

"What were you thinking?" Jorg demanded. "You buy a shield and a mallet, then go trotting off through town by yourself? I guarantee those rats have never had the amount of money between them that you spent on your shiny new toys. You're naïve, and it's going to get you killed." He spat the words, then rubbed his temples.

Ingrid grimaced and rolled her bottom lip between her teeth, closing her eyes. She wanted to say she was sorry, that she hadn't thought of it that way, but instead she kept her head down and let the foolishness of her actions go undefended. Too much was happening. Her brain and her heart were a swirl of questions and emotions.

Finally, Hagen broke the silence.

"You need to think about what you really want, and what you are truly capable of. Like I told you earlier: if you want to be a warrior, you can't worry about helping those you hurt. You are caught between two places, Ingrid. Figure out what you want. In the meantime, do not walk around alone." His voice was tender, reminding her of their father.

Hagen had grown up while she was still playing like a child. Pressing her lips together to fight the threat of tears, she only nodded. Hagen reached under her chin and made her face him.

"Promise me."

"I promise," she said. Her bottom lip trembled slightly, but she kept her face dry.

"This is behind us, then. We leave town the day after

tomorrow—none too soon." With that, he walked back to camp.

Jorg started to follow, but stopped next to Ingrid. He leaned down, and his lips brushed against her ear when he spoke, causing her knees to slip like sand on the shore. "You are important to me. And not because of Hagen." He said it too low for Hagen to hear, and then he continued on after his friend.

His lingering scent of fresh grass and woodsy pine made her heart race in a way that the surrounding forest never had. A rush of heat flashed through her body as she walked back to her tent and found Selby still inside. Her shield and mallet were propped against the side of the tent, cleaned.

She apologized to Selby, then told her about the conversation in the woods.

Jorg's statement, she kept to herself, however.

"You know it's because we all love you, right? We want you safe."

Ingrid made a sound between a grunt and a chuckle. "Hagen's right that I don't notice danger; everyone has always kept me safe. But I need to learn to protect myself. That's why I wanted to be here."

"You'll learn. Don't give up. We'll figure this out together."

"Yeah." A commotion of excited voices and the rattle of trenchers outside the tent, penetrated through the walls. "Sounds like it's time for the evening meal. I don't think I can get myself killed helping with *that*."

Pushing off the ground, she groaned. Her stiff shoulder muscles shouted in protest.

One more day, and she would be on her way home. Back to where it was safe and boring. Where she belonged.

After the meal, groups of men sat around the fire talking and laughing, while Ingrid and Selby collected trenchers and put away the skause. As punishment for coming on the trip uninvited, the young girls were made into servants at mealtime. Klaus told them it was initiation, and the girls acted like it bothered them, but in reality, they had fun listening to the bits and pieces of gossip they heard as they moved among the groups.

That night, however, Ingrid kept dropping things, or forgetting what she was doing. Her mind jumped from one issue to the next: the strange woman in the street, the girl she'd fought, the look on that girl's face.

More than anything else, her brother's perfect and handsome friend made her mind swirl. She snuck glances at him, and each time she did, his eyes met hers.

Why is he always looking at me? Why do I always look to see if he is?

It was dark by the time she sat by the fire to warm up before bed. The flames sputtered, flicking sparks into the air to dance like a hundred happy sprites. The smoke bending in the breeze filled the air with smells of pine and ash.

Selby plopped down next to her. "Great choice of where to sit. Not close enough for it to seem as if you are trying to be next to him, but in direct line of sight so you can stare at him without it being obvious. You are learning well, my apprentice."

Ingrid smiled and looked into her lap. "Stop. This is where there was enough room for both me and you."

"Uh-huh. Just accept it—it makes life more enjoyable. Take me, for example. I know that at some point, probably soon, Hagen is going to ask my sister to be his wife. While a part of me gags a little, another part of me says, 'hey, might as well enjoy the view while it's available.'" She nudged Ingrid and continued, "*You* are getting your looks returned. For that, my friend, I envy you."

"You're impossible."

Ingrid dared another glance, and grinned at her knees when she saw the smile returned across the flames.

"What do you think it is? We've known each other a long time. Why now? Part of me doesn't feel ready for this, but the other part wonders what took so long." She glanced at Selby, and they giggled quietly together.

"Well, I don't know. Maybe it's being out here, away from home. The adventure of it all. It's brought out your wild side." Selby laughed and gave Ingrid a slap on the knee.

Ingrid let the words settle in her mind. *What if that's all this is? He's just caught up in the excitement of the trip. I'm being ridiculous, now is not the time to think of these things. We'll see what happens when we get home and then I'll deal with it.*

Selby kept on talking, and Ingrid let the thoughts of Jorg and his intentions toward her bounce around in her brain. More questions came to mind each time she gazed through the yellow and orange glow.

In an attempt to clear her head, she looked up at the

plethora of stars overhead, letting herself become over-whelmed with how small her life was in relation to the heav-ens. When she brought her gaze back down, she caught a glimpse of someone standing by a tent near the tree line.

It was the woman from the street.

She motioned for Ingrid to follow her into the trees, and a tightness seized Ingrid's chest. She nodded her acceptance anyway. The woman turned and disappeared into the dark, and Ingrid clasped her hand over the amber bead hanging from her brooches. It was glowing the same as it had the last time the woman was near.

Interrupting Selby's continued one-sided conversation, Ingrid said vaguely, "I've got to go take care of some business. I'll be right back."

"Do you want me to go with you? It's pretty dark out there."

"No, I'm fine. I'll hurry." She gave Selby a smile and squeezed her arm as she stood to leave.

She looked over at Jorg, and this time, she held his gaze when he met her eyes. With a tip of her chin, she pointed toward the trees. He raised his eyebrows in confusion, but excused himself from the group.

Ingrid waited at the edge of the tree line for Jorg to show up. When he did, her breath jumped into her throat and froze in place. So much for dealing with all of her feelings about him later.

He acted as if he was going to walk by, but stopped and turned right in front of her. They stared at each other for a minute without saying anything. Ingrid was so overwhelmed by his presence, she couldn't form words. Her heart raced like a squirrel scampering up and down a tree, and her hands started to sweat—an impressive feat since they were ice cold.

Jorg took a step closer to her, his face neutral and unreadable. "Some might think it's a bit inappropriate to meet like this." A hint of a grin tugged at his lips.

Ingrid felt the heat rise from her toes to her face in an instant. She let out a nervous chuckle. "I made you a promise, and I'm trying to keep it."

"Promise? How's that?"

"You asked that if I ever saw the woman from the street again, I wouldn't go to her without telling you. Well, she's waiting for me in the trees."

Jorg's face instantly turned solemn and wary. He moved in front of Ingrid, and surveyed the tree line. Ingrid had to force herself not to reach up and touch his strong back as it crowded in front of her.

"I just wanted to let you know that I'm going to meet her now."

Jorg turned and stared down into her face. "No, you're not."

She furrowed her brows and glared at him for a second. "Yes. I am. I only told you to keep my word. You're welcome to wait here if you want."

More emotions than she could process swirled through his eyes. He cupped her face in his hand. "Please, don't go out there alone."

She lost all coherent thought. Swallowing hard, she felt her heart gain speed.

"I have to go. I don't think she means me harm." Somehow she managed to squeak out the words, barely above a whisper.

Keeping his hand on her face, Jorg glanced at the ground then back into her eyes, hesitating at her glowing necklace. "We have already established that you want to see the good in others, whether it's there or not. Your judgment in this can't be trusted."

"That's not for you to decide. I didn't say I thought she was good, I said I don't think she means me harm. You can wait here for me or not."

Jorg smirked. "You've got a feisty side." Cold like a winter wind blew over Ingrid when his hand dropped away.

"I guess so." She raised her eyebrows and jutted out her chin with a tight smile.

"I don't agree with this, but I'll be right here. I have excellent vision and hearing, so call to me if you feel the least bit threatened."

She nodded and knew the feelings in *her* heart had nothing to do with her stowaway adventure. "I will."

Stepping around him, she walked into the trees, not looking back in case she lost her nerve.

The forest reached an intolerable point of darkness. Ingrid was questioning her resolve and considering turning back until the woman stepped out from behind a tree. There was a glow around her that made her easy to see.

Unease washed over Ingrid.

"Hello, Ingrid. I've been waiting a long time to talk with you again."

"Again? Who are you?"

"I'm an old friend of your family. We first met when you were only five years old. I am the one who gave you that bead."

She pointed to the glowing amber bead in the center of Ingrid's necklace.

"Why haven't I seen you before today? I know you were the woman in the street. Why didn't you come up to me?"

"You have special gifts, Ingrid. You are just realizing them. More and more things will happen that will open your eyes to the abilities you hold inside. Embrace them. Not everyone will be happy about what you can do, and you need to be careful who you trust. A beautiful sword cuts as deep as a plain one, do not be deceived. The time is coming, soon, when you will need to help those you love and you must be ready. I will guide you. You must train and learn how to control your powers. Others will try to deceive you and change your path—guard yourself." She smiled and looked toward camp.

"I don't understand. What abilities? What is coming?"

"Your questions will be answered in time. For now, keep your eyes and your heart open, and what you need will come to you."

She reached out and gently rubbed her finger on Ingrid's cheek. An overwhelming sensation of warmth mixed with a torrent of emotions. Then the woman turned and started to walk away.

"Wait, I don't know how to find you. How will you guide me?"

The woman smiled at Ingrid, and, touching her shoulder, looked directly into her eyes.

Wait. How did she get in front of me so fast?

"When the time is right, you will learn how to find me. Know that I'm close and waiting. Now go back to the others.

He worries about you. We will meet again." She nodded over Ingrid's shoulder, making her look back.

No one was there.

When she turned back, neither was the woman.

Alone in the dark, Ingrid suddenly felt cold and scared. Turning back toward the sounds of camp, she hurried as fast as she could, stumbling occasionally but not falling. Just before she reached the tree line, she saw Jorg pacing back and forth where he'd waited for her. She made no attempt at being quiet, and he ran to meet her where she emerged from the darkness.

"Are you alright? Did you see her?" He was touching her hair and her arms, inspecting her for injuries. A giggle bubbled up through her at his efforts and she had to swallow it to keep her composure. His intentions were of genuine concern, but she could feel the heat of his hands on her, and enjoyed it.

He stopped and met her eyes, inhaling deeply, then smiled. His dimple burrowed into his cheek, and Ingrid's insides turned to mush.

"I guess you're alright, then," he said, but didn't move his hands from her arms.

"I'm fine. She was confusing more than anything." Ingrid smiled at him and didn't look away.

For a few seconds that felt like hours, they didn't move.

"We should get back." Before he let her go, he tucked a strand of hair behind her ear.

A streak of fire surged through Ingrid.

Jorg dropped his hands and walked back to the campfire. She stood alone for a moment, unable to move her feet.

Gathering her wits, Ingrid forced herself to return to her tent and to reality.

❧ 9 ❧

The next day, the camp bustled with activity. The shields procured and the meetings over, it was time to pack up and begin the journey home. It would take longer from this direction, as they needed to bypass the falls. Tighter packing was also needed, to make room for the extra food and supplies they had traded for or purchased. Three of the men were still unable to make the journey home because of the broken bones they had suffered during the fight in front of the king's gates on their first day—despite the healing they'd received.

Three of the king's men had volunteered to take their place and fulfill their duties.

With everyone and all the supplies finally loaded, the boats shoved off from the docks in the misty, early chill of the next morning.

It was hard going, rowing against the river every day. Even though it was slow and lazy in appearance, the current rippled under the surface like a giant rug being pulled out from under a table. Ingrid had positioned herself at the point of the bow, as she had on the first trip, so she could watch the horizon. She'd hoped her newfound courage would help her avoid her seasickness, but it did not. Her stomach didn't care what kind of skill she had with a shield or mallet; it refused to enjoy the gentle waves.

The men needed all the help on the oars they could get, so Jorg sat facing her as he rowed in unison with the others. Using him as a distraction from the rolling motion of the boat, she let her mind wander. *Most girls in the village are engaged or married by my age. Why don't I feel ready for that?*

She snapped out of her reverie when she noticed a knowing grin accompanied by the turn-a-stomach-to-porridge dimple directed at her. Finding the horizon line, she willed her stomach to a halt.

That's just what I need to do: throw up all over with Jorg looking at me.

"I saw that," Selby whispered.

"Saw what?"

"You staring and him noticing. He likes you. I'm happy for you."

"It's nothing. I can't think about that kind of thing right now."

"I think you already are." She crossed her arms over her chest. "Besides, if you don't show some interest, he might start looking around. If he wanted to kiss me, I'd let him."

Ingrid's heart paused, and her breath caught. "Mind your own business, and leave him alone." She said it a little harsher and louder than she'd meant, and a couple of the men closest to them glanced their way.

Selby lowered her gaze into her lap and gave a quiet giggle.

"That's what I thought. That made you jealous."

"It didn't. Just stop talking about this."

Ingrid scooted to the edge of the platform, letting her feet dangle and ending the conversation. When they stopped to make camp for the evening, she was all too happy to jump ashore.

Around midmorning of the third day on the river, they had to pull to shore and prepare to move the boats over land to avoid a strong section of rapids. Moving three large, heavy-laden dragon ships would take all-out effort. Everyone pitched in to help.

Ingrid cleared brush and debris away from the base of trees, which several men then worked to topple. Once the trees were felled, Selby worked to remove their branches. Like an unlashed raft, logs lay next to each other, waiting for the boats to pass atop them. Ropes and huge amounts of grunting effort would roll the ships across the ground.

It was more physical work than Ingrid had ever done.

She would wake in the mornings and not remember crawling into bed the night before. Her stiff muscles ached and begged to continue lying against the soft furs, but she hauled herself up to work on time with the others. While she didn't care for the strenuous tasks, she was happy to feel her muscles gaining strength through the exercise.

"Why the smile, Ingrid? Is this work too easy for you?" Her father's teasing voice startled her from her thoughts.

"No, Papa, not even a little. I've never been so sore in my life," she confided. "I was thinking about home."

"Did you enjoy yourself in the city?" he asked.

"It was much different from what I thought it would be."

"Yes, I'm sure it was. I'm also sure you weren't thinking to bring back such a large bruise on your jaw." Ingrid winced, but her father continued. "Hagen explained to me what happened. I understand that you did well."

"He had to help me, though. It—I didn't realize . . . "

She struggled with how to explain how she felt, remembering the look on the girl's face and her slack body as it hit the mud with a splat.

"He was impressed with your fighting skills, but he told me he has concerns about your ability to detach yourself from compassion in the middle of a fight."

"For a long time, I've thought about the excitement of battle, and the stories that are told when a great warrior defeats an enemy. But I never knew the impact of the weapon jars your arm so much it feels as if it will break, or how the smell of blood fills the air. I never understood what it's like to see another coming toward you in a rage." She hesitated and her voice grew quiet. "Or how they look when they fall. It was terrifying, Papa. Not the thrill I expected."

Tired from all the hard labor, she didn't have the strength to hide her true feelings. Not from her father, or from herself. Sadness, regret, disgust, shame; they swirled within her like an eddy in the river.

Nodding his head in agreement, Klaus gently lifted her downcast face to meet his eyes. "I'm happy to hear that it was not a thrill to you. Battles demand injuring or killing others; it is serious business. My sweet Meyla, you do not have the heart to put your feelings aside. I won't tell you that you cannot train with the maidens at home—that's up to you. You have proven yourself capable of it, but now that you know the requirements, search yourself and see if you are *ready*. Make sure it is the right decision, before you go down a path you can't return from."

The warmth in his voice and the gentleness in his eyes made her melt into his chest. Tears spilled onto her cheeks, and she didn't stop them. He held her tight and let her be a child a little bit longer.

When enough logs were laid out, the ships crept along, inch by inch, like snails. Once a log was cleared at the back of the path, it was carried to the front. Ingrid was too short to make a difference on the pulling ropes, and not strong enough to carry the logs, but Selby was helping. Ingrid kept out of the way and wandered along the edge of all the people, alone.

Useless again.

Several days passed at the painfully slow pace. One day, as Ingrid wandered around, offering help with any odd job, a faint odor of rotting flesh pinched her nose. It was coming from off the trail and she ducked between some grasses to investigate. A few feet away, lying in a bed of matted grass was the decaying body of an otter. The flesh was all gone except on the underside, next to the ground. It lay on its back, with all the bones of its skeleton exposed and complete.

She could see its long spine, curved into an S-shape, and the bones of its front flippers, which looked like human hands. She couldn't see any teeth marks or breaks marring the bones and it didn't seem like there had been a struggle.

She remembered the two otters playing on the shore her first day on the boat, and hoped this was a different one—a poor thing that was either old or sick. She said a quick prayer of blessing over the body, then turned back to rejoin the group.

Rushing out of the brush and onto the trail, she found herself rejoining her group's procession behind the three men from Jorvik who had offered their help. Their gravelly voices carried back to her, too deep in their conversation to notice her right away.

"You aren't paid to think. If she's one of them, then they all deserve what's coming for harboring her kind."

"What if she's not?"

"Who cares? We were hired to do a job. We'll need to heat the tar without being noticed—"

The speaker stopped talking as soon as he spotted Ingrid, sparking her curiosity.

Before she could wonder too much about their target, another one barked, "What are you doing this far back in the line, young lady?" He had a voice that sounded like a grinding stone.

"I had to step out of my place for a minute. Is there a problem?"

"No. But you should get back to where you belong."

"I can be wherever I want."

Brazen and bolder than when she left home, Ingrid wasn't afraid of him—even when he took a step toward her. His body reeked of odor, and he was missing most of his teeth.

A cloud of foul stench floated over her when he spoke.

"You're a feisty one, huh? You should add some sense to go with it."

"I'm sure I have more sense than you." Ingrid lifted her chin and stared into his eyes.

"Get movin'," his gruff and even fouler-smelling companion hissed.

Glaring at each of the men, she walked around them and headed for the front, trying to act casual. They did frighten her, and she didn't like the look of them. They were up to something.

What was it they had said? Heat the tar? She couldn't put it together, and didn't want to go to her father like a tattling child, so she walked on.

Later that night, as Ingrid emptied a pail of dirty wash water she heard muted voices near the boats. She snuck toward them, and saw three men hunched on the shadow side of one of the boats, her father's. She crept closer to see what they were doing. In the dark it was hard to make out, but she could see hemp rope in their hands.

She had started to crawl away to get her father, when one of them stood up and stared in her direction. She froze. The voices stopped, and the whole world stood still. In the distance, frogs croaked, and an owl hooted overhead, but Ingrid listened in the direction of the men.

The man that stood up stretched and then crouched back down by the others.

Ingrid let out a long, slow sigh. She lay down on her belly and scooted backwards as slowly and quietly as she could. One of the men was looking around while the other two did something near the bottom of the boat. She couldn't see their faces, but she was sure that they were the ones she had come across earlier. They could be doing some kind of repair, but she didn't believe that—the men she had talked to were not the helpful sort.

The air was heavy, and the ground was damp. She wanted to get up, to go and get someone, but it was as if her limbs were stuck to the mud.

"Ingrid!" Selby's voice rang into the night.

The men froze in the middle of what they were doing. Selby called again, this time a little closer, and the men crouched low and waddled toward the end of the boat. They reached the trees and bolted into cover.

Ingrid could hear the crack of branches and the thud of the men's boots as they ran away from camp. She picked herself up and ran back to Selby and the campfire, leaving the wash bucket abandoned.

When she reached the ring of light offered by the fires, Selby's eyes opened wide. "Where have you been?"

"I went to empty the wash pail, and saw men down by one of the boats. I hid until they were gone."

She looked down at herself and realized the reason for Selby's shock. Mud clung to her from chin to knees. She started to shake as the cold air hit her moist body.

"What were they doing?"

"I don't know, I couldn't see much in the dark."

"Should we tell someone?"

"Let's wait until morning, then I'll tell Papa."

Ingrid's dreams were filled with a sense of dread that night. She tossed and turned in a panic, feeling smothered by her furs.

The next morning was cold with damp fog and a mist that blew across the bending grasses like ghostly smoke. Silvery dew gave everything a slippery cover. A breeze drove the chill to the core of Ingrid's bones. Voices echoed back against the low sky, giving the impression that they were the last humans alive.

The incident with the men the night before was on Ingrid's mind as soon as she woke up. Klaus was hauling supplies to his boat when she found him.

"Papa," she called.

After he set down the heavy box he carried, he walked toward her. "Yes, Meyla?"

"I don't know if it's worth mentioning, but I saw three men by our boat after dark last night."

"Why are you just now telling me?"

"I couldn't see much, and didn't know if I should alarm you. But the men ran off, and I don't see them this morning."

"Tell me exactly what you saw."

Ingrid described the event to her father, and he strode off.

The hulls of all the boats were checked, but nothing out of the ordinary was detected. After the morning meal was eaten, the arduous task of shifting the boats to re-enter the river began.

Sunshine had burned off the foggy haze by the time the first boat slipped into the water. Irritated cranes flew up into the sky, and chattering chickadees scolded from the trees. One by one, each boat floated onto the river in position to sail, and they set the oars to work.

Ingrid lounged on her stomach, her chin resting on the rail while she watched little bugs zig and zag across the top of the water. Then suddenly they were gone.

She rolled over to see the oar workers struggling against bubbling water. They were entering a small set of rapids. Ingrid suddenly understood where the zippy little bugs had gone—straight into her stomach. She could feel them bouncing around, as if they'd been caught in a jar with no escape.

Remembering the techniques she'd been taught, she put her head down between her knees and measured her breath carefully. In through her nose, slowly out her mouth, counting. In one, two, three, four; out two, three, four. She kept her eyes closed, but not scrunched tight, and insisted to her hands that they not keep a death grip on her skirts.

The jostling picked up, and the boats had to spread out to keep the oars from crossing. From her vantage point, Ingrid was unaware of anyone else, focused only on her breathing. She imagined herself floating through the air like a butterfly when that daydream was suddenly popped by a commotion near the center of the boat.

Ingrid sprang to her feet in instant panic. Wide-eyed, she watched the flurry of activity as people started shoving barrels and crates away from the ship's center. Horrified, she saw what had caused the alarm: water was coming into the boat.

First it was a small seeping, but then there was a loud crack, and bubbling cones of water came through the bottom like fountains. Everyone grabbed whatever they could lift and threw it overboard to lighten the load. Within minutes, it was clear the boat was sinking anyway. It started to lurch from side to side, and people moved about, trying to save what they could. From the corner of her eye, she saw Jorg and Hagen push their way toward where she was.

Where's Selby?

Without warning, the boat was on its side; people, barrels, crates, ropes, shields, and weapons all spilled into the swift, icy river.

Ingrid caught a quick breath, and then she was tossed underwater. It was impossible to tell which way was up as her arms and legs flailed, and her long tunic and apron twisted around her, fighting to keep her under. Murky darkness surrounded her and blocked all sight.

Something hard and unforgiving banged against her head. Grasping for anything, her fingers found leverage on some type of wood, and she latched onto it with all her might. Determined, she pulled herself above the surface, and heaved her body onto the top of a broken crate. Most of her body still dangled underwater. Light danced in and out of her vision as she coughed up the gritty, foul-tasting water from her lungs. Exhausted, she could hear voices behind her, but did not dare let go of her support.

Oh, my head hurts . . . Hagen and Selby, that's who's calling me. I'll just rest a minute, and then I'll swim to them.

She closed her eyes, and drifted in the current, farther away from the others.

Bright light pierced Ingrid's eyes from beyond her closed lids, and she blinked them open against the unfamiliar sunshine.

The scent of honey and jasmine floated in the air as she lay in grass under a beautiful tree, with leaves that looked like they were made of glass—their thin edges tinkling together in the slight breeze to form a sweet melody.

As confusing as it was, she felt only contentment. Watching the beams of light throw green sparkles through the magical leaves, she wanted to sink down into the soft grass and stay for hours.

"Hello, Ingrid. I didn't expect to meet you so soon."

A gentle, dreamy voice came from her right. It took great effort to roll her head away from the beauty in front of her. Crossed-legged a few feet away sat a young girl with luscious, flowing, golden hair that spilled onto the grass around her. Not much older than Ingrid, her eyes were a brilliant sapphire blue and crinkled with her welcoming smile.

"I'm happy you are here, but we don't have much time."

Ingrid pulled herself up on her hip, propping one arm on the thick green ground beneath her. "Where is here?"

"Asgard."

She looked at the young woman with wide eyes, and pushed herself to her knees. Her mouth was suddenly dry, and her heart raced like a rabbit for its den.

"Asgard? Am I . . . dead?"

Smiling again and shaking her head, the woman assured her, "No, sweet girl. I've brought you here so I can explain a few things before you go back." She took hold of one of Ingrid's hands.

Where are my gauntlets? My hands don't feel cold.

"My name is Hnossa. I'm your guardian. You have special gifts, Ingrid, gifts that we have not seen in a millennia. Long ago, it was foretold that one would come who possessed the ability of sight as well as healing. One greater than Groa, wife of the morning star. That person would be necessary to stop a great tragedy in Asgard and Midgard, which could change the future for both worlds. You are that person, my dear."

Stunned, Ingrid sat frozen.

I must be dreaming. This can't be real.

"It is real, very much so, and I need you to listen. We haven't much more time," Hnossa said.

"I didn't speak aloud."

"Yes, I am sorry to intrude, but it is important that you learn who you are and what you must do." Releasing Ingrid's hand, she tucked a strand of hair away from her face and took a deep breath. "I wish I could tell you this in a gentler way, but it is not possible. There is a movement underway by unknown forces that threatens to destroy all the realms. You must develop your gifts, and stop them before they finish their task."

A cold chill skittered down Ingrid's spine.

"You must be mistaken. I can't do anything great. I can't be who you're searching for." She clenched and released her fists, clenched and released. She gasped in quick, shallow breaths.

"I know this must frighten you, but I am here to help you. You are not meant to be a shieldmaiden that is true, because your destiny is something so much more. You are the key to our survival, the only one who can correct the imbalance of our worlds. Develop your skills, but guard yourself. The abilities you own are powerful—there will be those who will want to use you for their own selfish gain. Be wary of those who speak in the shadows. We will see each other again."

Every muscle in Ingrid's body tensed. That was what the woman in the woods had told her, also. *How can this be?*

Before she could ask any questions, Hnossa pressed an index finger to Ingrid's forehead. Instantly she was freezing, wet, and terrified.

10

Back in the water, clinging to the crate lid, Ingrid tightened her grip on the rough edge, choking and coughing as the icy river sloshed over her face. The current tossed her small body as if it were a reed pulled from the root, and the rush of water muffled all sounds. Numbed hands made it hard to keep her grip. Pinching her eyes shut, she waited for her watery grave.

Seconds later, though, the swirling water subsided, and she floated calmly along. Seemingly tired of its own anger, the river pushed her toward the shore.

Eventually bumping against the soft mud and spongy reeds, she lay her cheek on the slippery wood and allowed her body to relax. Freezing, her teeth started clacking together as she rolled off the board. Using her elbows, she pulled herself up the bank and onto the mucky shore. Her lungs burned as she coughed up the slimy water she'd swallowed. Mud squished between her fingers and the smell of rotting leaves filled her nose. Insects buzzed around her ears and frogs croaked close by. Ingrid sat up but couldn't see over the reeds. Gray clouds covered the sun, muting all color and pressing cold further into her core. Her tunic was twisted around her legs, and she bent over to work them free.

A pungent, acrid smell burned the hairs of her nose, and Ingrid froze. Sucking sounds came from beyond the reeds, as if something moved toward the edge of the water. Biting down on her bottom lip, she kept as quiet as possible. Multiple sucking sounds told her that more than one body was getting closer by the second.

Hunched over, she tried to spy a quiet way out of the reeds. As she looked, the air grew thick like cold gravy. Nothing made a sound; it was as if the whole world held its breath.

Something warm and slimy dropped onto the back of her neck, and she instantly retched at the smell. She flailed around to get to her feet, but found herself lifted up and hanging sideways.

A spindly yet strong arm pressed her into a soft, sticky body. Heat rose off the form like a fog, blanketing all of Ingrid's senses, except the need to vomit. Fluids poured from her eyes and nose in response to the smothering fumes of rotten eggs and dead fish. Her insides compressed as thick, gooey slime oozed over her, and slid down her neck and into her hair.

Not even the Stinks are this disgusting.

Whatever had ahold of her met up with the others she'd heard moving, and they began to speak in a language she didn't understand. Their voices gurgled like boiling stew, and she could hear the dribbling of liquid as the words left their mouths.

Whoever, whatever, these creatures were, they were repulsive.

Breathing as shallowly as possible, not daring to open her mouth, Ingrid allowed herself to dangle along, bouncing into the squishy being, until she was dropped onto the ground, landing on her hands and knees with a splat. She tried to stand, but her feet slipped in the sticky mess all around her, and she plopped onto her backside. Lifting her hands, she watched as the sticky ooze rose with them, strings of the stuff stretching and clinging to every part of her like glue. She had to fight the bile rising into her throat every second.

Hair plastered to her face with slime, covering her right eye, she opened the other gingerly. What she found was a sight she was thoroughly unprepared for. Before her were three of the ugliest creatures, she'd ever seen. Not in any story that Hagen had ever told her, even when he'd been trying to scare her in the dark, had such vile, putrid creatures been described.

They towered over her as they stood in the shadows of several birch trees, their long, greasy, moss-colored hair falling over hunched shoulders. Each face was full of warts and moles alongside long, prominent noses that dripped long, stringy cords of snot onto their bare, rotund chests. Wide, frog-like mouths quirked up into fiendish grins as they stared up and down every inch of her. Ragged pants were visible from under their overhanging bellies, ripped at the ankle, exposing large, hairy feet. Between the four fingers or three toes on each appendage oozed more of the sticky slime. It leaked from their pores and caused trails along the ground wherever they shuffled their feet, the same, sickly yellow color as their skin.

Ingrid wiped her mouth against her shoulder, with little success. "Who are you?"

She would have held her nose to block the smell, but her hands were so covered in the stench and slime, she didn't dare bring them to her face.

The one closest to her spoke in the language she couldn't understand, then looked at her as if it was waiting for an answer.

"I can't understand you. My name is Ingrid, if that's what you are asking."

"You must excuse our use of the old language. We have not come across humans in a long time," the same one spoke as before. "My brothers and I have been away, but it is good to be back." His voice scratched like a wheel without oil and burrowed into Ingrid's ears. "Ingrid, you say is your name?"

She nodded. "Yes, and who are you?"

"Ah, a name is powerful. I will not give up mine as easily as you. We are trolls from the underground. From where do you hail, young Ingrid?"

"I live farther up the river, in a small village. If you allow me to pass, I will catch up to the others I belong with, and be away from your home."

"Oh, this is not our home. And we think it would be best for you to journey with us instead."

Feeling queasy from more than the smell now, Ingrid tried to devise a plan to rush past the large beings and hurry along the shore. They didn't look quick enough to keep up with her, especially if she darted through the small brush.

Finally, my size might be an advantage over an enemy.

Turning to his companions, the leader said something in

his strange tongue, and they stepped forward faster than Ingrid would have thought possible, grabbing each of her arms.

"Let me go," she wailed.

Not turning his head, the beast called back to her, "You will continue along with us for now."

With that, the conversation was over, and no matter what she said, or how hard she kicked, she was trapped, the sticky slime cementing her between her captors in the most disagreeable way.

Overloaded with sensory input, her head swirled, and, stuck as she was between the simmering bodies, she shivered with cold. Gooseflesh rubbed against her tunic, still wet from the river. Even though the late afternoon sun hid behind the clouds, the trolls clung to the shadows, making the cool breezes more frigid. Somewhere, Ingrid had lost one of her gauntlets.

Probably in the river.

As afternoon turned to evening and then to night, the trolls became more and more animated. Darkness was their sanctuary. Finally, they stopped and built a campfire, which Ingrid sat as near to as she dared, her chattering teeth and blue fingers happy for the warmth.

"Where are we going? I think I have a right to know," she said when the chill had eased.

"You will make a good servant, we think. We are taking you home to see. If you don't work out, oh well. None the worse for us." The two that never spoke to her made gurgling noises that she took for amusement. "It is time for fun now," the leader declared.

All three got up and walked into the night, talking among themselves and leaving Ingrid alone by the campfire.

I should run, but which direction?

She stood and turned in a slow circle, trying to get her bearings. The landscape had not been familiar to her all day, and a sinking feeling washed over her.

That's why they don't need to worry about leaving me here untied. I can't go anywhere, anyway.

She sat back down with force and thought about her options.

The trolls were obviously happiest at night. Even during the day, she'd noticed that they never strayed into the light, always staying in the shadows as they walked. Hagen used to tell her and Selby stories when they were little, tales about how trolls couldn't stand the light.

How did those stories go? Light and what? Ugh, I need to figure this out.

Standing up and pacing, she urged herself to remember.

It burns or turns them to stone or something . . . that's it! If I can make it 'til morning, then maybe I can work them into the light, and it might give me a chance to run.

The breeze blew from behind her and brought with it the foul smell of rotten eggs. The trolls were on their way back.

Ingrid sat down by the fire again, fidgeting with her fingers while her mind raced with possible escape routes.

The trolls crashed back to the campfire holding several dead rabbits, which they threw at Ingrid's feet.

"Prepare those for our supper, girl," the leader snarled.

"I don't have a knife."

"Use your hands. You have those."

"I can't. You must prepare them yourself, or give me a knife." Ingrid stood and faced the looming monster.

After they talked in their gurgling language, the shortest of the three glared at her and spit words in her direction, then grabbed the rabbits and walked away from the fire. Ingrid sat back down and faced the flames, willing herself not to smile.

Not long after, the roasting meat sent a spasm to Ingrid's stomach. She hadn't realized how hungry she was until the sweet smell overpowered the stench of troll, and made her mouth water. When it finished cooking, she ignored her own stench and filthy fingers, and tore into the meat with troll-style ferocity.

Devouring the meat, she continued to think. She smiled. *Maybe all those years of enduring Hagen's teasing will come in handy.* It had to be good for something. "Yum, rabbit and mead, nothing better!" she raised her hand in a mock salute to the trolls, as if she held a horn of mead.

The slurping stopped as the trolls stared at her. Drool and slime hung from their fingers as they held pieces of meat halfway to their mouths.

"You don't have any mead," the leader pointed out. The others peered at her sideways.

Ingrid raised her eyebrows. "I do, it's right here." She took another sip. "What? Oh, you want some, too?"

The leader eyed her with a menacing scowl, but the other two nodded their heads with enthusiasm. Ingrid made as if she were going to pass her "horn" to them, but hesitated.

"It's magical mead, you know. I can't just give it to you. You have to earn it."

The two gurgled at her and gestured for her to share.

She pulled the horn to her shoulder and shook her head. "No. If magical mead is not earned, terrible things will happen."

"How did you get it? I didn't see you do anything to earn it," the leader said.

"Oh, but I did. I earned it a long time ago, and now, I can have it whenever I want." She raised her eyebrows and let out a sigh. "I wish I could share with you, I really do."

"What do we have to do to earn it?" As eager as the other two, the leader leaned forward, his eyes bright with anticipation.

"Well, let's see. There are feats of strength, stealing from a dragon, performing magic, or winning a game of wits. At least, those were the choices offered to me when I earned mine." She took another drink from her invisible cup, and licked her lips.

Wide-eyed, the smallest troll mimicked her by rolling his long, pointed tongue along his wide, amphibious lips. Ingrid clenched her teeth together to control her gag reflex, while a pained smile stayed plastered on her lips.

"What did you choose? Surely, we can do anything you did." The spokesman stood and put his hands on his hips.

Gurgles erupted from the other two as they talked over each other. The leader joined in, and Ingrid sat back, waiting as they argued amongst themselves for a few minutes. When they stopped talking, they all faced her, and the leader spoke again. "We will tell you our choice when you tell us what you chose."

"Magic." A genuine smile and a cock of her eyebrow kept the three silent as they stared.

Their meal forgotten, they looked at each other, and arguing broke out once again. The hissing, gurgling, and spitting that accompanied their language was impossible to understand, but Ingrid picked up on a couple repeated words.

Names. I bet those are their names. Interesting.

"We don't believe you. If you could do magic, you wouldn't stay with us. You are lying."

Ingrid stood up, her mouth a tight line of white, and her eyes narrowed as she huffed air in and out through her nose. Warmth spread throughout her chest when the leader flinched and the others took a step backward. "How dare you accuse me of lying? Now you have insulted my honor, and I won't share with you at all."

"Well, it's too late. You have made the offer, and we can make our choice and still have it." The troll poked out his bottom lip, his eyes darting back and forth while he shifted his weight from one foot to the other. "If you can do magic, prove it."

"You dare to challenge me?" Ingrid forced herself to stand tall, clenching her fists so they wouldn't see the tremble in her hands. *Now what? I don't know any magic.* She sucked in a quick breath as an idea popped into her thoughts. The trolls were all shifting on their feet and making grunting noises from their throats. "Are you sure you want to do that?" she asked and stared at the two weaker ones, who looked from their leader to her and back again.

"Yes." It was a statement, but the tone no longer held the menace it had before.

"Fine. Do you see this mark on my face?" She tilted her

head and allowed them to look at the mottled purple bruise on her jaw. They all nodded at her. "Watch."

She closed her eyes and laid her hand on her face, covering the area. Concentrating, she felt her hands grow hot, and a pleasing warmth settled into the skin below her palm. There was a tingle at the same time that reminded her of the time she'd snuck a kitten into her bed and it had slept next to her face, purring.

It ended too soon. When the sensation faded away, she opened her eyes and pulled her hand away from her face, knowing that the bruise was healed.

Another eruption of chatter between the three trolls gave Ingrid time to regain her composure. The bliss she'd felt while the healing took place left her swaying and drowsy. "I've proved myself, now state your choice."

The troll in charge turned away from the others, and they all stood silent. "We are no longer in agreement."

"That is a problem for you, then. If you can't choose, I will do it for you . . . I choose a game of wits. I will make up a riddle, and you try to guess what it means."

"No, you could trick us and change the answer."

"I've already proven that I don't lie." She gave them a smug grin. "We can make it easier, if you need it. How about I answer a question that only you would know the answer to?"

All the trolls laughed and jumped up and down with excitement, causing an unfortunate explosion of flatulence. A particularly ripe gust floated toward Ingrid.

Ugh. I didn't think they could be more revolting. "So it's agreed?" A sour taste coated her tongue from the fug that hovered in the air. Her stomach wobbled, and her jaw muscles clenched as saliva built up behind her teeth, but she swallowed hard and spoke again. "I choose to guess your names."

For a second, there was total silence. Then a roar of laughter from all three made her turn her head away to avoid the drops of slime that flew from their mouths like sparks from a campfire.

"You will never guess. That was a poor choice, but we are sure to win now, so go ahead." The leader's eyes were bright and glistening with his anticipated victory.

Ingrid paced in front of the fire and tapped her chin with her fingers as if she were thinking. The trolls giggled and danced around. She turned and faced them.

"I've got them."

None of the trolls moved, and even the breeze seemed to hold its breath.

"Borku."

She said it slowly and deliberately, watching their response.

"Forgo."

"Stop!" the troll who had done all the talking screamed, while the other two howled as if in agony.

Their dancing turned to writhing and bouncing into each other. The screams and howls grew louder until the largest one stopped. His eyes rolled into the back of his head, and his body shook violently. The middle troll fell to the ground and rolled back and forth, and the smallest stood still, ragged breaths heaving in and out of his chest.

At first, Ingrid thought they were acting dramatic because they didn't want to lose. Then a horrendous popping sound rang out. She wanted to run, but her wobbly legs wouldn't allow it.

The largest troll shrieked and exploded, blowing Ingrid to the ground. Seconds later, the middle troll emitted an even louder roar, and went the way of the other one, turning into a cloud of debris. The remaining troll spun in circles, screaming in confusion, before he took off at a run straight for Ingrid.

She was on her hands and knees, and he tripped on Ingrid's huddled form, knocking the wind out of her and sending them both flying several feet away. The troll rolled when he hit the ground and landed back on his feet, barely breaking stride as he kept running.

Ingrid watched as he disappeared into the trees, and gulped air back into her lungs. Standing, she forced her legs to run in the opposite direction.

11

Gulping huge amounts of air, Ingrid's chest heaved from her uncontrolled, panicked flight.

Pull yourself together. They will not find you again, they are . . .

She couldn't finish the thought as bile rose into the back of her throat. Having no idea where she was or what direction she was heading as she stumbled through the darkness, she kept moving. No plan—other than to put as much distance as she could between her and the trolls—spurred her forward.

When she tripped for the third time, landing again on her battered knees, she stopped.

I need to wash, and I can't think in the fog of this troll stench.

While she tried to breathe through her mouth and come up with a plan, a sound echoed through the brush behind her. Still as a deer, she sat and listened. It came again, distinct and deliberate. Something was getting closer to her, whether animal or another troll, she wouldn't wait to find out. Having had the rest and time to gather her wits, she kept the moon behind her left shoulder and headed—she hoped—west.

Her mother had taught her how to use the stars as a guide at night, showed her how to find the North Star and several constellations to mark positions. It occurred to Ingrid that she didn't know how her mother came to know such things. For that matter, she didn't know much about her mother at all, never having taken the time to see her as anything other than the woman who loved and took care of her. A sudden tightness gripped her chest.

Curling one arm around her middle, she pushed away thoughts of home and hurried her pace. A break in the undergrowth allowed her to see her surroundings clearer and move faster, without the scratches from broken branches and thorns. Peeking out from a cloud, where it had been playing hide-and-seek, the moon illuminated the open ground, giving Ingrid a chance to stop and get her bearings. There wasn't any sound of running water, so she figured she must be too far from the river to make it there in the darkness, and she couldn't smell anything familiar past the rotten-egg scent of troll.

Deciding to continue on her original path, she walked only a few steps before she heard movement inside the brush from where she had emerged. As fast as she could, she ran ahead through the clearing, diving into a thick clump of brush and scampering on her hands and knees until she found a place she could get on her feet.

Before she could take a full step, however, a body slammed into her from behind, knocking her to the ground.

Screaming, she wiggled and punched out at her attacker, connecting once and causing a loud grunt and an increase in the pressure against her.

"Get off of me!" she yelled, turning herself sideways so she could lash out again with a leg and a fist.

"Ingrid?" a familiar voice asked and rolled away from her. "Ouch. Stop kicking."

When the pressure on top of her lifted, Ingrid pushed off the ground and rushed forward on her hands and feet like a bear. Hearing her name didn't register at first, and when it did, she stumbled and lost her balance, falling on her elbow against a rock. Standing, she turned around to face whoever it was.

The light was dim inside the undergrowth, and she could only make out the shape of something—human, she hoped—heading toward her. Then a second one emerged and bolted toward her.

Ingrid lowered herself into a fighting position despite the pain in her elbow.

"Ingrid, we found you!" Selby's voice rang out, and Ingrid wilted, scooped into a hearty hug by her best friend. Almost as quickly, she was pushed away as Selby groaned.

"I know, I smell like a midden heap," she said with a scrunched face.

"You walk with trolls, you smell like trolls," Hagen said, laughing, from where he and Jorg stood behind Selby.

Ingrid grunted. "Not something I intended to do, I assure you. Nor do I ever want to see one again, thank you very much."

"I can't believe trolls are here. I've heard stories of them, but never heard of anyone seeing any in recent times," Jorg said.

"They haven't been around. They told me that they had

been away, and I was the first human they had seen in a long time."

"You spoke with them?" Jorg asked, a curious expression on his face.

"Yes. Only one spoke in a way I could understand; the others used their 'old language,' whatever that is."

"Why don't we go back to the clearing, where we can see better and there's more space," Selby suggested, giving Ingrid a sheepish grin.

"Where I can stand downwind, you mean."

"I was trying to be nice about it, but *ugh*, you stink. I want to hear how you ended up with those disgusting things in the first place."

They fought their way back through the thickets to open ground, and Ingrid moved so she stood against the breeze.

"How's this? Am I more tolerable if I stand over here?"

"That's fine. We should get a fire started and get warm before you start to tell of your adventure. This looks like a good spot to spend the rest of the night, anyway," Hagen said.

Always in charge. "Are we far enough away from the other one, do you think? One ran away." Ingrid wasn't sure if she felt comfortable stopping before daylight.

"We found the broken crate along the river with your footprints and followed the trail. The trolls aren't careful enough to cover their tracks. When we caught up with you earlier, we fell back to decide how to get you away from them and then we heard the noises. The survivor ran in the other direction, so we'll be safe here," Jorg assured her. She gave him a weak smile and nodded acceptance.

After they gathered wood and got a good fire going, Ingrid

sat on the downwind side, continually waving smoke out of her face. The others sat huddled on the other side, as far away from her as they could get.

"Are we anywhere near the river?" she asked. "I would rather plunge myself into the cold water right now than keep smelling like this or fighting this smoke."

"I'm afraid not. We'll have to work our way closer to it in the morning," Hagen told her.

"Alright. I don't suppose you have a flask of water or anything that I could use to at least wipe some of this off?" Even to her own ears she sounded whiny, but fatigue had caught up to her.

"Here, you can use my hangerok, it's still damp from being in the water earlier," Selby said and unpinned her apron, handing it around the fire to Ingrid.

Wiping her face and neck, her mood was instantly relieved without the stinging stench of rotten eggs assaulting her nose, and the breeze cooling her cleaned, damp skin.

"That feels better." A sigh escaped while she worked at getting more goo out of her hair.

"Can you tell us what happened?" Hagen asked.

"Well, let's see. I was onboard the boat, and then I was fighting to keep my head out of the water."

"We think the boat was sabotaged from those men you saw, but it was checked before being put into the river, so that's just our guess. We came after you right away so we don't really know," Hagen said.

"Oh."

"It was worth it, don't worry about us. Just tell us what

happened," Selby said and gave Hagen a disapproving glance with a quick slap on his shoulder.

Taking a couple slow breaths and waving the smoke away, she told them, "The trolls found me along the shore almost as soon as I crawled out of the water. I didn't know what they were, and couldn't see—their smell made my eyes water so bad."

"They didn't hurt you, did they?" Jorg interrupted with a look on his face that pleaded for the answer to be no.

Ingrid smiled at him. "No. They carried me for a while, and then crowded me between them while we walked. I couldn't help getting their muck on me, even before the end. I kept thinking of how to escape, then while we were eating," Ingrid shuddered at the memory of the slime-soaked rabbit she'd devoured in her hunger, "I remembered the time you teased Selby and me about having magical bread. How you made us do all kinds of stupid stuff to 'earn' ours." A smile broke across her face, squishing her cheeks into her eyes. "I convinced them I had magical mead, and that I would share it if they earned it. I thought maybe if I won, they would let me go. I suggested that we play a game where I would tell them their names. I'd listened to them talk among themselves enough that I thought I had them figured out . . . I didn't know it would destroy them." Staring blankly into the fire, she let silence take over.

"We heard something loud, almost like thunder," Selby said in a low voice.

"Their bodies shook, they roared, and then . . . " She opened her hands and swept them into a wide arc.

"That sounds horrible." Selby put her hands over her mouth and wrinkled her nose.

Ingrid fidgeted with Selby's apron, still trying to wipe sludge off herself. "How long do you think it will take to get to the river in the morning?"

"Not too long. We can head there first thing before we start for home. A bath would be a good idea for all of us," Jorg said with a wink.

Ingrid lifted the cloth to her face again, stifling a groan of embarrassment.

"Can we follow the river and meet up with the boats again?" Selby asked, and Ingrid was grateful for the change in subject.

"The boats will be too far away by now to reach on foot, and I think we should get away from the river. We would do better to pick our way through the forest and the moors than run into any more slime monsters," Hagen said.

"Do you think anyone from home might be searching for us? Maybe we should stay by the water so they can find us," Ingrid said.

"They'll search around where the boat went down, but you were washed too far away for them to find us," Hagen answered.

"I agree. If we head north and turn west in about three days, we should come to the village about three more days after that. I traveled through this area once with my father," Jorg said.

"So tomorrow, we wash and then we walk." Selby shook her head in agreement with the plan. "For now though, I don't know about you guys, but I want to keep the fire bright and make sure that other troll doesn't come back around."

"Little Ugly wasn't the bravest of them," Ingrid said without emotion, watching the flames of the fire dance.

"Little Ugly?" Selby asked with a snort.

Ingrid looked up at her and grinned. "That's the one that ran away." She let the smile grow on her face, and bit her bottom lip before she added, "He was also the most disgusting. He farted more than Hagen." She laughed at her own joke, and Selby joined her when Hagen threw a small clump of mud at Ingrid.

Hearing the laughter of her friends made Ingrid believe that everything would work out, and they would make it back home.

The night was clear, and millions of stars blinked over the camp like a sparkling blanket. Ingrid lay on her back watching them. She should sleep, she knew, because she would need rest for the walk home, but she couldn't. When she closed her eyes, she either saw trolls or the images from her vision on the river. As hard as she tried, she couldn't tell anymore if it was real or something she dreamed while nearly drowning.

Something small hit her in the arm, and she brushed at it, thinking it was a bug. Another something hit her under the chin, which she grabbed and realized was a piece of twig, and not the spider she had feared. Sitting up, she saw Jorg smiling at her.

"You're supposed to be asleep," he said.

"How do you know I wasn't, and you didn't just wake me up?"

"I guess I don't. Do you normally sleep with your eyes open? Because that would be strange."

She narrowed her eyes at him in mock annoyance, then scooted closer so their voices wouldn't wake the others. "I can't sleep."

"You've been through a lot."

"I can take watch, if you want to rest," she offered. *Please stay awake and talk with me.*

"Nah, I'm not able to sleep either."

They sat in silence for a while, content as they kept the fire stoked. The worries and fears that had plagued Ingrid earlier slipped away.

"Do you know much of the nine realms?" she asked, twiddling a small stone in her hands.

"I don't know. As much as anyone, I suppose. Why do you ask?"

"Hagen knows more about them than me. Papa tells the stories of all the gods and their worlds, and he's paid more attention than I have. I know who the gods are of course, but not much about the realms themselves. Do you think a human can go to any of them?"

"I don't know, probably not. Some of them wouldn't be possible, like Muspelheim or Niflheim—they are all fire or mist—but with the others, I don't know if a human could travel there."

"What about Asgard—the Bifrost connects it to our realm, right? Isn't that why it was made?"

"First, Heimdall controls the Bifrost, and he wouldn't open it to humans, I'm sure of that. It's a road only the gods travel. Second, and most important, no god or goddess would allow a human to enter their world. What's this all about, anyway?" He glanced sideways at Ingrid, then back to the fire.

"I don't know. Nothing, I guess." She let it drop. *It had to be a dream.*

"Do you think that's what's bringing the old things back here? Like the trolls? Because I've been trying to figure that out, too."

"Yes, that's partly it." Images of the beautiful woman and her sweet voice from the river haunted Ingrid's memories. *She seemed so real. But was she?*

They continued in silence again, then Jorg reached over and took Ingrid's hand, the bare one, and rubbed it between his large hands. "Did you lose the gauntlet for this one?" he asked. "I can't believe how cold your hands get."

"I don't know if I lost it in the water or after," she answered distractedly as she watched his hands caress hers.

"Maybe we should tear off the bottom of your apron and wrap that around your hand—would that help, do you think?"

Jolted from her dreamy stare, she flashed a quick grin. "Probably, I didn't think of that." Reaching into the purse attached to the belt around her waist, she found her scissors, and cut a wide strip from her apron. "I forgot I had these. The trolls wanted me to prepare the rabbits they caught for dinner, but I didn't have a knife, so they made the smallest one do it." She chuckled. "I'm glad they didn't make me empty my bag."

"You don't have a knife?"

"No, *that* I lost in the river."

Pulling a knife from his boot, Jorg handed it to Ingrid. "Take this one. You should never be without something to defend yourself."

"What will you do if I take this one?" She took it from him even as she asked the question.

Smiling, he shook his head. "Don't worry, I have more."

"Oh." She turned the knife over in her hands. The bone handle had beautiful carvings in it, and supported a blade about as long as Ingrid's hand. "Did your father make this? The carvings are so intricate." Swirls of vines and leaves twisted in a delicate lace pattern on both sides of the handle.

"No, I made that one. When I was younger, I used to get into a lot of trouble for wasting time, dulling blades by making shapes and designs on things. Now, my father uses my creations to get a better price for his ironwork. It's funny, because I never got the hang of forging, though my father has tried to teach me, but making the handles and doing the carvings, that comes naturally."

Ingrid watched his face as he spoke, noting the sadness that crossed his features as he talked about his father. She'd heard his story from Hagen once.

Orphaned, Jorg had been found as a baby in the forest by the woman he knew as his mother. With no children of her own, she brought him home, and convinced her husband to keep him, even though he believed Jorg was a changeling left by the faeries. They later bore several daughters, but no sons, and his father reluctantly accepted a relationship with him.

"It's beautiful, thank you." She gave him a smile before tucking the knife into her belt.

"Here, let me help with that." Jorg took the strip of fabric from Ingrid and gently wrapped it around her wrist and up over her hand, tucking it at the end to keep it in place. "That should hold for a while," he said, but he didn't let go of her hand, and she didn't pull it away.

Never had her heart beat so fast, and as she smiled, an involuntary shiver rattled through her limbs.

"Are you cold?" Jorg asked.

Not waiting for an answer, he scooted around to Ingrid's side and tucked her under his arm. Instant heat flushed her face as she enjoyed the sensation of his strong arm around her shoulders.

Unsure of how to respond, she sat very still until Jorg pulled her closer to him, and she let herself sink into his side. Letting her last view be the dance of the flames in the dark night, Ingrid closed her eyes, her heartbeat calm and steady, all thoughts of their situation or what lay ahead of them lost in the peaceful moment.

Twittering birds in the still, gray, early morning dawn teased Ingrid awake. Stretching, she yawned. She was thankful for the sleep, but stiff from lying on the hard ground. The birds were the only sound, as the rest of the group had not yet started to stir; even Jorg had found sleep at last, over on his own cloak.

When did you go back over there? A smile spread across her face as she remembered the feeling of being close to him.

She was eager to find a place along the river to wash. The odor coming off of her body burned her eyes like skunk vapor, and she felt sticky all over. Reaching out her foot, she nudged Jorg's boot.

"Ingrid, it is not nice to wake a man who only just fell asleep."

"Well, it's not nice to tell a girl there's a place to take a bath, and not show her where it is, either."

He smiled before opening his eyes. Taking a deep breath, he sat up and stretched. "Is it only me that has to take this abuse? You're just going to let those logs continue to be useless?"

She looked over at the other sleeping forms, then pumped her eyebrows at Jorg with a mischievous grin. She tossed Selby's soiled apron over Hagen's face, and then dropped to her knees next to Selby, giving her a hug.

"Good morning," she said in a singsong voice.

Hagen and Selby both pushed from the ground in a hurry, muttering unkind words in her direction. When everyone was up, they kicked dirt over the fire, then followed Jorg into the bushes.

They reached the river about an hour later, and Selby announced that the girls would wash first; no one objected.

"You guys take off for a while, and find a good spot to build a fire, where we can dry our clothes and get warm."

"Bossy," Hagen said, turning back toward the way they came. "You'd better be wearing your clothes when we get back."

Jorg laughed. "We'll get the fire ready. Come on, Hagen. Let the princesses have their baths." Hagen snorted and followed him away from the water.

Ingrid smiled, but wasted no time in getting her filthy clothes off and jumped into the freezing water.

"Oooh. This. Is. So. Cold," she said between shivers.

"Wash fast," Selby answered before scrubbing her face and neck while standing on the bank.

Ingrid scrubbed as well as she could and then pulled her soiled clothes into the water with her, doing her best to rub off the gunk. Climbing onto the bank, she slipped her wet shift over her head, then wrapped only her apron around her, not wanting to put the heavier tunic on before it could dry.

"Can you see through this?" she asked and turned a slow circle for Selby to look it over.

"That works. Hopefully the fire is huge so you dry fast."

Grabbing Ingrid's other wet clothes, they hurried back to the boys. High over the fire, a flat rack was already built and waiting to dry the clothes. The fire was burning well, and the girls crouched in front of it as soon as they arrived.

"Thank you for building this," Ingrid said between chattering teeth, gesturing to the rack.

"We didn't want to wait forever for everything to dry. It won't be enough, but it will take the chill off," Hagen said. Then added, "It was Jorg's idea."

"Oh good, for a minute I thought you had gone all considerate," she teased.

Deciding that they should bathe as well, the boys headed to the water. Steam rose from the clothes as both girls stayed as close to the fire as possible. They'd barely warmed through by the time the boys were back.

Ingrid tried to avoid looking at Jorg, because the boys were wearing only their breeches. They carried their shirts over, laying them atop the fire with the girls' things. Losing the battle and peeking through her hair at him, she felt her face warm, and she looked back toward the fire.

"Your face is red," Selby whispered with a giggle.

"Shhh, it's just the fire," Ingrid answered with a grin.

"One hour, and then we leave, no matter what," Hagen announced.

"Now who's bossy?" Selby rolled her eyes.

True to his word, Hagen made sure they were dressed and walking north an hour later. Still damp, and now hungry, with no provisions, attitudes threatened to turn bleak until they found a large patch of bilberry bushes. They stopped to pick their fill.

Helped by the sweet fruit, they continued ahead, leaving the forested valley and entering the moors by early afternoon. Yellow gorse blossoms, bright against the soft, gray sky, dotted the rolling hills. Strong breezes bent the grasses in a dance and brought a fresh, clean scent into the air. Picking their way around boulders and through deep ravines, they made good time on the squishy, moss-covered ground.

As they climbed to the top of a gentle rise, smoke rose on the horizon in a puff of black and gray. The breeze brought the smell of burning wood and something else that Ingrid couldn't quite make it out—or rather, she could, but didn't want to believe it.

"Do you think it's a pyre?" she asked, fiddling with her beads.

"No, there's too much smoke. It's a whole settlement," Jorg answered.

Keeping an eye out for invaders or worse, they approached

the village with caution. They searched everywhere that wasn't smoldering or still burning, which wasn't many places. By the time they finished investigating, it was clear that all the villagers were dead.

A few lonely sheep and chickens wandered about aimlessly. The stench of burning flesh and wood filled their noses and stung their eyes. Most buildings were rubble, and there wasn't anything they could do to stop the few flames that remained.

Whoever had done this was long gone.

Ingrid and her friends stood in what had been the center of the village, stunned and silent, listening to the occasional cracks and pops of the dying fires. The smoke in the air thinned out, making it easier to breathe.

"As awful as this is, we should try to find anything that can help us. Food, cloaks, maybe even a dead chicken or two," Hagen said.

Ingrid and Selby looked at each other and nodded at him. "We'll search this way, and meet you back here," Ingrid said.

"Call out if you find anyone alive. It would be good to know who did this."

They scoured the village. It felt disrespectful to be gathering the belongings of those still sprawled on the ground. Some were burned in their homes, while others had died from vicious looking stab wounds or broken necks.

No one wanted to talk as the group stood with their findings. Sitting down, they mindlessly ate some pieces of dried meat and hardtack while their nerves settled.

"Hagen," Jorg eventually sighed.

"I know. Let's get to it, then."

"What is it? Get to what?" Ingrid asked.

"We can't leave these people where they lay. They can't enter the afterlife until they have been buried and prayed over," Hagen answered.

"Oh. I'll help. I don't want to walk away from here without doing everything we can."

"Agreed," added Selby.

"This is difficult work, Ingrid. And I don't mean just the digging." Hagen frowned at her hard, his eyes narrow and his mouth set in a straight line.

"I know," she said. "I understand what it means, but I want to help these people find peace. Don't you dare treat me like a child." She looked him in the eye, her jaw tight.

"Fine. We'll dig first, then gather the bodies." He and Jorg had found shovels, and he handed her one, then they walked over to a large, open area of flat ground. Hagen dragged his shovel in a large rectangle. "We'll start with this and see if it's enough."

They spread out and jammed their shovels into the cold ground.

Hours later, Ingrid's arms were wobbly, and her hands could barely straighten from gripping the handle of the shovel. Selby hadn't fared much better.

They had buried all of the people they could find. There were twenty-three of them, all in a row.

The four friends stood at the side of the mass grave, and Hagen said a prayer to plead the gods to open the doors to the place of the dead and let them find peace.

🦋 12 🦋

It was growing dark by the time they finished, and there wasn't time to move away from the village to sleep. A goat pen they had searched earlier still had usable straw, so they bedded there for the night.

Ingrid didn't sleep well, waking at the slightest sound. When she did sleep, her dreams were filled with images of bodies and fire. Smoke stung her eyes and choked her throat—swinging swords barely missed her head. Sweating and out of breath, she'd wake, peer around quickly, and relax when she found the comfort of her brother and friends nearby.

The latest time she woke, they slept peacefully as before, but fear continued to tingle the hairs on her arms. Moving as little as possible, she scanned her surroundings. By the corner of the building about ten feet away, she saw motion.

Reaching out her hand slowly, inch by inch, she touched Hagen.

He didn't stir.

His face was turned to her, so she inched her finger from

his arm to his nose. He batted her away as if she were an annoying fly. She touched him again. This time, his eyes opened.

She quickly put her finger to his mouth and mouthed, "Shhh."

He squinted his eyes and silently asked, "Which direction?"

With the slightest of movement, she nodded over his head.

Wrapping his hand around the hilt of the dagger at his side, he pointed his eyes toward Ingrid's knife for her to do the same. Deliberate and steady, he pretended to roll over in his sleep for a better look.

The intruders weren't fooled, and slunk from their hiding position around the corner.

Hagen and Ingrid both jumped to their feet, calling to the others. Wolves as big as ponies stalked closer, with bared canines and bright, hungry eyes.

Jorg rolled on his shoulder and came up on one knee, axe in hand, while Selby crouched with a spear in hers. Hagen was slightly in front of Ingrid, and Selby moved to Ingrid's side behind him. Jorg positioned himself with Hagen, in front of the girls.

Ingrid rolled her eyes at his protective move. *He needs to get over this, I can take care of myself, thank you very much.*

Ingrid startled when Jorg darted a glance back at her and grinned.

What was that for?

No words were spoken, but with a spurt of speed, Hagen and Jorg dashed forward to engage the wolves, while Selby fanned to the right.

Confused at whether to follow the boys or stay with Selby,

Ingrid lost her grip on her knife, and it fell to her side, just out of reach. Dropping to her hands and knees, she snatched it up and scrambled toward the back of the pen. In the darkness beyond her vision, she smelled musty, wet fur.

Coming toward her were a pair of glowing, yellow eyes.

A loud growl rumbled from deep inside the wolf's chest, and drool hung from wicked-looking teeth that were longer than Ingrid's fingers.

In one silent motion, the wolf jumped.

Diving to the side, she rolled away from its snarling jaws and flung her arm straight up from the ground, her knife meeting the shoulder of her assailant.

The vibrations rocked her entire arm, and she couldn't pull the knife free.

Refusing to lose the gift from Jorg, she held onto its handle, and the wolf pulled her to her knees as it struggled. The beast yelped in pain as it yanked itself free, then backed away, keeping his eyes focused on Ingrid.

When their eyes met, Ingrid froze, every muscle locked and immobile. Panic bubbled in her center as she realized how vulnerable she was, standing there in the middle of the melee. Then images flashed through her mind, one after another. The fight still persisted in her peripheral vision, but ahead of her stood a man, not a wolf. His eyes were glaring and angry as he bled from his shoulder.

"Who are you?" Ingrid yelled at him, but the image dissipated.

The wolf was still there. It lowered its head and prepared to lunge at her. When it sprang, Ingrid dodged and added a long slice along its side to the still-bleeding shoulder injury.

Yelping, the wolf fell to the ground, its sides heaving. Seconds later, it staggered to stand, turning to face her once more.

Suddenly appearing by Ingrid's side, Selby raised her spear, readying to throw it at the injured animal.

"No, don't!" Ingrid pushed the wooden shaft to deflect it as Selby let go.

"Why did you do that?" Selby kept her eyes on the wolf as she yelled at Ingrid.

"We need to keep it alive," she said calmly.

Hagen and Jorg rounded the corner meeting up with the girls. Before they could rush the creature, Ingrid moved in front of them.

"We need to keep this one alive, apparently," Selby answered.

"Why?" Hagen sounded as confused as Selby.

"Ingrid doesn't think it's a wolf."

Worry lines creased Jorg's forehead as he turned to Ingrid. "Is this true?"

"We're not facing an animal . . . it's a man in wolf form," she told him.

"I know a way to find out."

Moving faster than any of them had seen him, Jorg reached the wolf and pinned it to the ground with his knee at its throat. Blocked by Jorg's back, Ingrid screamed when she saw him bring his knife down on the wolf.

The three friends stared in shock as Jorg stood holding what looked like a torn cloak made of wolf skin, while a man lay curled up on the ground at his feet.

Turning to the group, he threw the cloak to the side and pulled the man to his feet. "It looks like Ingrid was right."

Ingrid felt numb. Her skin was cold and clammy, and she did not understand what to do next. Standing before them was the man she'd seen in her mind—the man who, seconds earlier, had been a wolf.

"We need to tie him," she croaked, needing too much effort to get the words passed her throat.

Why is this happening? What is causing all these beasts to surface?

Then, breathing hard and needing to get away, Ingrid turned on her heel and walked out of sight, around the corner. Once hidden, she bent over and wretched.

They had eaten little in the last few days, so only the acid taste of bile passed her lips.

A hand lifted her hair away from her face and held it for her while she heaved.

When nothing more would come, Ingrid wiped her mouth and stood upright.

Selby let go of her hair and rubbed her back. "Feel better?"

"No."

"I wouldn't either."

"I need something to rinse out my mouth."

"This way, I know what you need." Selby took her by the hand and led her back to the goat pen where they'd slept. Picking through the pile of supplies they had gathered, she found a wine skin. "Here, drink this."

Without concern for what the blackened pouch might contain, Ingrid pulled the cork and took a long draw. The bitter taste made her cough, but once past the first couple of swallows, she found it more pleasant. Warmth flared against her raw throat and wound its way to her stomach, spreading through her insides.

"That's enough. You need to take it slow." Selby raised her eyebrows as she pulled the leather flask away from Ingrid.

Feeling instantly relaxed, Ingrid plopped to the ground and sat with her legs straight out and her arms slack on her thighs.

"Hmm, that might have been a mistake." Selby crouched in front of Ingrid and rubbed her arm, tucking some of her hair behind her ear.

"I'm okay. What am I supposed to do, Selby? How do I know these things? That wolf was—is—a man!" She threw her hands in the air and let them fall again into her lap. "This is too much." She closed her eyes and shook her head back and forth, as if she could erase her surroundings.

Footsteps sounded behind her, and she heard the rustling of straw as Hagen and Jorg sat down on either side of her, leaving enough space so that no one touched.

"What did you give her?" Hagen asked as he looked up at Selby.

"Wine. Want some?"

"Sounds like a great idea." Taking the flask, he drank deep before passing it to Jorg, who followed his lead.

Ingrid intercepted it as Selby was about to take it back, and downed several more swallows. All three of her companions reached out to take it from her and voiced their concern.

"NO."

"Whoa!"

"Wait! Oh, Ingrid." Selby pried the nearly empty flask out of her hands and put it out of reach. "You've had enough."

"It doesn't matter. I think I'm going crazy, anyway."

"You're not crazy," Jorg sighed. "You were right. That beast was a man, under some kind of mask or veil. How did you know?"

"I have no idea!" She threw her arms up and let them fall into her lap again as she squealed. "I saw him in my mind. As a man—like he wanted me to see him inside my head. I don't know how that's possible." She closed her eyes and shook her head, letting it droop to her chest.

Her breathing slowed, and she relaxed.

"Ingrid? Did you fall asleep?" Jorg asked.

Tilting her head at him, her eyes glittered, and she smiled a sleepy grin. "No. No-ot ye-et," she sang.

"I see. I think you should. We can talk more in the morning." Jorg put an arm around her in an attempt to help her lay down.

"You are so handsome," Ingrid said as she reached up and touched his jaw with one finger while snuggling into his arm.

"You need to sleep," Jorg said gently, trying to keep a straight face.

Selby and Hagen both snickered. Ingrid heard them, but didn't care.

"Where is your dimple?" she asked, drawing her brows together and pushing out her bottom lip.

Jorg closed his eyes and drew in a deep breath, still trying not to smile, while his mouth tugged at the corners to defy him.

"I want to see it." Ingrid put her finger on Jorg's cheek where the dimple hid.

He lost his battle and grinned at her, causing her to giggle.

"There it is!"

"You really need to rest."

"Oh-kay." She clutched the fabric of his shirt, pulling herself closer to him, and laid her cheek on his chest before closing her eyes.

Hagen stood, putting his hand on Jorg's shoulder. When his friend looked up at him, he said, "Remember, she is my little sister." He winked. Walking away to check on their captive, he snickered under his breath, and motioned for Selby to follow him.

Jorg closed his eyes and shook his head, then held Ingrid a little closer, shuffling them both backward until he could lean against the side of the pen.

Ingrid wasn't quite asleep. She could hear the others talking, but she was too preoccupied with the strong muscles next to her cheek, and the bicep under her hand.

With her wine-induced courage, she drew in a deep breath to fill her senses with the grassy pine scent surrounding her before sleep pulled her away.

Cold crept into every crevice of Ingrid's body. A pre-dawn fog spread across the ground. Opening her eyes, she saw nothing but a white mist surrounding her, and for a moment, she wondered if she'd died. The smell of straw and the lumpiness under her back made her hope she hadn't.

I expect a much softer and more comfortable place to lay down in the afterlife. A noise assaulted her ears, and she smiled. *The gods could not be so cruel as to force me to listen to Selby's rattling snores for all eternity. How did I get here, though?*

For an instant, she felt a sliver of panic as she struggled to find her memories. There had been arms around her, a soothing hand rubbing circles on her back, then she must've fallen asleep. Panic rose up again as she pleaded with her subconscious to tell her it had been her brother or Selby who had comforted her, but she knew it wasn't—she was keenly aware of Jorg's presence, as his face flashed before her eyes. The last thing she'd seen before laying her head against his chest and closing her eyes was his hand coming down and brushing the hair away from her face.

Sensations tingled in her chest while something skittered around in her stomach. Mortified, she remembered the events before she slept.

What in Freya's name are these feelings? This can't happen—not now, in the middle of all that's going on. No matter how cute that dimple is. Oh, I remember telling him that! You need to get a hold of yourself, stupid girl!

How she was going to face him again, she didn't know. She was sure he would think she was the biggest baby. Before she could continue her thoughts, she heard a rustle of straw, and froze.

"How are you feeling, Ingrid?"

She slammed her eyes closed as she heard Jorg's whisper. *Maybe he'll think I'm still asleep.*

"I know you're awake," he said with a quiet chuckle.

"I'm fine," she whispered.

The air between them felt alive with an unseen energy. She could tell her breathing was louder than it should be because her chest was so tight, and she could barely get any air into her lungs. After a few minutes of silence, she relaxed. His presence near her felt comfortable.

"Thank you," she whispered, needing him to know she knew he had helped her.

Without a word, he threaded his fingers through hers. A smile betrayed her resolve, and she drifted off to sleep again in complete peace.

The sound of someone clearing their throat made Ingrid's eyes pop open with a start. Turning her head toward the sound, she saw the smiling eyes of Selby staring at her. The fog still hovered around them, but had lightened with the early rays of morning.

Wordless, but with a devilish grin, Selby moved her eyes down to the hand lying on Ingrid's stomach.

Was he always laying this close?

She looked back at Selby and rolled her eyes, trying to make it seem like it was no big deal, and Selby's eyebrows almost reached her hairline. She wasn't going to get out of this quietly. Her friend would have all kinds of comments, if she knew her. The best she could hope for was to deal with it as quickly as possible and move on.

Maybe just a minute longer.

As she finished the thought, Jorg's fingers tightened their grip on hers ever so slightly. Again she was struck with the feeling that he had somehow perceived her unspoken thoughts. That sent a shiver of unease through her whole body.

Ignoring Selby, Ingrid turned her head as little as possible until she could see Jorg out of the corner of her eye. He lay on his side, facing her, with his free arm folded under his head, and the hint of a smile on his face.

She suspected he was awake and enjoying her embarrassment.

Frustrated by that, and the little snickers bubbling up from Selby, she tried to roll away from the muscled arrogance holding onto her. She removed her hand, but his tightened even more when she rolled, and he followed closer as if to snuggle tighter together.

That brought a loud snort and cackle of laughter from her so-called friend before she could get her hand up to cover her mouth.

This ends now.

She jumped up and exclaimed that it was time to get and up and get moving for the day. The words came out much louder and higher-pitched than she'd intended, causing heat to rise in her cheeks, and she wanted to find a place to hide.

That was more than Selby could handle, and she burst into a roaring laughter, doubling over on herself and choking from lack of air. Jorg rolled over onto his back, put both hands behind his head, and smiled at Ingrid, making her face flare hotter.

Stomping off to find privacy, she almost tripped on Hagen, who'd started to sit up. His hair sticking up, he wiped the drool from the side of his mouth, confused about the abrupt awakening. Selby laughed harder, but rushed after Ingrid, still snorting in humor.

Ingrid pretended to be looking for firewood, wanting to be away from everyone for as long as possible.

"Ingrid!" Selby halted her mid-stride with an intensity to

her voice that no longer held any humor. "Don't go that way," she said much softer.

In the fog, she'd had no sense of direction, but she instantly understood. Her whole body shook as she walked toward Selby. "Is he still tied up?"

"Yes. Let's go back. There's no way we'll be able to get a fire going in all of this mess," waving her hand around at the fog.

She knows me too well.

"We'll have some biscuits and salt pork before we deal with that." Putting her arm around Ingrid and leading her back to camp, Selby was the perfect best friend again, knowing exactly what to do without making Ingrid feel stupid or weak.

By the time they got back, the boys had packed up the blankets and pulled out the cold food that was to be their breakfast. Without looking at Jorg, Ingrid picked up a couple pieces of dry bread, and sat down on the straw to eat.

Her stomach wobbled and protested against the food; eating wasn't such a good idea. She nibbled a few bites, then stored the rest for later.

Breakfast took only minutes, and then they sat quiet. Ashes and the smell of smoke floated in the air as a reminder of the day before. The morning's antics aside, no one wanted to talk about what they should do with the man-wolf tied around the corner.

"We're going to have to figure out who and *what* he is," Hagen finally said.

"Yes, and then?" Jorg asked.

Ingrid kept her eyes focused on her lap. A quick glance out the side of her eye told her that Selby was doing the same.

Hagen let out a long breath and stood up. "Let's see what he says first, then decide what to do with him." Jorg nodded and rose to go along. "Ingrid, you stay here. I don't want him influencing you again. Selby . . ."

Ingrid and Selby both looked at Hagen when he didn't continue speaking.

"What?" Selby asked.

"Stay with her. Got it?" He cocked an eyebrow, waiting for her response.

"Yeah," she sneered at him. "Did you think I would leave her sitting here by herself?" She looked away and huffed.

Ingrid smiled at her friend, then looked up at the boys. "Be careful."

"We will. I mean it; stay here," Hagen said with his brows raised and eyes pleading rather than stern.

Ingrid forced a smile that looked more like a grimace and nodded.

Jorg looked at Ingrid, and the muscles in his jaw tightened. Then he gave a quick nod and strode after Hagen.

Confused, Ingrid looked at Selby for help.

She only raised her eyebrows and shook her head.

Ingrid couldn't help glancing in the boys' direction every couple minutes, fidgeting with her fingers and her skirt. Selby caught her eye, and they looked at one another without speaking.

Together, they jumped up and scurried toward the corner of the building. Ingrid dropped to her knees, and Selby crouched over her as they peered around the corner. They could see the three men, too far away to hear. The captured man sat against a tree with his legs extended; his arms were tied behind him, around the trunk. Hagen crouched at his side, eye-level with him. He must have been the one talking, because Jorg stood tall on the man's other side, his legs slightly apart and arms folded over his chest.

Ingrid watched the way his nut-brown hair fell loose onto his shoulders, with the top pulled away from his face and tied at the crown, his perfectly shaped eyebrows and straight nose clearly visible.

He is so strong and handsome. She sighed.

"I don't think you're looking at what I am," Selby whispered.

Ingrid felt a flush rise into her cheeks, and when she looked back, Jorg was facing them. He narrowed his eyes and jerked his chin slightly, urging them to go back. Ingrid swore she saw a slight tug on his lips before he resumed his guardian stance. A nudge to the back of her shoulder said Selby noticed it, too.

Scooting back a couple feet on her hands and knees, she knelt down again on the other side of the building. Selby followed her, remaining hunched over.

"What do you want to do?" Selby asked in what passed as her quiet voice.

"I think we should go back to our things and wait."

"I was afraid you'd say that."

They sat back down among the gathered supplies and waited. Selby wrapped and unwrapped a piece of straw around her fingers. Ingrid tucked her legs between her arms and bounced her toes nonstop. Birds chirped, and a mouse scurried through the straw a few feet away from them, as if it were any other, average day.

"Ugh, I hate waiting with nothing to do," Selby whined and paced.

Both of them stopped moving and watched the corner when they heard footsteps approaching, sighing in relief when only Hagen and Jorg rounded the corner.

"What did he say?" Ingrid's mouth was dry, and her nerves jumped all over her body.

"A lot of nonsense," Hagen mumbled. Anger radiated off of him like a riled bull. "Why isn't all of this stuff packed so we can leave?" he snarled.

She ignored him and looked to Jorg. His lips were pressed into a tight, white line offering no help.

"What did you do with him?" Selby asked.

"Left him."

"Tied to the tree?"

"I smell smoke," Ingrid cried, and started to run toward the prisoner.

Jorg grabbed her arm and stopped her. "It's the burning cloak, nothing more," he said, holding her stare until she nodded acceptance. "Pack up. He'll be fine."

Selby and Ingrid looked at each other, then helped with a mutual understanding that it wasn't the best time to push the boys for information. Within minutes, everyone had packs secured to their backs, and they were on their way.

Cold settled over Ingrid, and she pulled her cloak tighter around her shoulders. Without looking back, they worked their way out of the village and back onto the open moor.

The long, mournful cry of a lone, sorrowful wolf pierced the air. Ingrid's breath hitched as she waited to hear it again.

Silence answered, thick and heavy.

❧ 13 ❧

Walking single file, they picked their way along, watching for hidden bogs.

Caught up in thoughts of wolves and fires, Ingrid stumbled and lost her balance. Before she got halfway to the ground, Jorg's strong arms wrapped her in an embrace. He pulled her to her feet and held her back against his chest, but he didn't release her.

Without looking up, she said, "Stop catching me." Her voice came out feeble and unconvincing.

Leaning down, he rested his face near her ear, and his breath brushed against her cheek as he whispered, "I will always catch you."

Standing tall, he finally released her, and she took a step forward, but he didn't move. When she forced herself to look back, his gaze was all-consuming. It took all her concentration to keep her breathing steady and her face neutral. Finally, he stared up at the sky and closed his eyes. When he looked back at her, he smiled and walked ahead, brushing past her to catch up to Hagen.

Unable to move, she willed her thudding heart to slow down. Then she took a few shaky steps forward.

Selby sidled up to her and walked by her side without a word. Ingrid closed her eyes for a second and bit her lips together for strength—a quiet Selby was never a good sign. Anything brewing inside of her never stayed there for long.

"Do you think a man will ever look at me that way?" she finally asked quietly.

Not what I expected. "What are you talking about?"

"The way Jorg looks at you. And don't tell me you don't know. I've seen you looking at him, too."

"Oh." She wasn't sure how to answer that. "I don't know what's happening with him and me. But I know you are smart, beautiful and . . . fun." She couldn't keep the snicker out of her voice. The man who won Selby's heart would have his hands full.

Ingrid expected Selby to laugh also, but she kept her eyes focused on the ground and sighed.

I've been such a bad friend. "I was only joking. Everything will work out, you'll see." She wrapped an arm around Selby's waist and leaned into her.

"That's really all I want." Selby kicked a rock out of the way. "I'm not like you."

"I know. You are brave and strong, and there's barely anyone who can defeat you in training."

"But I don't want any of that like you do. It isn't what's important to me; it's what's expected. And I'm good at it."

They walked in silence while Ingrid thought about her words. What could she say? *'I'm sorry I haven't paid any attention to you or your dreams because I've only cared about my own?'* That's what she should say, but she felt too guilty to let the words come out.

"What *do* you want?"

"To be a wife and a mother. Live on a bit of land, and farm. Quietly."

"Why haven't you ever told me that before?"

"Didn't seem right, I guess. But we'll take care of each other, no matter what, remember? Glory and honor and all that." She smiled over at Ingrid as she mocked the conversations they'd had so many times.

"Of course you can always count on me. I understand what it's like to want a life different from what's expected. You know that."

"I do. Because of that, I will always be at your side and support you. It doesn't matter anyway."

"Don't say that. I'm beginning to question my desire to fight in battles to earn glory. Maybe you have the right idea." Ingrid touched her jaw, remembering the fight she'd had in Jorvik. "Besides, you're the one with all the curves. Men will be falling at your feet in no time."

Selby snorted a laugh and peered sideways at Ingrid. "Well, that's true enough—about the curves, anyway." Exaggerating the swing of her hips as she walked, she made them both giggle.

In complete confusion, the boys looked back at them, increasing the girls' laughter.

Linking arms, they walked on together through the squishy

peat and grassy meadows of the moor, following the confused boys.

Using the bow and arrows he found in the village, Jorg hunted for their dinner while the rest of them set up camp for the night. Thanks to his uncanny vision, even at dusk, they were roasting two rabbits in no time.

"How is it you're the same age as Hagen, yet your face stays silky smooth, while his looks like something you'd use to scrub a pot?" Selby asked Jorg.

Directing a glare at her, he lowered his dinner and clamped his lips into a tight white line. As he worked to keep his composure, Ingrid watched his muscles tense and his nostrils flare.

"You're being rude, Selby," she said, trying to defuse the situation.

"I wondered, that's all."

"I. Don't. Know," Jorg answered through clenched teeth. "It's the way it is for me, I guess."

"There's nothing wrong with it. Besides," Selby flashed a grin at Ingrid before looking back at Jorg, "it shows your dimple easier, and I know someone who enjoys that."

Heat crept across Ingrid's face, and she tried to shrink into the darkness. The corner of Jorg's mouth twitched, but he softened his eyes toward Selby.

"You're not a very good friend." He popped a piece of meat into his mouth and shook his head at her.

"What? I'm the best!" Selby put her hand to her chest in feigned outrage.

Ingrid groaned. "Not always," she muttered. She shook her

head, while finding the folds of her skirt increasingly interesting.

Hagen stood and aimed to change the subject. "Ingrid, come with me, I need to talk to you."

"About what?"

"Come with me for a minute."

"Why can't you talk with me right here?"

"I was trying to save you more embarrassment, but fine." Sitting back down, he pinned her with his stare. "You were stupid when we were fighting off the wolves, and your careless-ness is exactly the reason you should stop trying to be a shield-maiden," he said.

"I was not stupid! You take that back."

"You stood frozen and didn't even try to fight."

Ingrid could feel tension spike into Selby's muscles next to her, as they sat on the same rock, and she caught the motion of Jorg leaning forward.

Jumping up to defend herself, she did her best to seem taller. "I was not just standing there. There was a wound in the man's shoulder, did you see? I did that, but then something happened between the wolf-man and me. I . . . I don't know what it was, but I couldn't hurt him anymore." *So much for my defense.*

"What do you mean?"

"You'll think I'm crazy." *Everything about this situation is crazy.* "We connected somehow, me and the wolf. I saw things in my head. I saw him standing there as a man." Out of habit, she rolled her lip between her teeth.

No one said anything. A quick peek at Selby found a wide-open mouth, with a half-chewed bite of rabbit in full view.

"You were drunk and making excuses when you mentioned seeing him inside your mind," Hagen said, his eyes wide and head shaking. "That's not possible."

"It is."

Startled at his support, all eyes turned toward Jorg.

"There are those with the gift of sight who can connect with many things from nature. I've heard it talked about before," Jorg said, looking at Ingrid with soft eyes. Kind, accepting eyes.

Hagen glared at his friend. "Don't encourage this. Ingrid's not a völva." Angered by Jorg's comments, he stepped closer to his sister. "You froze, and you could have been killed."

Ingrid did not falter as he came closer. What happened to her was too intense for her to allow him to dismiss it as impossible. Maybe she wasn't a seer, a *völva*—the stories she'd heard of women with the gift to use Freya's seiðr magic scared her—but she would not let him decide that for her.

"Hnossa and the woman in the woods both said that I have special gifts and should embrace them."

"Who is Hnossa?" Jorg asked, his brows nearly touching as he stood.

"What are you talking about?" Hagen glowered back and forth between them, clenching his fists.

"I wasn't sure I wanted to talk about it. But when I was in the river, before the trolls caught me, I had a vision. I met a woman who called herself Hnossa. She told me I was in Asgard, and that she'd brought me there so she could help me develop my gifts. We didn't talk long. I thought it was a dream, but I don't think so now. Not after the wolf."

"My mom's aunt lived in a village where a woman claimed

to be a seer," Jorg told them. "She would go out in the woods alone for days, and when she came back, she'd say she had talked with the goddess Freya, and learned what the village should do next."

"So you think Ingrid should go off into the woods by herself so she can talk to wolves before they eat her?" Hagen growled. He looked as if he could shoot arrows out of his eyes.

"No, of course, not. But I am saying that maybe she has a gift she didn't know about before, and we should help her with it instead of ignore it."

"Wait, a seer?" Selby joined the conversation. "Do you think you can do magic like Freya?" Selby's voice rose in pitch with excitement, but her eyes were wide with fear.

"I don't want to talk about this anymore. I can't see the future, and I can't do magic. I'm sorry I didn't fight the wolves like you wanted, Hagen." She plopped down on the rock, hoping they would all let it go, but she knew that wasn't going to happen.

"Maybe that's why your bead was glowing," Selby offered.

"My bead? What are you talking about?"

"Your amber one; it was glowing while you and the wolf-man were staring at each other. Did either of you goats see that?" She raised her brows and looked at Hagen and Jorg.

"I saw it," Jorg said.

Ingrid didn't know what to think about any of it. The experience with the wolf was not one she wanted to live through again.

Tears stung the back of her eyes. Staring at the fire, she forced her mind to clear.

"Behind the wall, when you got sick, your hands were

warm, too. Then as you calmed down, they started getting cold again," Selby related in a calmer, gentler voice.

"My hands were warm, too?" She sighed and absently rubbed her hands together.

At a loss about why her life had spun out of control, she retreated inside herself, blocking out the others' voices and focusing on the rhythm of her pulse and the orange and yellow of the fire that flickered against her closed eyelids.

Alarmed by a gentle touch on her shoulder, she gasped and opened her eyes.

"Are there other times when your bead glows?" Jorg asked, breaking her meditation.

"At weird times. I haven't paid attention to it enough to notice a pattern."

"I bet it happens when your hands get hot, too. Like when you help someone who is sick." Selby sat up taller, an eager glimmer in her eyes. "Remember last fall, when you brought those herbs to Einar when he was sick? You made him tea, and he complained when you handed him the cup that you'd made it too hot and you could've burned your hands. But you didn't." Selby bounced, recalling the incident.

"When we get home, we should talk to father about this," Hagen stated. "He'll know who we should ask about it. Maybe we shouldn't try to figure it out just now." He walked away, toward the other side of the fire, and spread out his cloak to sleep on.

Ingrid watched as his muscles tightened in his back and he kept clenching his fists then releasing them. *He doesn't know how to fix this. Neither do I, big brother.*

Selby kept talking. "But this could be huge. Maybe you

have other gifts that are just starting to wake up or something?"

"Let's just go to sleep. I *don't* want to talk about it anymore."

They exchanged looks for a minute, each daring the other one to give in. With a big sigh, Selby gave up. Thankful for the reprieve, Ingrid lay down on her cloak and rolled away from the others. Tied in knots, her stomach ached.

According to Hnossa and the woman in the woods, her gifts were special. If they were right, her life would never be the same. Each had warned her about trusting others, as well.

This is all too confusing.

In the blackest of night, sleep finally gave her peace.

They were walking toward home before the first tangerine and rose-colored rays of sunlight filled the sky. If they walked hard and stopped as little as possible, they could make it home in another two days.

Clear and sunny, the day had started out with promise, but the horizon showed an outline of black clouds brewing. Shelter became the top priority as they picked up their pace. Unfortunately, out on the moors, there wasn't much available, but for a time, they thought they could manage. They pulled up their cloaks and pushed on when the rains started. Fast-moving and looking angrier by the minute, the storm caught quickly up to them. Soon, rain soaked through their cloaks, and before long, they heard the low growl of thunder.

When it ended, there was not a single sound—not a bird

chirping or a rodent scuttling. It was eerily quiet. A tingle danced through the hair on Ingrid's arms, and a squeal flew from her throat when she noticed the wisps of hair floating up from everyone's heads.

Several large boulders jutted out over a small ravine not far ahead of them; the group scrambled for them as fast as they could against the wind. In her hurry, Selby caught her foot against a small stone, and tumbled down. Hagen turned back to help.

Crawling on his hands and knees, he shoved her toward the rock shelter, as a bright light and a deafening, hissing sound cracked through the air near them.

Blinded to all their senses, Jorg and Ingrid fell into the gully. With another boom of thunder, rain poured down harder, creating a black veil so dark, they couldn't see but a few feet in front of them, and the rushing sound of the water caused their voices to slam back when they tried to locate each other.

Further away, another flash of light gave a view of their surroundings. Two dark figures lay on the ground where Ingrid had last seen Hagen and Selby, but there was no movement.

Rushing to the slumped bodies, she was flooded with relief when Selby moaned. As gently as possible, she helped her friend roll over, then bent over her to block the rain from her face. Ingrid's bead created a soft glow when she brushed Selby's hair away from her eyes. Closing her own eyes, she kept her hand in place until the glow dimmed and Selby took a long draw of breath.

A few feet away, Jorg hovered over Hagen as he lay at an

awkward angle. Even soaked from the rain, his cloak was smoking, and his hair looked like it had been singed in a fire.

Concerned and fighting her rising panic, Ingrid crawled over to Hagen and put an ear to his chest. Small and fluttering, his heart beat persisted, confirmed by the slight rise and fall of his ribs.

Disoriented, Selby made her way over to the others and made a feeble attempt to rouse Hagen. It was clear that he would not wake, so Jorg heaved his listless body over his shoulder, and they trudged to the rock shelter. Once settled, Jorg broke off small branches from some nearby bushes to fashion a small windbreak.

Ingrid sat on her knees next to Hagen, closed her eyes, and concentrated on calming her heart rate by rubbing her hands together. When she opened her eyes, she could feel the warmth spreading from her core through her arms and into her fingers. Pressing her hands directly over Hagen's heart, she felt the pulse deep within herself pushing into her brother. Lost in the rhythm of energy flowing out of her body, she lost sense of time and space. It was like she floated, not seeing anything in the darkness except a blinding light, which she somehow knew was her own body.

As the light faded, and cold settled deep within her bones, she fell against Hagen's chest. Jorg grabbed ahold of her shoulders, and helped her into a sitting position. She leaned against him while she regained enough strength to open her eyes.

Her mouth was dry. In fact, all of her felt dry, like she was a withered flower on a hot day, even though she was soaked to her skin. Burned hair and wet wool overpowered the smell of rain and mud within the small space.

Leaning down once again to listen to Hagen's chest, she found that his heartbeat was stronger and his breathing even. Still, his eyes didn't open. She hadn't healed him.

Why didn't it work? This can't be happening. It's like the vision of the baby girl.

Traitorous tears slipped down her cheeks, and she slapped them away, falling to the ground on her backside. "I didn't fix it."

"That was lightning, Ingrid, direct from Thor's hammer. I'm sure you've helped. Maybe he just needs more time." Selby tried to sound convincing, but Ingrid could hear the wobble in her voice.

"You did what no one else could have done. Selby's right, let's rest and give him time," Jorg said.

Ingrid lay on her side and watched Hagen's chest rise and fall, ignoring the attempts made to reassure her. Tears silently slid down her cheeks while she concentrated on her brother's unconscious form.

Hours later, she rubbed her face and sat up. Rain still poured down, but the skies were lighter and no longer rumbled like an angry herd of horses pounding through a meadow. Selby sat propped up against the back of the rocks, but Jorg wasn't in the shelter. Scrunching her forehead, she peered out into the rain.

"He needed to step out for a bit."

"How long has he been gone? Is everything alright?"

"If we don't count that Hagen won't wake up, or that we have been shipwrecked, battled with trolls, attacked by some wolf-shifting man, and are now stuck under some rocks, yeah, it's all great."

A weight pressed down on Ingrid as she moved over to wrap her arms around Selby. "I don't know what to say. This is all my fault. I don't know why I can't help him." As she watched Hagen lying on the hard, cold ground, her heart felt numb.

"It's not your fault, and you know better than that. Hagen and I would have followed you down that river no matter what."

"I wish I could have gotten to shore before that happened."

"I think we all do." She stopped short, then after a second, said, "I didn't mean that. I'm sorry I'm acting like such a toad. I'm cold and hungry." She hesitated, and then whispered, "And scared." An attempt at a smile pulled at her mouth, and she rested her head against Ingrid's shoulder.

Squeezing her arms tighter around her friend, Ingrid could not remember ever hearing Selby say she was afraid of something. It was comforting, in an odd way—like they were equals for the first time. She used her free hand to stroke Selby's hair, and they sat in silence for a while.

"Why do you think Jorg came after me? In the river, I mean."

Selby made a noise in her throat that sounded like a cross between a grunt and a snort. "You are so cute and so lovable, but you have to catch up when it comes to men, my friend. That boy likes you. Maybe as much as you like him."

"I know," she said with a shy smile. "I mean, it seems sudden. Why now?"

Selby sat up and looked Ingrid in the eye. "He has liked you for a while, you just didn't notice. He was subtle. I think maybe with everything that's happened, and the things you can do, things have been brought out in the open."

Ingrid sucked in her lips, but couldn't hold back her smile. "He's really cute, don't you think? He smells like a fresh pine tree, and I get all wobbly when he flashes that dimple at me."

"You get all flushed and red when he smiles, too."

"Don't say anything. I feel bad even thinking about stuff like that while we're stuck in here, so far from home, and Hagen is . . ." Her voice hitched, and she swallowed hard before continuing. "How are we going to do it? Get him home, I mean?" The reality of their situation put an end to her musings about Jorg.

"We'll have to carry him somehow."

Just then, Jorg ducked back under the rocks, dropped some branches on the ground, then left again. The girls looked at each other, and Selby shrugged. Jorg entered again and dropped another set of branches on the ground.

"It's getting better out there," he noted. "Not as rainy. But we're going to have to stay the night. I thought we could build a litter to haul Hagen on while we're waiting for the storm to pass. Some of the wood might even be dry enough to start a small fire to warm it up in here."

"That's a great idea, but how do we build a litter?" Ingrid asked.

"If we strip the bark off these smaller branches, we can use it as binding to wrap around these longer ones, then we tie a cloak over the frame, lay him on top of it, and drag it behind us."

"It's better than sitting here doing nothing," Selby agreed, grabbing a piece of wood.

"How will the cloak support him? Won't he fall through?" Ingrid asked.

"No, I'll strap some smaller pieces across before putting the cloak down."

"Have you had to make one of these before?" she asked as she set to work pulling the white bark off a branch.

"Once. One of my uncles got hurt while we were out hunting; it worked really well to get him home. He complained the whole way, but it seems like Hagen will be fine with it." He lifted his mouth a little, trying to grin.

"Funny," Selby said. "But you should leave the jokes to those of us with the gift." She winked at him while pulling on a long section of bark.

"It's okay, I don't have the knack, either. Be careful, though —if you are the object of her humor, she can be brutal," Ingrid warned.

"No chance to avoid it. Anyone as serious as this guy is a constant supply of material. Besides, it's an honor to be one of my victims."

"Oh? How's that?" Jorg asked.

"I'm super funny."

Ingrid shrugged her shoulders at Jorg and kept working. "I'm sorry, she's uncontrollable, but she grows on you."

"Hey . . . ! Alright, that's fair."

Jorg snorted, and a smile stretched into his eyes.

I could enjoy that smile every day. Ingrid sighed then forced herself to concentrate on the bark she was pulling.

When she glanced up a little later, Jorg was looking at her. He smiled and winked. Ingrid studied her branch with more intensity, and tried to control the flutters in her chest.

14

Ingrid sat in the dark, holding herself together by the thinnest of threads as she reviewed the events of the day over and over. The rain had stopped, and once they'd finished the litter, everyone had gone to sleep. Except Ingrid.

Her thoughts raced and tormented her. *How can I not heal one of the most important people to me?*

Hagen, the biggest pain in her life, and her biggest treasure, was always at her side when she needed him. Sure, he picked on her, gave her a hard time around his friends—at least before this trip—but that was part of being a big brother. Not once had Ingrid questioned his love or loyalty to her. She'd grown up under the illusion that life could be whatever she set her mind to, that it would happen because she wanted it.

All of those beliefs lay shattered around her.

How could I be so naïve? My nightmare is happening all over again because I've learned nothing. I am as weak as everyone has always thought of me.

Looking at the tiny group huddled under the outcrop, she sighed. The damp ground seeped through her clothes, and her gooseflesh tingled against her linen tunic. In an attempt to warm herself and clear her mind, she decided to head out for a short, brisk walk. Sleep was not an option, and her legs were aching, needing to stretch from the cramped quarters.

"Ingrid!" Jorg shouted in a loud whisper, trying not to wake Selby.

Turning, Ingrid stopped and waited while Jorg jogged toward her. "What?" she asked, keeping her voice low as he neared her.

"Where are you going?"

"I can't sleep and I'm cold. I'm going to walk around a bit."

"You shouldn't go alone, you know that."

"I'm not going far. I need to move so I can clear my head. Go back and sit with Hagen." She looked down and kicked at the ground. "I'll sit with him when I get back."

The concern in Jorg's eyes was one more item to add to her thoughts.

"Don't go far, promise? Stay within shouting distance." He stared at her and touched her arm so she would look at him. She shivered at his touch, and he noticed. "It's warmer when we sit close together; you don't have to walk around."

Being close to you is why I have to walk around! She shook her head. "I'll be fine."

A wince flashed in Jorg's eyes, but he recovered quickly. "Yell out if you need help," he said through tight lips.

She rolled her eyes with a hint of a grin. "I won't need help, but fine. Now go back and watch Hagen. I know Selby isn't doing it, I can hear her snoring from here." She smiled.

Looking over his shoulder, he huffed a smile, then turned serious eyes back to her. She turned to walk away, and when he didn't also move to leave, she shooed him with her hands. Hesitating, he turned and walked back to the rumbling alcove.

Ingrid walked straight ahead then turned left, keeping the outline of the rocks in her view. Her intention was to make a large circle but stay close, as Jorg had asked.

A faint glow, like a campfire, flickered off in the distance to her right. She stopped and wondered whether she should go back and tell Jorg.

I'm sure it's nothing. I'll tell him about it when I get back.

Determined, she walked toward the glow. There would not be any cowardice from her. Life was dangerous; she knew that now better than ever. Whatever she found, she'd tell everyone when she returned.

With heavy clouds still blocking the stars, she tried to use landmarks to guide her, but on the moors, one clump of bushes or rock jutting out looked no different from the next. Even though she'd walked for a long distance, she was no closer to the mysterious fire. For a moment, she contemplated turning around and giving up. That consideration only fueled her need to find the source. She walked faster.

At last the light grew bigger, and her steps quickened again. The land sloped down in a small depression, and she saw that the light was over the next rise. Vaguely, she thought it odd that the smell of burning logs hadn't reached her yet, but she pushed it aside.

When she arrived at the top of the next rise, she froze. Her blood lurched in her veins, and a thick ball of fear dropped into her stomach. What she saw in front of her was not the expected campfire—it was a large, shimmering oval, like a looking glass suspended in midair. Within the light, blurry images appeared, moving, dancing, and beckoning her to another world. While she stood unable to move a muscle, the images cleared, and she recognized the landscape: the lake and the tree with glass leaves that she'd sat beneath while talking with Hnossa in Asgard.

Without another thought, she stepped through the shimmering portal.

Melodic birds blessed her ears, and the sweet smell of flowers graced her senses. A familiar voice called to her. She turned to see Hnossa walking toward her through a serene meadow.

"Hello, my dear. I'm so glad you found me."

"How is this possible?"

"It was imperative we speak, so I created a doorway for you."

"But I have to go back. My brother needs me . . . Wait, shouldn't there have been a bridge?"

"Don't fret, Ingrid," Hnossa soothed. "Heimdall doesn't always need to know everything. I'll make sure you get back to your brother, but there are more important issues to discuss first." For a second, a shadow passed behind Hnossa's eyes, but then her sunny smile returned and radiated warmth around Ingrid. "Come with me." Hnossa took Ingrid's hand and tucked it into the crook of her elbow.

"Where are we going?" Ingrid let her gaze float around to the unnatural sights around her. "Everything is so beautiful here."

Leaves played melodies as they brushed against each other,

yet there was no breeze. Butterflies left splashes of pink, orange, and lavender as they bounced from one flower to the next against the glimmering aquamarine sky. Vanilla and berries scented the air, with a hint of pepper tingling in the background. Ingrid realized that while the day was brilliant and clear, it had been night when she left.

"How is it daylight?"

"Asgard is not on the same schedule as your realm, dear. We do not need the same sleep cycles that mortals do, so we have far more sunlight."

Mesmerized, Ingrid stopped, eyes wide, when around a corner, the path opened and ended at a palatial home. "Wow! Is that where Odin lives?" she whispered to Hnossa.

Hnossa laughed with a sound like beautiful crystal chimes. "No, silly girl. That's my house."

The '*house*,' as she put it, was made of a cream-colored stone that reflected so much light it should have blinded Ingrid, but instead it was soothing. Golden shutters graced both sides of each window and matched the solid gold front doors, which opened on their own, welcoming them inside. The opulent marble entry tile shone like glass beneath her feet, and golden handrails with intricate scrollwork edged the spiraling staircase to the upper levels.

Hnossa patted Ingrid's hand, and she breathed again. "Let's keep walking, dear. I will show you around if there's time after we're finished talking."

Still gawking, Ingrid followed when Hnossa pulled on her arm. The soft sounds of a harp followed them as they walked down a wide hallway flanked on either side by beautiful art hung within paneled walls. There were no sconces anywhere, yet light illuminated every corner. Hnossa stopped in front of a set of double wooden doors that rose so high, Ingrid couldn't touch the top even if she stood on Selby's shoulders.

Removing Ingrid's hand from her arm, Hnossa opened both doors to show a room like nothing Ingrid could dream. The ceiling was higher than the large oak tree outside of the village, and shelves lined two of the tall walls from floor to ceiling, every inch of them filled with books. Large, comfortable-looking chairs were scattered atop a rug that squished with softness underfoot. Along the second long wall stood floor to ceiling windows that opened out onto the fields they'd walked through.

Intrigued by the crystal clear glass panes that kept out the weather, Ingrid touched one with her finger, leaving a smudge, and gasped as she watched the fingerprint fade away. Overwhelmed, she turned once again to soak in the sights of the room, her eyes scanning the thousands of leather or cloth-bound books.

With panic written on her face, she turned to Hnossa and clutched her stomach. "I don't know how to read," she whispered.

"That's fine, don't worry yourself. You wouldn't be able to read these, anyway; they are written in the language of the gods. I only brought you here because we can talk in this room without being overheard. It is enchanted with a protection that makes eavesdropping impossible." Hnossa pulled Ingrid into an embrace. "Relax, my special girl. Let's sit over here on the couch, and I will tell you what you need to know." The two settled into the soft cushions, and Hnossa wove a tale for Ingrid.

"Long ago, the Vanir ruled as the gods of all realms. Jealous of the growing power of Asgard, the goddess Freya used her enchanting spells and charms to enter their realm and cause discord among their people. Odin declared her an enemy for her manipulation of his home and family—rightly so, don't you think?" She smiled at Ingrid, who nodded.

"The Æsir tried to kill Freya, but they could not, and only succeeded in angering her Vanir family. The two sides fought a fierce and destructive war, neither side earning an advantage over the other, and the war stretched on without an end in sight.

"Eventually, the two groups of gods and goddesses reached an understanding, as it became clear that there would be no true victor. As part of the truce, each side exchanged wards to ensure fair treatment of everyone.

"Downtrodden after the war, most of the Vanir left Vana-heim and settled into a quiet existence on Alfheim."

"I have heard much of this from sagas," Ingrid admitted. "But most of the stories are of Odin and Asgard, not Vanaheim or Alfheim." She looked to Hnossa with her forehead furrowed. "Though I've heard occasional mention that the elves of Alfheim chose not to associate with any other realm, especially Midgard."

"Yes, that was true. The elves viewed humans as an inferior race of creatures, and could not understand the Asgardians' affinity with them." Hnossa smiled with tight lips, and a look of pity, or something darker, swirled in her eyes for a moment, and then was gone.

"I'm not sure what all of this has to do with me."

"You will. Let me have some juice and sweets brought in

for us. Tales are always better with a snack." Hnossa's cheerful smile was back in full view as she rang a bell that tinkled a soft chime.

How could anyone hear that in this large house?

Seconds later, a wizened old gentleman opened the door, carrying a tray with golden goblets and a plate full of decorated treats that Ingrid had never seen before. Hnossa handed her a goblet.

"May I ask what this is?" Ingrid asked.

"It is only juice," Hnossa answered with a confused expression.

"Just checking. I would like to stay away from wine"

"I would never serve you wine from the gods. You will have no ill effects from our food or drink here. Shall I continue?"

Ingrid could only nod because her mouth was full of the sweetest bread-like treat she had ever tasted.

"That's my favorite cookie, too," Hnossa winked, then launched back into her story. "The Vanir and the elves share a heritage from the beginning of the realms, which is why they are so close. Not everyone agreed about a truce with the Æsir. They desired to continue the battle and defeat the Asgardians, keeping their rightful place as the true leaders of all the realms.

"Eventually, it caused a split in Alfheim. Those who sought ways to overpower the magic of Freya and Odin moved into their own lands, and learned the power of the dark arts. Known now as the dark elves, they traveled throughout many of the realms gathering resources and making allies among the enemies of Odin. The weaker, passive elves stayed within Alfheim, associating only with the dwindling Vanir, until both retreated deep into secret, hidden lands, rarely to be heard or seen."

She reached over and patted Ingrid's hand. "This is where you come in."

Ingrid's eyes widened, and she sat up taller.

Hnossa continued. "Enlightened with the knowledge of more powerful magic, the dark elves sought to restore Vanaheim, and heal the rift on Alfheim at the same time. Odin learned of their plans and, working with Freya, cast a spell around Midgard and connected it to Asgard. It protected the weaker humans, but it also increased Asgard's power and position against the other realms."

Ingrid felt her chest constrict, and her heart pounded against her temple. She swallowed a gulp of juice and waited for Hnossa to continue.

"Freya devised a plan to tether the protection in place forever by stealing a piece of thread from the Norn, Skuld. Woven within the magic thread is the fate of a human. Born with the ability to heal like Eir, and use the gift of sight like Frigg, that person would add the strength of Midgard to the powers of Asgard, binding the spell until the end of time."

Hnossa looked deep into Ingrid's eyes, making sure she had the girl's full attention. "That magic is weakening; that is why beasts not seen for centuries are once again within your world. But the one prophesied has been born! It is you, Ingrid."

Ingrid choked on the cookie she was eating and jumped off the couch, gulping air into her lungs.

Hnossa sat quiet and waited.

Guzzling down the rest of her juice, Ingrid squared her shoulders and shook her head at the woman.

"I can't be that person. I'm not a healer, for starters; my brother lays unconscious because I can't do anything for him. I can barely hold anything in my hands without dropping it, and my muscles are too weak to hold a regular shield. There is no way that I have magic like you describe."

"My dear child, I know it is hard to believe, but you must. The elves are failing, and if they do not restore the equality of magic to the Vanir, the imbalance will destroy your realm and mine. Giants, goblins, and dwarves, to name a few, will roam your world, taking all of mankind as slaves or killing them. No one will survive. Eventually, Odin and Freya will fail to hold Asgard, and evil will prevail with no hope for anyone. You must control your abilities; learn to harness your power so it cannot be used to harm anyone. Right now, you don't know how, which is why your brother still suffers, but you can *learn*."

"No, this is too much. It's not me." Ingrid paced back and forth in front of the couch. Her heart beat like a war drum, and she felt dizzy. She bent over, put her hands on her knees, and tried to catch her breath. "Why would Odin and Freya put all the realms at risk? They guide and protect us. And why would you think I am this person?"

"The gods are as emotional as humans, and can lose their way when they let greed and power cloud their judgment. This is a lot for you at once, I know; perhaps you should go back and rest. When you've had time to think over all that I have told you, we can speak again. In the meantime, you must not tell anyone of your trip here. We cannot risk the information of who you are getting into the wrong hands. No one can be trusted, do you understand?"

Ingrid shivered as a cold chill spread throughout her insides, but she nodded in agreement.

"Remember what I told you before: be wary of anyone who comes to you in secret, working in the shadows. They will only try to deceive you."

"I understand. I would like to go back now, please. I'm worried for my brother. I shouldn't have left for so long."

"You needn't worry. I am here to watch and guide you, sweet child." Hnossa stood and again wrapped her arms around Ingrid.

A bright, warm, and soothing light flashed in Ingrid's eyes, and she felt herself floating until everything disappeared.

She cracked open her eyelids, and peered out cautiously. Darkness surrounded her, and she lay on the hard ground, where something sharp poked into her back. Cold pierced every inch of her body, making the smallest movement painful. Little by little, she brought her knees up and, with monumental effort, pushed herself to standing.

Now what? I've never felt so cold. Ingrid's body felt numb, but her teeth chattered so hard, the sound echoed behind her eyes and pounded in her ears. Gone were the light, airy, sweet smells of Asgard, replaced by the assault of mud, moldy grass, and juniper.

Wrapping her arms tight around her middle, she tried to look around after her eyes adjusted to the dark, but nothing looked familiar. Whether she was in the same place where she'd found the portal earlier, she didn't know. Not too far away, she saw a clump of bushes.

It has to be warmer under there.

Slow and steady, she shuffled her feet until she reached the shelter and pushed her way into the brush, collapsing into a tight ball once she was as far in as she could go.

After a time, when she could not get comfortable or warm, she got back to her feet. *I may as well walk. It's better than freezing to death where no one will find me.*

She walked in the darkness, listening to the scampering of rodents as they scouted for food and hearing the occasional hoot of an owl. The night air was clean and fresh, washed anew from the earlier storm. While she walked, a gap opened between clouds, and she gazed up into the stars revealed overhead. Smiling, she noted that the North Star shone bright and steady, giving her the guidance she needed to get back. Oddly content after the day's events and her conversation with Hnossa, she let the emotions wrap around her like a shawl— until she saw a tall mass of angry male headed straight for her.

As he closed the distance between them, Ingrid noticed the tight fists by his side, the flared nostrils and straight line of his mouth. For a brief second, panic fluttered through her, and she thought about turning to run away—just as quickly, she set her feet and waited for Jorg's approach. The corded muscles of his arms were bulging under his shirt sleeves.

What is his problem?

Well within her personal space, he stopped and towered over her, saying nothing. She lifted her chin to look at him, knowing her eyes were too wide and that the hard swallow she took belied her false confidence.

Jorg grabbed ahold of Ingrid's upper arms and shook once, tightening his grip before letting go. Ingrid wanted to yelp, but kept quiet, daring a glance down at his fingers, which were flexing in and out as if he was trying to regain control.

"Where have you been?" he asked from between clenched teeth.

"Walking."

"I have been searching for you for two hours."

Did I really walk that far? "I can take care of myself. I was on my way back, you didn't need to come searching for me."

Jorg drew in a deep breath and let it out slowly. Ingrid used the opportunity to shift her weight into her heels, gaining an inch of space between them.

"You said you would stay within shouting distance."

"If I recall, *you* requested that, and I only implied my agreement. I needed to be alone, so I walked further."

"*Implied!*" he roared. Silence filled the air as all creatures within earshot halted.

"I'm not lost, and I'm not a child." Her own voice gained volume, and the quickening of her pulse made her hands shake.

Anger billowed off of Jorg like steam, but she kept his stare without flinching. Growling, he turned away from her, walked a few steps, and then returned, only to turn around and do it again. Ingrid watched him pace and willed her feet to stay where they were.

Jorg stopped again in front of her, not quite as close this time. "How do you know you're not lost?"

Without moving her head, Ingrid directed her eyes at the star still shining brightly between the gap in cloud cover. Focused again on Jorg's face, she raised an eyebrow, begging for his response.

He reached up and ran his hand over his face before dropping it to his side.

"Do you have a plan for where you'll sleep? Even if you keep walking, you won't make it back to the others before dawn. Unless you don't need sleep . . . since you have everything worked out, and all."

Ingrid rolled her eyes. "I didn't think about that. It's not a problem, though. I can find a safe spot, and rest for a while wrapped in my cloak before going forward."

"Hmm. Well, since you have a plan, I'll leave you to it." Turning, he strode off toward their camp.

"Wait. You're just going to leave?"

He stopped and twisted back toward her. "You said it yourself—you're not a child. You don't need me."

"I never said I didn't need you," she whispered, unsure if she wanted him to hear her or not.

Within a few strides, he'd closed the distance between them, and once again stood before her.

"I mean, I need Hagen and Selby, too," she rushed out. "W . . . we all need . . . each other." She stammered over the words, not looking him in the eye.

Nice, Ingrid, way to sound like an idiot.

Earthy pine scents tickled her senses, and she tried to keep focused anywhere but on the imposing figure in front of her. A strong finger pushed her chin upward, and a pair of hazel eyes swirling with green and gold bored into hers.

"That is true. So stop trying to prove how brave you are by yourself. We already believe in you. How about we both rest, and walk back together?"

Mesmerized by the starburst of colors in Jorg's eyes, Ingrid realized it was the first time she'd noticed them. *I'm sure they must have always looked like that. I wonder why I've never noticed.*

"Ingrid?" Jorg's voice snapped her out of her thoughts. It also seemed like he was struggling to keep from grinning.

She stepped away from his touch, and brushed her hands on her thighs. "Yeah. That sounds fine." Her voice sounded squeaky in her ears.

"I passed a good place to stop about ten minutes from here. How does that sound?"

Shaking her head and setting out in a brisk walk, she concentrated on the ground. "Sure."

Jorg moved up to her side, and they walked together in silence.

By the time they found the spot he'd mentioned, Ingrid's muscles were sore, and all the information Hnossa had shared with her had given her a headache, so forcefully it had battered her thoughts.

"We would both be warmer if we shared my cloak," he offered. Leaning toward her, he winked. "It's bigger."

Ingrid felt the heat rise up her face and into her ears.

Jorg flashed her a glimpse of his dimple, then sat down on the ground. Lying down on his side, he stretched the fabric so that there was enough room for Ingrid to lie next to him and still be covered. She sucked in a small breath, lowered herself down next to him, and wrapped the warm wool over her shoulders.

She flinched when his arm pressed around her middle.

"At least Selby isn't here. You can relax, and not worry about what she might say." His breath tickled her cheek as he spoke, and she bit her lip to keep from smiling, without success.

"I'm sure she'll have plenty of comments, anyway."

Jorg huffed, then shifted forward and pressed a light kiss to her cheek. "Goodnight, Ingrid," he whispered and leaned back, tucking his free arm under his head.

Stunned, she held her breath and didn't move. If Jorg's arm wasn't holding her down, she might have floated away.

Her cheeks squished into her eyes as she smiled against the elbow under her head and relaxed.

15

Something tickled Ingrid's nose, pulling her out of sleep. Hoping she could ignore it and fall back to sleep, she twisted, and wiggled her face to relieve the itch. It didn't work. Just before she could brush her hand across her face, her arm was held down tight. She stiffened and snapped open her eyes.

"Shhh. Don't move or make a sound," Jorg whispered in her ear.

It sent a thrilling shiver down her spine, making it hard to follow those directions—then she noticed the hare. It must have hopped next to them without realizing what they were.

Fast as an arrow, Jorg's arm shot out and grabbed the small animal. In his attempt to jump to his feet, Jorg pulled the cloak tighter against him, flipping Ingrid over onto her stomach, as he did everything he could to avoid falling on her.

Squealing, she covered her head with her arms, and Jorg landed hovering over Ingrid: one knee on her left side, with the arm not holding a squirming rodent braced against the ground near her right. While his other knee had bumped her back, he'd managed not to put his weight into it. There wasn't much choice but to straddle her while he gave the rabbit a quick death. Then he shimmied out of the cloak and scooted away.

Ingrid peeked out from under her arms to find Jorg sitting on the ground, laughing, and she joined him. The predawn skies were pushing away the darkness, and it was time for them to head toward the others, anyway. She stretched her back and rolled her neck, while Jorg secured the hare to his belt.

"We'll have breakfast now, at least," he said, still smiling.

"You do make mornings eventful."

He snorted then reached for her hand. "Let's go."

Hesitating for a second, she peeked a glance at their joined hands, smiled, and walked with light, happy steps.

After about thirty minutes of walking and neither saying a word, Jorg cleared his throat.

"Where did you end up yesterday? How far did you walk?"

Ingrid didn't know how to respond. Should she tell him about Hnossa, and where she'd really been? Would he believe her?

He won't. And I'm not supposed to tell, anyway.

"I don't know exactly. I just kept going until I felt better, then turned around," she lied. Gooseflesh rose on her arms, and she tried to convince herself it was the morning breeze making her shiver.

Peering at her sideways, he squeezed her hand. "Don't do it again." It wasn't a question, nor was it a strict command. More like a plea.

She squeezed his hand back, but didn't dare say anything. It wasn't a promise she could keep.

Selby came running up to them once they were in sight of the overhanging rocks they used as camp. With hair sticking out in all directions, her braids were a more of a mess than a simple night's sleep could achieve. A wild look in her friend's wide-open eyes grabbed hold of Ingrid's stomach and squeezed.

"What is it? Is it Hagen? Did something happen to him?" She ran to Selby and pelted her with questions.

"No," Selby pushed out while trying to catch her breath. "He's fine, but where were you?"

"I went for a walk to clear my head, and got farther away than I planned. I'm okay, but it's obvious you're not. Tell me what's wrong."

Bending over and resting her hands on her knees, Selby took long, deep breaths before she spoke again. "There was a raiding party last night."

"What?" Jorg laid his hand on her shoulder and looked her in the eyes. "Where? Did they see you?" Concern seeped from his words.

"You two are quick with the questions but not quick to listen." She pulled her arm out of Jorg's grip. "Let's go back so Hagen isn't alone, and I'll tell you all about it."

"Sure. I'm sorry I left while you were sleeping, and didn't make sure you knew where I was," Ingrid said as they walked over to where Hagen lay.

Selby glanced at her from the corner of her eye, then slipped her hand through Ingrid's arm. "Don't do it again."

I'm hearing that a lot. Ingrid leaned into her friend and knew everything would be fine between them. "Deal."

"And don't think that because I'm terrified right now I will let you get away without telling me how your night with Pretty Boy went," she whispered, and pumped her eyebrows.

Selby's whispers were never quiet, and Ingrid saw Jorg turn his head away from them, but not fast enough for her to miss the grin he tried to hide.

When they reached the campsite, they sat down, surrounding Hagen.

"How is he?" Jorg asked.

"There's no change. He's been the same since you left."

Ingrid gazed at her brother and wiped her hand over his forehead. For a moment, she thought she felt her hands warming, but she was wrong.

Pulling her hand away, she let it rest in her lap. "So? Tell us about this raiding party."

"I fell asleep for a bit after Jorg left to find you," she shot a mock scolding glare at Ingrid. "So I don't know how long it had been, but I woke up to add a log to the fire, and heard singing. Loud male voices, singing and laughing." Ingrid reached out and held her hand. "I smothered the fire and listened to see if there was any change in the songs. There wasn't, so I crawled to the top of the outcrop and peeked over. Off in the distance, there was a glow of fire, just beyond the ridge. Since I was downwind, I made sure Hagen was warm, and then I set out to see who belonged to the voices."

"You should not have gone by yourself," Jorg told her in a soft voice.

Sure, he yells at me, but with Selby, he sounds all worried.

Jorg met Ingrid's gaze. "It's different."

Ingrid sat up straighter and sucked in her breath. A slight panic pounding inside her chest, she brought her brows together. He shrugged a little, and Ingrid let her mouth fall open for a second, then pulled her hand away from Selby to wrap both arms around her middle.

"Am I missing something?" Selby asked.

Ingrid didn't realize Selby had stopped talking. "No, just go on. Please." She needed the distraction so the panic of what Jorg had implied couldn't take over.

Selby shook her head. "We'll get to what's going on here," she motioned her finger back and forth from Ingrid to Jorg, causing Ingrid's insides to twist tighter, "after my story. Well, I went by myself, obviously. I was careful, and when I got close, I crawled behind a bush and hid. On the other side was a large group of men, or so I thought." She glanced quickly down to her lap before she continued. "It was hard to see all of their faces in the dark. Only a few were close enough to the fire for me to make out their features, but . . . they weren't men. They had long, pointed ears, and pale complexions; when the fire lit up their faces, it was like they glowed."

"Maybe it was just the shadows of the campfire?" Ingrid tried to sound hopeful.

"I think they were elves, from the stories I've heard, except those stories talk of a friendship with humans. These were dangerous, on a mission to find and take someone to their leader. I was too afraid to stay longer, so I snuck back here and made sure Hagen and I were both hidden in the shadows."

"Did you see which way they went when they left?" Jorg looked at her, concern creasing his forehead.

"Yes, they headed the same way we're going."

"Do you think they're headed toward our village?" Ingrid asked.

"Yes," Jorg answered.

Selby and Ingrid exchanged looks, and shifted closer to each other while Jorg walked off to prepare the rabbit for breakfast.

After breakfast, they set off, but walking was slow. Jorg and Selby took turns pulling Hagen in the litter, but wouldn't let Ingrid help.

"I need to at least *try* to help," she insisted. Coming to a stop, she put her hands on her hips. Selby's legs were moving slower and slower, and the red flush highlighting her face was beaded with sweat. "Stop pushing me aside."

Selby lowered Hagen to the ground with care. Pulling up part of her apron, she wiped her face. "Fine, go ahead."

"It's my turn, just keep walking," Jorg said, and tried to push past Ingrid.

"No! I'm sick of you doing that. I can't heal him, so I don't know what I'm supposed to do now." She grabbed ahold of Jorg's arm, intending to get only his tunic, but her grip was so tight, her nails dug into his forearm.

"Fine, but pull back your claws, wildcat." He smiled at her, and let out a growl like a wild animal. Ingrid rolled her eyes but let go.

Well, I got my way. And he looks heavy . . . great. She wasn't about to give up the battle she'd won, though. "Stand back so I can get a grip."

She turned to stand between the handles of the litter, and squatted down to the ground so that her backside nearly touched the dirt. Encircling the branches with her hands, she laughed to herself that the covers on her hands would at least make the work more comfortable. Then she pushed from her thighs, and stood with ease.

Yes! That wasn't as hard as I thought. I can do this.

Shaking her hair from her face, she took a step. Her body bounced back when the litter didn't budge. She refused to look at Jorg or Selby, although she could see both out of the corner of her eyes, and they were trying not to watch her, either.

"Don't. Say. A. Word. I can do this," Ingrid growled.

Jorg and Selby both spoke at the same time.

"Yes, you can."

"Wouldn't think of it."

Ingrid pulled in a deep breath and held the branches tighter while she tightened her stomach muscles and leaned into her first step. The litter slid a small amount, and she pushed forward with more intent. Slow, steady steps made forward progress. She looked up and cocked an eyebrow at her friends before looking straight ahead with determination.

Jorg and Selby walked on each side of Hagen, staying behind Ingrid. She was glad for it, because she knew the strain was making her face contort in unflattering ways.

I'm doing it, but it's costing us so much time. Do I give up? Or wait until they force me to stop?

The guilt for slowing down their progress ate at her insides. There was a party of some kind heading toward their village, and instead of going as fast as they could, they were crawling along for the sake of her pride.

She stopped walking and sighed. Lowering her legs, she set Hagen onto the ground and turned around to face Jorg and

Selby. Jorg crossed his arms over his chest, and bit the inside of his cheek, but stared at the ground. The look in Selby's eyes almost made her cry, because her best friend looked like she wanted to run to her and hug her. Ingrid had seen the same softness in her mother's eyes when she tried to pretend she believed in Ingrid's dreams.

I've fooled no one more than myself.

"I think it's time for me to stop. We need to move faster," she said.

She wasn't sad or angry about it, she just finally understood that there were some things that—no matter how much she wanted them—she wasn't physically capable of doing.

"It's not right for me to be so selfish. You were right."

"It wasn't selfish. You need to help just like we do." Selby smiled. "So hauling some heavy oaf around the countryside isn't your skill, lucky you."

Jorg snorted and walked over to her. "Step aside, and let me take my turn. I don't think I've ever known that one," he nodded over toward Selby, "to stay silent for so long. I'm sure she has at least a thousand words ready to spew out at you. Help her, before she explodes and we have to carry both of them." He stepped between the litter poles, lifted Hagen, and walked off with a strong, brisk stride.

"Well, for a man, he's pretty perceptive," Selby said as she looped her arm through Ingrid's.

Ingrid giggled, relieved to have such good friends by her side. Then, true to Jorg's prediction, Selby chattered away about so many topics that Ingrid had to snicker as they hurried to catch up to Jorg.

When they stopped for the night, it was painfully clear

that Ingrid's little stunt had cost them too much time. At the speed that Jorg and Selby could walk, they probably would have made it to the village by the following evening. Now, they would need at least one more night to get home.

Determined to make herself useful, Ingrid gathered broken branches and started the campfire. Jorg went to hunt for dinner, and Selby settled Hagen as much as possible, rolling him to his side and straightening his clothes to make him more comfortable.

"I know he'll wake up, but it's hard to see him like this."

Ingrid swallowed the lump that jumped into her throat. "Yes, it is," she said, her voice just above a whisper.

"I didn't mean anything by that. You did amazing. But no one is stronger than Thor, and it was his lightning that caused this."

"Yes, but that doesn't make me feel any better. I thought if I wasn't meant to be a shieldmaiden—which, let's face it, I'm not—then maybe I was called to heal. When the fighting broke out right after we landed in Jorvik, I was so afraid. Then when I saw the first injured man, it all faded away, and I couldn't stop myself from going to him. I helped so many that day, and some were so bad off they may have died if I hadn't. Why was I able to heal them, but not my own brother?"

"I don't know. We have to believe that there is a reason for this, though, and it will show itself. Besides, I've never been able to stare at his handsome face for so long before without getting caught. Gods take, gods give, I guess." She pushed against Ingrid's shoulder, and Ingrid shook her head and smiled.

"You're hopeless."

"It's a good thing he can't hear all of that. His ego is big enough as it is," Jorg said behind them, making both girls jump. He sat down and whittled skewers to spit the three squirrels he'd caught.

Ingrid giggled, and Selby snorted. "He deserves it," Selby said. "He's brave, strong, and will be the leader of the village one day."

"I'm hungry, and I want to keep my appetite," Jorg said.

"Fine, but I speak the truth. You seem happy to follow him everywhere he goes. Maybe I'm not the only one with a crush on him?"

Ingrid let her mouth fall open and pulled her eyes wide. Even with the twinkle in Selby's eyes proving she was teasing, it was a bold thing to say.

"You are lucky you are not a man right now," he growled.

"Want to arm wrestle me to see who loves him more?"

"You know he is in love with your sister, right?"

"Yes. What's your point?"

"You shouldn't lust after someone that isn't available to you. I hear Sten thinks you're . . . 'quite womanly,' is, I believe, how he put it."

"One of the Stinks? No thank you." Selby made a fake gagging noise and scooted closer to the fire.

"I don't know. He would never interrupt you when you talk too much because he wouldn't even understand you, and you could get him to do anything you wanted, since he doesn't bother too much with extra thought—it could be a match from Asgard, and you aren't even looking into it."

"Oh boy," Ingrid said under her breath as she rolled her eyes.

"Listen, pretty boy, you tell him next time you see him to keep his grimy eyes off me. I can't think of anything worse for my life." Selby was about to burst out with a tirade when she noticed Jorg biting his lip to keep from smiling. "You think you're so funny. Laugh it up. Maybe I'll find a handsome prince someday, and shut all of you up."

"Don't bring me into this!" Ingrid exclaimed.

"I wasn't laughing at you, I just like being called 'pretty boy.' Although, I prefer 'handsome', 'strong', 'god-like' . . . something along those lines, if you can remember that for next time."

"Not going to happen. From me, at least." Selby smiled at Ingrid, but turned away when a glare as sharp as daggers flew back at her.

Jorg chuckled and rotated their dinner.

Later, Selby had rolled over to sleep and was breathing slow and steady, but Ingrid couldn't manage, and sat up to stare into the flames. Jorg was lying across from her on his side, and met her eyes through the orange glow.

"Can't sleep?" he asked.

"No. The others have made it home by now, don't you think? From the boats."

"I'm sure they have. It would have only been a couple more days on the water. Even if they stopped and looked for us for a couple days, they'd still be back by now."

"That's good."

"We'll make good time tomorrow."

"I'm sorry for holding us back today."

"You needed to do it. I'm glad you tried."

"Why, so I could make a fool of myself?" She picked up a

twig and poked the logs of the fire. Little sparkles of orange took flight like a flock of sparrows.

"No. Because you needed to know we support you."

Ingrid looked up at him. His eyes were serious as he sat up, and he never stopped holding her gaze. "Thank you."

"Always."

Ingrid tried to smile, but it came out more like a grimace. "I think I should hurry ahead tomorrow. I can run and get there faster than we can as a group. Then maybe everyone will have a chance to be ready and not let those men Selby saw surprise them."

"They are too far ahead of us. We should stay together, it's safer."

"You don't think I can do it." She said it as a statement, but lifted her voice enough for a question.

"I know you can. It's better if we stay together, though."

"You and Selby can carry Hagen; I can't. I can run, though. I'm fast, and I'll make it."

Jorg stared into the flames, and his foot tapped in the dirt. "I believe you. I just don't want you to go."

Really? He probably means something else.

"You're important to me, Ingrid. I thought you knew."

She narrowed her eyes at him. It wasn't the first time it had seemed like he heard her thoughts, and she didn't like it. "I do."

He got up and walked around the fire to sit down next to her. "I don't think you do. When I couldn't find you the other night, my gut twisted into knots. If something were to happen to you, I couldn't live with it." He stared directly into her eyes, and she swallowed hard.

His piney scent washed over her, and she felt dizzy. Without thinking, she reached up and brushed the hair away from his face, tucking one side behind his ear.

Jorg's brows came together, and his shoulders stiffened, but then he relaxed and waited for her reaction.

"Oh," she gasped and looked back into his eyes.

Jorg put his hand over hers and closed his eyes. "That's not something I let anyone see." His voice was a whisper, and the pain in it broke Ingrid's heart.

"I think they're beautiful. You are still the same to me, nothing would change that," she assured him.

He snapped his eyes to hers. "Do you mean that? Even after what Selby saw and heard?" He hadn't let go of her hand, and he squeezed it as he held his breath, waiting for her to answer.

"I mean it. You aren't like that." She smiled when he let out his breath and his shoulders came down at least two inches. "I need to tell you something, though." She pulled her hand out of his, and traced the outline of his ear up to the small, pointed tip, feeling him shudder.

"What?" The worry spread across his features again.

"Twice I've been told that elves are part of my future. We might be in for some trouble."

Jorg's face split into a wide grin. "I'll take my chances."

"Good. Me, too."

He took hold of Ingrid's hand again, and reached his other behind her head.

He's going to kiss me. My first real kiss. Oh goodness.

Jorg grinned enough for his dimple to show, and brought her closer to him, but instead of what she hoped, he leaned his forehead down and rested it against hers. Sighing, she closed her eyes and enjoyed the warmth of his touch.

"Please don't say anything about me to anyone. Hagen doesn't even know, and I'd like it to stay that way."

Ingrid was so caught up in the feel of his hands and the smell of his unique scent, she didn't comprehend what he said at first. "Huh? Oh. Okay."

"We need to get some sleep now. Some other time, when we can talk by ourselves, you can ask me all the questions I'm sure you have. Not that I'll be able to answer them—I've got a list of my own that no one has answered. But I'll try." He sat up and let go of Ingrid. She felt cold and alone the instant his touch was gone. "Lie down and I'll cover you up. It's getting cold."

You could curl up to me again. Let's see if you hear that.

Biting his lip and keeping a neutral expression, he pulled her cloak over her shoulders as she lay down.

Mm-hmm. That's what I thought. I'm going to figure out how you're doing that.

Turning to the fire, Jorg stoked it and added another log. Without looking in her direction again, he walked back to his own spot, wrapped himself in his own cloak, and closed his eyes. "Goodnight, my sweet girl."

"Goodnight." Ingrid noticed the possessive statement, and fell asleep with a smile on her face.

❧ 16 ❧

They were up and walking by the time dawn stretched from its slumber, painting lavender streaks against the soft, gray sky. Ingrid stopped walking, twitching her hands next to her sides while she fiddled with her skirt.

Jorg was leading the group; he checked over his shoulder for the others and stopped when he saw Ingrid standing far behind. Selby trudged behind Jorg with her head down, pulling Hagen, and didn't notice Jorg halt.

"Hey, watch out," he said with a low chuckle, as he darted aside before she ran into him.

"Sorry, I . . . why are we stopping?"

"I don't know." He nodded his head toward Ingrid, as she still stood staring at the ground behind them.

She stepped closer and kicked at a clump of grass, but kept her eyes downcast.

"Why'd you stop?" Jorg asked.

"At this pace, we'll never make it to the village in time to warn them. I'm going ahead now. If I run most of the way, I might make it by nightfall."

"Ingrid, we talked about this last night. You need to stay with us," Jorg said and tightened his lips into a white line. "And it is still more than a one-day walk—even at a jog, which you can't keep up the whole time. The others have at least a day on us, anyway."

Selby stepped away from the litter and looked between them for a couple seconds. "I don't know what happened *last night*," she stared hard at Ingrid with a slight grin teasing her lips, "but I think I agree with Bossy. You shouldn't take off on your own. We're safer together."

Jorg snorted and rolled his eyes before he leveled them at Ingrid again.

"I remember what you said last night. All of it." She met Jorg's eyes and didn't flinch as he inhaled a deep breath to keep his calm. "I might not make it in time, but I have to try. Neither of you can go, because as we all know, you're the only ones who can carry Hagen. I'm not asking either of you—I'm offering you the opportunity to support me before I leave."

"Wow." Selby drew out the word while giving Ingrid a smile.

Ingrid smiled back and knew she had her friend's support. Looking back at Jorg, she raised an eyebrow as she crossed her arms over her chest.

Closing his eyes, he growled in what Ingrid recognized as frustration. Despite his emotional state, she liked the deep timbre of his voice when he made that sound.

He walked over to Ingrid in measured strides and stood within her space. He took two deep breaths, then put his hand behind her head. Tingles shot throughout her body as he leaned toward her and kissed her cheek near the corner of her mouth. A tiny squeak escaped her throat.

"Be careful. I expect to find you well when we arrive home," he whispered before pulling away.

Ingrid blinked several times before answering. Jorg's warm breath on her face flustered her thinking. "Uh-huh, I will."

Jorg then walked over to Hagen. "I'll pull for a while," he said to Selby without looking at her. He readied the poles in his hands and looked blankly at Ingrid. "Go then, if you're going. Use the daylight, and get as far as you can." His voice was cool, unwavering.

"Can we call this official now, or are we still going to pretend nothing is going on between you two? Because that looked a lot like something just now," Selby said, bouncing her head and waving a finger between the two of them.

Ingrid could see Jorg's profile as he stared straight ahead.

I know you're mad. His eyebrow rose slightly, and he pulled in a deep breath through his nose. *Okay, really mad, but I can do this.*

Ingrid didn't know how he could hear her thoughts, but she wanted to say it so he would know it was just for him.

"I'm not super happy about being left with a fussy, lovesick puppy, but hurry home." Selby walked up to Ingrid and gave her a big hug.

"Try to be nice," Ingrid whispered into her ear.

"What? I'm always nice. Now go." Selby turned Ingrid around and slapped her behind to move her forward.

Ingrid shook her head and peeked once more at Jorg. He was looking off to his right at nothing.

I'll be okay.

She wasn't sure if she was convincing Jorg or herself, and she trotted away at a fast pace before she could think too much more about it.

After running for a couple of hours and only taking small amounts of time to walk and catch her breath,, Ingrid's stomach rumbled, reminding her that she needed to take a real break. Sitting against the base of an ash tree, she pulled a hard biscuit from her apron, and nibbled on it. There hadn't been any fresh water along the way to fill her flask, and it was running low. She took small sips to conserve the rest, and distracted herself by thinking about how Jorg could hear her thoughts, and musing how long he'd been able to.

A squirrel skittered down the trunk of a neighboring tree and stopped, frozen except for the twitching of its tail every few seconds.

"How do you think he does it? Do squirrels read each other's minds?" She smiled at the rodent, enjoying its peaceful companionship while she rested. "I don't think he's always been able to do it. I mean, he's always been nicer to me than Hagen's other friends, but he's never paid any attention to me. No, I think it's just been since we left home. Of course, I don't know for sure. Maybe it's part of his heritage, and he can read everyone's thoughts? If that's true, he won't like being alone with Selby."

The squirrel ran farther up the trunk, then stopped again, clinging to the bark as it faced the ground. Dark, unblinking eyes watched Ingrid—or, more likely, the biscuit in her hand. She smiled at the little creature. "How do you stay so still upside down like that?" Ingrid twisted her head this way and that at the squirrel, garnering her a couple quick tail flicks in response. "Don't worry, I'll share a bite with you, but you have to stay and keep me company. Deal?"

Breaking off a small piece of the hard bread, she tossed it toward the base of the squirrel's tree. After a few minutes, it darted down, picked up the crumb, then scurried back up the trunk to sit on the first branch and stuff its little jaws.

"If you like that, you should have tasted the cookie I had in Asgard; you would faint and fall out of that tree from bliss. I've never tasted anything so delicious."

Sitting with her knees pulled up, she closed her eyes for a minute and tried to remember as many details from her time with Hnossa as she could: the gem-like blue of the sky, the sun warming her skin, the sweet fragrance of lavender, lilies, and lemon, and the slight breeze that made the leaves twinkle.

With a warning screech, the squirrel zipped away in a flash, which startled Ingrid out of her respite. On alert, she pulled her feet under her but stayed in a crouched position as she looked around for the danger.

Nothing moved except the grasses, swaying in the distance. From behind her, a shadow passed overhead, darkening the sky momentarily. Then a noise pushed Ingrid's heart to beat so hard she could feel it against the fabric of her tunic.

It was like the flap of a giant eagle's wings, only these carried the weight of thunder as they snapped.

Too afraid to look up, she slapped her hand over her mouth to stifle the scream wanting to escape, and watched the shadow move away from the trees and onto the grasses beyond. *Oh, Freya, please don't let this be real.*

An ear-piercing screech shook the ground under her and confirmed her fears.

High above the ground, but low enough to see in full, was the biggest beast she'd ever seen. The hunting party had described the dragon they'd witnessed, but it didn't compare to the vision before her eyes.

Larger than a horse and cart, the dragon glided through the sky with an eerie grace, occasionally flapping its wings before floating along on the current. Its huge head swept slowly back and forth as it surveyed the ground. Scales like shards of glass flashed colors that changed from blood red to dark blue to deep purple. It was terrifying and beautiful at the same time. Its wings looked delicate, as they spread out against the overcast light. Thin sheets of red between dark outlines of bones, but the vicious claws at their points stole their innocence. The dragon's massive body undulated side to side as it swam through the air, its long tail acting like a rudder as it steered the beast in a lazy circle. Ingrid caught the glint of light that flashed off the sharp spikes on the end of its tail.

Pressing her back into the rough bark, Ingrid held her breath and sat as still as possible, every muscle tensed and ready to flee, but she had nowhere to run. The small clump of trees she sat under comprised of three or four midsize ash and birch trees and several gorse bushes; a short distance away from the inadequate shelter were only tall grasses and peat bogs. In truth, she could crouch and hide among the grasses better than someone taller, but it wouldn't protect her from being spotted from overhead. Additionally, the dragon would spy her if she tried to run, so her best bet was to keep herself as small as possible and wait.

Farther away, the dragon kept making wide, serpentine movements as it hunted. Criss-crossing in overlapping patterns, Ingrid thought it odd it would hunt in such a methodical manner. Most of the beasts she was familiar with either wandered around until they smelled the musky scent of their prey, or they followed a routine route through their territory, catching whatever crossed their path.

As she watched, the dragon spread its wings, and made a wide, sweeping arc. Then, with a giant thrust that cracked through the sky like thunder, it glided straight toward Ingrid.

Quick, shallow breaths pushed her chest in and out rapidly, and she slammed her eyes shut, squeezing her arms tighter around her legs to hold as still as possible. Swallowing the cries that wanted to tear from her throat, Ingrid willed her racing heart to slow, and worked to control her breathing, hoping that the sweat on her brow would not create a strong enough scent to draw the beast now bearing down on her position.

Calm down, breathe, it will pass by.

The sun was behind the monster, so the dragon's shadow reached Ingrid first, coating her in another layer of darkness. Unable to close her eyes anymore, she watched the hunter approach—unhurried, scanning, the spiky whiskers on its muzzle wavering in the breeze of its flight.

It wasn't hunting, it was searching—Ingrid realized with a start.

Its eyes were roaming the ground for something specific, or some*one*. Another flash of tremors rippled through her body.

The dragon flew over her, then circled back. The air was growing warm from the heat radiating off the massive creature. It scanned her hiding place before continuing past her. Sweat dripped off Ingrid's chin onto her arm, but she didn't dare move to wipe her face.

Frozen in place, she lost track of how long it had been since the dragon's last pass. Unwilling to look for it and risk being seen, she stayed put. A scratching noise came from the tree near her. Looking over with only her eyes, she spotted the squirrel once again clinging to the trunk, staring at her with its big brown eyes, and twitching its tail as if nothing unusual had occurred.

Ingrid let out a slow breath and unfurled her legs, wincing at the tingles as blood flowed through them again.

"I suppose you wouldn't be back if danger still lurked in the sky, would you?"

In her hand, she still held the biscuit she'd been nibbling on, though it was broken and crumbling from being held so tightly. She tossed several little pieces toward the squirrel.

"Here you go. I've lost my appetite, but I'm glad you still have yours."

Pushing herself to stand, she tucked away the larger chunks of the remaining hard bread for later and brushed the crumbs off her hands. Not wanting to leave the protection of her cover, but needing to continue the journey to her village, she stepped out of the shadows with slow, cautious movements. The squirrel sat on its high branch, pushing biscuit pieces into its cheeks. She smiled at it, then took a deep breath, rolled her neck from shoulder to shoulder, and jogged into the tall grasses.

Late afternoon shadows stretched long, telling Ingrid she should keep her eyes open for a spot to rest for the night. Making it to the village before morning looked unlikely; the exhaustion of running for so long was catching up to her. She'd sleep for a few hours, and then head out again.

"Ouch! Oh . . . arrrgh!" she growled out as she stubbed her foot on yet another rock and nearly fell.

Covered in burrs and mud splatters, she was irritable and feeling sorry for herself. A light drizzle started, and she closed her eyes, listening to the patter of the rain as it landed against the damp soil. When she opened her eyes again, she saw two grouse scurry out from under a bush near her and dive under another one several feet away.

"Find shelter—maybe that will help my mood," she said to the wind.

"What's wrong with you?"

Ingrid spun around at the harsh, gravelly voice.

A man no more than three feet tall stood in front of her. A hat was pulled low on his brow, and it flopped over the back of his head so she couldn't see his hair. Plenty grew on his face though; he had huge, bushy eyebrows and a beard that sprawled down to his waist. Beady, dark eyes next to a large, bulbous nose were the only features visible. Some kind of pack rested on his back, and he held a large walking stick.

Ingrid narrowed her eyes at him. "I've been through a lot today, and I'm tired. I don't think you want to mess with me right now."

"Mess with you? I've got no use for a daft human standing out in the rain. You're in my way, and the sooner I put you behind me, the better." He walked toward her, clearly intent on pushing her aside.

She held out her hands. "Wait."

"Why?" He glared at her and moved his stick into a more guarded position.

Ingrid took a breath to calm herself. "Do you have shelter nearby? I would like to get out of the rain for a while before I continue on my way."

"Yes and no."

"What does that mean? Do you have shelter or don't you?"

"I do, but you aren't invited. There wouldn't be anything in it for me."

"What? Have you not heard of hospitality? A kindness just for the sake of kindness? Maybe you should try it."

"Kindness doesn't get you anywhere in life. Do you have anything you can offer me in trade?"

Ingrid thought about what she had with her: some dried fish, hard biscuits . . . nothing of any value. Then she remembered that, in the bottom of her pack, she had stashed something she'd picked up off the ground back in the burned village.

That feels like months ago. This journey will never end!

Tamping down her growing prickliness, she removed the small pack from her back and dug through it.

"I have this."

She reached out her hand and opened it to reveal a golden brooch. It bore an intricate filigree pattern, but the clasp was missing. She'd thought it would be a nice keepsake to remember those who had been lost, but it seemed better as a bargaining tool, under the current circumstances.

The man's eyes opened wide as he stared at her hand. Stepping closer, he reached up to take the object, but she closed her fingers and pulled back her hand.

"Show me your shelter first."

"I didn't agree that I'd bargain."

"Fine. If you don't want my gold, I'll continue on." She turned her back on him and started walking.

"Don't be so hasty. I'll take it. For one night's lodging and no more—I'll not give you anything to eat. You're too big, and would eat everything I have stored, most like."

Ingrid stopped walking and turned to him with a neutral expression. "Deal, but you have to provide me with something warm to drink and a dry blanket."

"Fine, but let me hold the gold now."

"No, you'll get it when you uphold your end of the bargain."

"You are bossy and you stink. Follow me."

Barging past her, he walked faster in his limping gait than she would have expected. She smiled to herself at her bargaining skills. Part of her knew that to trust this little man was a bad idea, and to make a deal with him was worse. Everything as it was, however, she accepted her choices.

"How much farther?" Ingrid wasn't sure, but she thought she'd seen the same boulder with a jagged crack through it more than once. *Is he trying to get me lost? If he is, he won't like how I use that stick he's holding.* She rubbed her temples, trying to put aside her bad temper.

"Not far."

"A man of many words."

He turned around so fast she almost bumped into him before she could stop herself. Gawking at him, she waited for him to explain.

"I'm not a man! Don't insult me again, or the deal is off."

He turned and resumed walking.

Ingrid watched the not-a-man waddle as she considered this. He wore homespun pants and tunic with a leather belt and leather shoes. Nothing about him screamed 'Other Realm'. Maybe his attitude, but there were a lot of men in Ingrid's village with equally poor conversation skills.

"What are you, then?"

"Humph."

"Helpful. Listen, I don't know what you are. I would like to know, but if you don't want to tell me, that's fine. But I'm not in the mood for games. How much farther? It seems like you're walking in circles."

"You haven't asked me my name."

Ingrid thought for a minute, and a prickle of warning pierced her, remembering the trolls.

"I don't want to know your name until I know what you are. You never asked me my name, either."

"That's the first smart thing you've said."

"Are you going to answer my question?" Ingrid chose to ignore his comment until later, when she was somewhere warm and dry.

"Just over that rise."

"Thank you. That wasn't so hard now, was it?"

"No wonder you travel alone. You're prickly."

"Not usually, but like I said, it's been a long day. Besides, you're traveling alone, too. And I don't think your attitude is temporary."

"Humph."

Ingrid shook her head and kept following the whatever-he-was, noticing that their path took a different slant, and they didn't pass the same boulder again after their talk. As they made it over the small rise, she looked out over the land. The ground sloped away into a dale, and the shrubs became denser. Gorse bushes bloomed in their happy yellow coats, giving off their woody smells. Any other time, Ingrid would have smiled to see them. Now, however, she only saw too many places to hide, get caught in undergrowth or stuck with no way out. What she didn't see was any kind of dwelling.

"I thought you said it was just over this rise? I don't see any house or hut or whatever you might live in."

"That's because you can't. I don't go around inviting snivelly little humans into my home on a regular basis."

"Well, you did today. So where is it?"

He narrowed his eyes and bit the inside of his cheek. "You sure you won't tell anyone?"

"No."

"No you won't, or no you aren't sure?"

"I won't tell anyone. Since it wasn't part of our deal, that's for free, to show you I'm not so hard to work with." She nodded to him and gave a fake smile.

"Humph."

Ingrid snorted. "I bet you could have a whole conversation only using that sound."

He ignored her and waved his walking stick and free hand around in circles. Words in a language she didn't understand came out of his mouth in a kind of sing-song, and part of the hillside, just a few feet down in the dale, played tricks with her eyes. She rubbed them, thinking her vision was blurred. Then the grasses glowed and faded in a rhythm, and little flashes of light danced around. Finally, there was a loud pop.

Ingrid blinked, then blinked again. It wasn't a house exactly. The ground lifted like a rug, and under it was a small, wooden door, rounded on the top to match the curve of the risen earth. Next to the door was a single, circular window.

The little man—Ingrid couldn't think to call him anything else—puffed out his chest, and cocked one of his bushy eyebrows at her. "Beautiful, isn't it?

"Amazing. How did you do that?"

"None of your business. This way."

"Humph." Ingrid smiled as he glared at her for mocking his favorite noise.

She would need to bend over to squeeze through the small door. *I hope it isn't that short inside, too.* She hesitated to follow him until he yelled at her from inside.

"Are you coming in or what? I don't mean to invite anyone else in here."

Bending at the waist, she took small, deliberate steps as she crossed the threshold. It was so dark, she couldn't see a thing, even with the door still open. There should have been light coming through the window, but darkness covered her eyes like a cloak. There was a smell of freshly turned soil in the air, but it wasn't damp or cold, it was homey and comforting.

"Do you have a torch or a candle or something? I can't see a thing."

"Oh, I forgot about that."

A small air current swirled around her, and she guessed that the same motions he'd performed outside were necessary again inside. When another pop sounded seconds later, the room materialized in front of her eyes.

❧ 17 ❧

It was a small, simple room. A round, braided rug in muted greens and browns lay in the center of the floor, and a fireplace nestled along one wall, with a single rocking chair sitting in front of it. A table with one chair rested against the far wall, and behind her, a short bed lined the wall next to the door.

At least that means there shouldn't be anyone else sneaking around. "It's nice," she said, still mostly bent over. Slipping down to her knees, she sat back on her heels while she continued to look around. "So you live here alone?"

"Yes. I like it that way."

"Do you ever get lonely?"

"I don't need to answer your questions." Walking past her, he reached under the little bed and pulled out a blanket. "Here. Now hand it over."

She smirked at him, but dug the gold out of the pocket where she'd stashed it.

"There you are." She took the blanket as he took the

brooch. "Would you be kind enough to turn around so I can get out of these wet clothes? They need to dry,"

"What?"

"I want to change. Turn around."

"Change into what?"

"Discussing anything with you is impossible. I will wrap myself in the blanket while my clothes dry before the fire."

"But you will still be human?"

It was Ingrid's turn to be confused. "Of course. Why would you ask that?"

"You said 'change'. I thought maybe you were a changeling and had tricked me."

"No, I'm just a regular, human girl. Now please turn around."

Before all the other strange beings she'd met recently, she would have thought his concern odd. Now she understood it more than she'd like. He turned around with a few noises that told her how annoyed he felt about such a request.

"Thank you, I'm finished." She laid out her clothes on the hearth the best she could, chuckling at how large her things looked in the cramped space.

"I'm going to have something to eat," she told him. "You said you had your own food, right?"

"Yes, and don't ask for any."

"You are grouchy. I'm not. I wanted to be polite, and not eat in front of you, but you wouldn't notice good manners, anyway."

He scowled at her the way he had outside—like she was planning to steal his secrets. "You turn around, now. I need to do something."

"What are you going to do?"

"None of your business. Turn away."

She drew in a big breath and let it out slowly as she contemplated her options. "Fine, but I'm trusting you to behave. I will not tolerate any tricks."

It was hard to tell under all the facial hair, but she thought he smirked.

"Understood."

What have I gotten myself into? 'I will not tolerate' . . . like I could stop him from using magic. What kind of creature uses magic? She nibbled on a biscuit and kept her back to him while she thought about what he might be.

A slurping sound drew her attention, and she dared a peek over her shoulder. He was sitting at the table with a bowl of soup in front of him. The smell of carrots and potatoes wafted toward her, making her mouth salivate.

I almost forgot—he owes me a warm drink!

She turned around and faced him. A little grin raised one corner of her mouth when she saw him hug his bowl a little closer to his body.

"You still owe me one part of our deal."

"No, I don't. You can stay here and you have your blanket."

"Yes, but I'm also owed a warm drink."

He glanced at her. "Look away again."

"Why? I know you use magic; why not let me see you do it?"

"You are annoying." He swished his arm around, and another steaming mug appeared on the table. "Take it, and we're finished."

"Thank you."

Ingrid sniffed the liquid, and it smelled delightful. It was a floral tea of some kind, with honey. She took a small sip, and felt the warmth trickle down through her chest and into her middle. A groan escaped despite herself.

"This is delicious."

He nodded, and she caught a quick smile before he resumed eating his soup.

After a span of silence, Ingrid risked another attempt at conversation. "I'm going to take a guess here; I think you are a dwarf. But I thought dwarves lived in groups, not in cute, little, magical houses like this. Is this house connected somehow to Svartalfheim?"

He jumped up from his chair, knocking it over, and stared at her, confirming she was right in her guess. "You need to be careful what you say." He lowered his voice before he continued. "It is not always a good idea to speak every thought that comes into your head."

"What's wrong with what I said?"

"Like names, some *places* have magic associated with calling upon them. You would be smart not to name the realm I'm from again."

"Why do you live alone?"

"Why do you ask so many questions that are none of your business?"

"Human." She pointed a finger at herself.

"Humph." As soon it came out, he looked over at Ingrid, and a small chuckle snorted from his nose. He tried to control it but couldn't, and before either of them realized it, they were both laughing.

"Thank you, I needed that," she told him.

It felt good to release some of the tension that had been building up inside of her. Never in her wildest dreams did she imagine she would someday have tea and laugh with a dwarf. After the last couple of weeks, however, it seemed almost normal.

"I was kicked out," he answered her initial query. "I never fit in with my kin, and I made some choices that were deemed unworthy of the realm. So I was sent here."

"I'm sorry. It must get lonely to live all by yourself."

"Not really. I like the peace and quiet. Do you have a big family?"

"No, just my parents and my brother."

A twinge of guilt stabbed through her at the mention of Hagen. She looked at the warm fire, and tightened the blanket around her shoulders.

"Well, I had plenty more than that. There's never a place to sit by yourself or hear yourself think. Someone's always pushing or shoving, and it's a fight to get enough to eat at every meal. I like it here."

"You still have your magic, so that's nice, right? Wait. I thought dwarves couldn't be out in the daytime?"

"That's true. As part of my banishment, most of my magic left me, but there's a different reason why I'm safe in the sunshine and I don't want to talk about it." Snorting, he looked off into the distance, lost in a memory.

Whatever kept him from turning to stone, she figured had to be a benefit, and didn't worry more about it. "You still have enough magic to hide your house, though. Can you do anything else?"

"Not really, just tricks mostly."

Ingrid nodded. "Having magic would be helpful."

"Why?"

"Have you noticed anything strange lately? Like dragons returning, for example?"

"I heard one flapping its wings earlier today. What has brought them back?"

"It's a long story, but it has to do with a failing protection spell that Odin and Freya placed on Midgard."

"The one that can only be strengthened when the human healer is born?"

"You know about that?"

"Everyone from the other realms knows about it. We were all here when it was put into place. Dwarves were stuck in their realm, unable to do business with Asgard for a long time. Then a deal was made. No one creates beautiful works of art like a dwarf, you see, and the gods like their beautiful things. If the spell is failing, that means the healer has been born, or will be soon. Don't worry—it will be resolved."

"Just watch out for fire-breathing reptiles and slimy trolls and men cloaked in wolf forms until then, right?"

"You've seen all of that?"

"And more."

The dwarf stared at her. He didn't move for so long, she thought maybe he'd been wrong about turning to stone—except he still looked alive, and wasn't gray.

"My name is Plintze."

Ingrid gasped and threw her hands over her mouth. "Why did you tell me that?" she asked from behind her fingers.

"Because you are the healer. You are meant for great things, and will not misuse the power you hold."

Ingrid's shoulders sagged as she let his words sink in.

For as long as she could remember, she'd proclaimed to all who would listen that she would do great things and that there would be stories told of her; a shieldmaiden worthy of sagas that would be told to future generations, stories about how she stormed the battlefield. Using feline-style grace, she would twist and turn, leaving a wake of defeated bodies in the mud as she avoided injury. Then she would stand in the center, shrieking victory, her hair blowing in the wind.

All the exhaustion of the day flooded her, and the weight of responsibility pressed in. The backs of her eyes stung and, as hard as she fought it, they filled with tears. Blinking, she took deep breaths until she'd reabsorbed them, and her heart rate slowed.

"I don't know how or why I have been born for this. I haven't wanted to believe that it is truly my fate, but I know it must be." Ingrid sighed as Plintze nodded his agreement. "I'm Ingrid. It's nice to meet you, Plintze." She smiled a genuine smile and held out her hand.

Plintze shook it with reverence, his eyes soft and crinkled as he smiled.

"I like your smile. It makes me happy," she said.

He peered at her sideways. "Humph."

Ingrid laughed. "Thank you."

"For what?"

"Your friendship. I haven't had a good experience when making new acquaintances lately. I'm glad I met you."

"You need to be careful. There are many who will not like that you have arrived, and will seek to stop you from your destiny. You shouldn't have risked coming here with me. If I were any other dwarf, you'd be in a cage, waiting for the highest bidder right now."

A feeling of dread skittered down her spine; she knew all too well he was right.

"I do have a habit of trusting when I shouldn't, but I was right about you." Hesitating, she bit her lip, trying to decide if she should ask him the question that had been bothering her. "Plintze, do you know anything about the dark elves?"

His bushy eyebrows drew together, covering his eyes. "Stay away; that's the best thing I can tell you about them. Why do you ask?"

"I know they are called dark because of the magic they practice, but do you think if they use their abilities to restore the Vanir to be of equal position with the Æsir, that it would be a good thing for all the realms?"

"No. Dark magic never has a good purpose, and only someone trying to deceive you would say so. The dark elves wouldn't want to make Vanaheim equal to Asgard; they would want to make it more powerful. To destroy Asgard would be to destroy all the realms. The Vanir accepted their fate long ago, and are a peaceful race. Who have you been talking to?"

"I can't say, or I'm not sure if I should right now. The power of a name, and all that. I'm confused though, because the one who told me how I fit into all this madness is the one who told me the dark elves were trying to help. She said that if the spell is bound for eternity, it would create such an imbalance in magic that *that* would destroy all the realms."

Plintze inhaled a deep breath. "The Æsir gods are a temperamental bunch. They can be selfish, greedy, and pompous, but they love Midgard. They would do nothing to hurt the humans. The dark elf leader is powerful, and not to be trusted; he is to be feared. If he believes that you will work on his side, he will keep you safe, but most likely lock you away. If he doesn't get your help, he will destroy you."

Ingrid stared into the teacup resting in her lap. "My friend saw a group of elves talking around a campfire the other night. They said they were looking for someone to take to their leader. They were looking for me, weren't they?"

"Probably. I guarantee that if the dark elves know who you are, they won't stop until they find you, and everyone around you will be in danger."

"That means I've put you in danger now, too. I'm sorry."

"Ach, don't worry about me. My house is glamoured, and no one knows I'm here." Plintze paced between the fireplace and the table, making growling noises and muttering under his breath.

Wishing he wouldn't have taken me in, I'm sure.

"I don't like it," he blasted out, surprising Ingrid into sitting tall, "but if you want to, you can stay here to hide. No one will find you if you stay in the house." He stood in front of Ingrid with his hands on his hips, and a scowl creasing his forehead.

Ingrid relaxed and settled back onto her heels again as warmth crept into her heart. Plintze wasn't so gruff after all.

"Thank you for that offer. I know it would be hard for you to give up your peace and quiet for me, and I appreciate it with all my heart. But I have to go home and warn my family. My friends are carrying my brother home right now, and I could not live with myself if any harm came to them because of me."

"That's your choice, then."

He looked toward the fire, and then at his dishes still on the table. He walked over and put his chair upright. Ingrid watched as his mustache twitched, and she tilted her head to the side as a slow smile edged across her face.

"If I wasn't here, what would you do for the rest of the evening?" She had the distinct impression she was keeping him from something, but she couldn't figure out what.

"Nothing. None of your business." He snatched the dishes off the table, set them in the sink, and then came over and grabbed the teacup from her hands. "Check your clothes." The command was gruff, but if she didn't know better, she'd guess he was nervous—like he didn't know what to do with her now.

Rising to her knees, she scooted over to the hearth. Her clothes weren't completely dry, but enough so that she could get dressed, which would make her feel more comfortable, anyway. She kept having to adjust the blanket to stay covered.

Guess this is one time I should be happy I'm short.

She looked toward the sink, where Plintze had his back turned to her. "Stay turned around, and I'll get dressed."

"Humph."

Ingrid giggled under her breath, and changed as quickly as she could. Wrapping the blanket around her shoulders, she stayed next to the fire. On the mantel, a box caught her eye, and she rose to her feet, keeping her knees bent so she could take a closer look.

"Don't touch that!" Plintze yelled, giving her a start.

"I wasn't going to, I just wanted to look at it. Did you carve it?"

Pushing her to the side, he pulled the box down and sat with it on his lap in the rocker. Ingrid sat on the far edge of the hearth, putting enough space between them to help him relax.

"I made it as a boy, a place for my mother to keep her needles."

"How kind of you. I'm sure she loved it."

Ingrid could see it better in the firelight. The top had snow-capped mountains, and a valley with a river running through it. Each side looked to have a different scene. She could see two: one had a tree with falling leaves and a many-pointed buck standing on a hillside, and the other showed a lake with a large eagle, talons out, ready to grab a fish out of the lake.

"Do the sides represent the seasons? They are so detailed."

Plintze nodded, but didn't look at her, keeping his eyes trained on the dancing flames of the fire. The orange glow flickered in his dark eyes, and he looked lost in thought.

Ingrid turned her face to the fire as well, letting them share the peace of the warm room and the companionable silence. The logs in the fire burned bright and warm, but as she watched, she realized they didn't turn to ash. There wasn't any smoke rising from them, either—only an earthy peat smell. Dipping her head, she peered under the mantel, and saw that there was no chimney.

She quickly sat back and adjusted the blanket around her shoulders, and Plintze's voice broke the silence.

"She had never seen the above world, but she always wished she could. I snuck out at night and wandered around because I wanted to know what it was like so I could describe it to her. One night, I met a sprite—temperamental those creatures, never know if they are friend or foe. This one was young and hadn't met a dwarf before and, out of curiosity, wanted to talk to me. We developed a friendship, of sorts. I would tell her about my world below, and she would tell me of the world above.

"My mother was always dropping her needles out of her apron, so I thought I'd make her this box, and let her see some of the above world at the same time." Plintze stopped talking and resumed staring into the flames.

Afraid to disrupt the mood that made him willing to talk so much, Ingrid stayed still and quiet. As the room fell into silence, she bounced her knees, and her mind wandered to Jorg, Selby, and Hagen.

I wonder how far they made it today? I hope they didn't see that dragon.

Gasping, she stood up too fast and hit her head on the ceiling. "Ouch!"

She fell back to the hearth, and grabbed at her head with both hands.

Plintze looked at her with a mixture of a scowl and confusion in his eyes. "What was all that?"

"I was just thinking about my friends. What if they run into that dragon I saw today? They won't be able to run away because they are pulling my brother. I have to find them and warn them." She wanted to pace, run out the door, do *something*. Here she was, sitting and watching a warm fire, and listening to stories, while they were outside, heading toward a beast that would eat them. Her stomach was in knots.

"There's nothing you can do. One way or another, they will

have to travel through the same area you did, right? What difference would it make if you were with them or not? Also, dragons don't hunt at night. They have terrible vision in the dark."

"Are you sure about that? Is it dark out now? I can't see anything out your window."

"My window is glamoured, inside and out. It makes me feel like I'm back home. It is late, so it is dark out, rest assured," Plintze said.

"You know for a fact that dragons don't hunt at night?" Ingrid strained to see out the window despite knowing there was nothing to see.

"I know it for a fact. Besides, if the dragon is searching for you, which I would bet my life that it is, your presence would be worse for your friends, not better."

His words were spoken in a matter-of-fact tone, not intending to cut into her heart, but they did. Ingrid sat still and let it sink in.

They're safer without me. Slumping her shoulders, she exhaled a long breath and nodded. "You're right. I will stay here tonight, but I'm leaving first thing in the morning. That way, the dragon, or the elves, or anything else sent to find me will be drawn toward me instead. They'll make it home safe that way." She looked at her host, a half-smile tugging at one side of her mouth while she nodded. "Thank you, Plintze, for everything. You are wonderful, and I'm so happy I got to meet you."

He stared at her, saying nothing, but his mustache twitched again. "We should get some sleep." Standing up and putting the box back on the mantel, he walked over to his bed along the wall and sat down.

Ingrid kept her eyes on the box. "I'm sorry about your mother."

"What?"

Turning toward him, a wash of empathy flooded over her. Banished from his home and alone, she wanted to give him a hug.

"If she was alive, I don't think you'd have her box." Selfishly, she'd interrupted the end of his story.

Clasping his hands together in his lap, he stared at the floor. "She isn't dead. When I gave her the box, she lit up with the biggest smile I'd ever seen. It was one of her greatest treasures. When I was banished, the High Council forced her to give it back to me and renounce me as her son. If she hadn't, she would have been banished, too. I couldn't allow that."

A tear slid down Ingrid's cheek. Not caring if he'd like it or not, she flung herself across the room, wrapping her arms around his shoulders in a tight embrace.

At first, he stiffened and pulled against her, but she didn't let go, and she felt him slowly relax until his head leaned into hers. Comfort seeped both directions, filling loneliness they each wanted to ignore.

Releasing him, she sat back and looked him in the eyes. "Your mother still loves you in her heart no one could take that away. I know it is true because you are a good man, Plintze."

He made a noise in his throat, and picked at a thread on his pants. "Humph, I'm not a man," he said, but his eyes had a sparkle to them. "Get some sleep." He lay down and covered himself with a blanket.

Ingrid smiled and scooted over to the fire, curling up in her blanket with her back to him. The flames shrank down to small, glowing embers, but the room stayed cozy and warm.

Before dawn began to lift the veil of night, they were standing outside of his door. Plintze handed Ingrid her pack, which felt heavier as she settled it on her back.

"You know the way to go, right?" he asked.

"Yes. You've been clear, and I'm confident I know the way. My pack feels heavier; did you do something to it?"

"I made sure you'd have enough to eat. You are scrawny."

Ingrid smiled at him, and grabbed his shoulders for a hug too quickly for him to duck away. He sighed in exasperation, but patted her back and returned her gesture for a quick second before pulling away.

"I will never forget our friendship. Be safe. I hope we see each other again," she said to him when she pulled back.

He nodded to her and shuffled his feet. "Now go. You need to hurry."

She turned and jogged off toward home, her heart full and renewed with hope.

❧ 18 ❧

Walking in a valley, alongside a creek, Ingrid enjoyed the company of twittering birds as they created happy melodies against the light blue sky. Absent of rain, clouds floated aimlessly overhead like light-hearted reminders that all would be well.

She stooped down to fill her flask from the bubbling water before heading up the hillside. On a different journey, if she had time to explore, she might have kept following the creek, winding its lazy way toward the village. But this was not the time for such pleasures. She held a firm grip on her anxiety as she hurried along at a steady pace, ensuring she'd have enough strength to make it home before nightfall.

Carried on the breeze, the scent of burned wood from an extinguished fire reached Ingrid's nose. Still miles away from the village, she couldn't imagine it was anything more than a wildfire, likely started by a spark off Thor's hammer. Catching her breath, she thought of Hagen, and her friends pulling him toward safety.

When she reached the top of the hill, a view of more knolls and valleys stretched before her, marking an end to the marshy moors, and signaling harder walking ahead. Then the blackened earth caught her attention. Trees like charcoal sentinels stood bare and gnarled, dirt so scorched that nothing would grow or thrive on it for years.

It could not have been a natural occurrence. It held the sinister tingle of magic, with a hint of rotten eggs and a beast that roamed the skies and torched on a whim.

A bead of sweat trickled down Ingrid's spine like a spider. She shuddered and forced her knees together to keep them steady. Looking heavenward, she scanned for any signs of a dragon, but found nothing but a few strands of clouds, pulled thin like fleece.

The birds won't even fly over this.

Here and there, surrounded by desolation, trees and shrubs stood untouched as lonely reminders of what once was. The entire landscape looked as if a toddler had had a nasty tantrum and thrown its toys in a random frenzy.

Exposed and vulnerable, she would have to pass through the dark barrenness no matter which direction she chose to walk.

Keep walking, Ingrid, and don't think about anything else. Just get home.

Muscles tight and eyes alert, she pushed her shoulders back and focused on the first patch of unscathed brush, striding forward with long, smooth steps. Within feet of her goal, a deafening screech pierced the sky behind her, and she squeezed her eyes shut as tremors rolled throughout her body.

Running the last few steps, she dove into the brush and

clawed her way as deep within the twisted branches as she could. Wedged beneath the flimsy cover, she struggled to roll over and peer through the leaves into the sky.

Circling low, a dragon larger than the last one glided overhead. Black scales shimmered with green and blue in the light, like boiled tar. Horn-like spikes protruded from the massive head like a crown, and ruby red eyes glittered in Ingrid's direction. Where the first dragon had wings that were thin enough for light to flow through, the skin between the bones of this beast was thick like dark leather, and longer, sharper claws tipped the ends like swords.

Making a lazy circle over Ingrid's hiding place, it flew away from her, and she held her breath, hoping she'd been lucky again. But then it turned on itself, and came back with a thunderous flap of its wings. With a gentle exhale, the taloned feet landed on the ground, and the dragon, folding its wings into its body, stood facing Ingrid on all four massive, muscled legs. A heavy breath, barely a whisper, would be all it took to fire the thicket she hid within.

Sweating and dizzy, her heartbeat thrashed inside her ears while she searched for anywhere else to hide. An ash tree rose high into the air about ten steps away; it was large enough to better shield her. If she could untangle her legs and move faster than the flames that were sure to come.

Blinded by a flash of light, Ingrid threw her arms in front of her face. A metallic taste entered her mouth when she screamed, and the scents of pepper and cinnamon washed over her. Unscathed and confused, she peeked over her hands when her eyes had adjusted to the daylight again.

The dragon cocked its head and curled its lips, as if in a

smile, exposing its gleaming white teeth. It slid its tail in a slow arc from one side to the other, carving away the soil underneath with each pass.

"Hello there, I've been searching for you for quite some time," a voice, oily and dark, seeped into her thoughts.

The dragon hadn't moved its mouth and, as detestable as it was, the sound didn't match the creature. There was something else to this monster. Imbued with a spirit that didn't belong to it, the massive body was veiled by shimmering waves of evil. Ingrid could feel its presence. Unlike the cloak worn by the wolf-man, this was not a borrowed skin, but a vessel.

"Who are you?" she asked with more strength than she felt.

"I could be a friend, if you'll allow it. We can do great things together, you and I. There is a purpose we both share, my lady, and I would be honored to have your presence by my side." The words threaded a blackness into her brain, even as they were spoken like a nobleman. Strange and menacing, a power seeped into her consciousness.

Ingrid shook her head, unable to form words, her breaths coming too quick and shallow as she stayed in hiding.

"There, there, don't be so afraid, child. I used this beast to search for you, but it won't hurt you if I don't allow it. Unfortunately, you are not near enough to me for a personal introduction, so we must speak through our friend, here." Sticky, like black honey, the voice oozed into Ingrid's head, pushing against her consciousness, making her wince.

Digging deep into her willpower, Ingrid crawled forward out of the brush and stood tall, yet her knees wobbled and her hands trembled. The wrapping on her hand that Jorg had tied for her had come unraveled and now hung by her side.

"I'm no one special. Why would you look for me? You must be mistaken," she said, hoping it was true, but knowing it wasn't.

A laugh, throaty and deep, flooded her senses. "I'm sure you are who I seek. Surely you don't think I'd be that easy to fool? Ingrid, sweet child, you have so much to learn."

"You know my name?" she whispered, and sucked in her breath.

"Of course I do. I've had many helping me to find you. I'm pleased to meet you, albeit in this awkward manner. My home is far from here, but I would like to invite you to join me so we can discuss our shared destinies. I will have my scouts come escort you to me—that way your safety can be insured."

"Who are you?"

"My apologies, I have been remiss in introducing myself. I am Jarrick of Alfheim, crowned prince and brother to Thelonious, King of the Elves. At your service, my lady."

Ingrid shook her head when the dragon seemed to bow its head slightly. The words were spoken in a manner of someone highborn and noble, true enough, but evil simmered from the beast in front of her. No one with pure intentions could ally with such a force.

"Why would you introduce yourself by name?"

"There is power in a name; only the weak can be controlled by it. Be careful whose advice you take, Ingrid. A simple mind cannot possibly understand the responsibilities of those like us, who are charged with greatness. You will learn that when you come to train with me."

Everything Hnossa told her crashed against the words shared by Plintze: *The dark elves sought to restore Vanaheim and heal the rift on Alfheim', 'Dark magic never has a good purpose; only someone trying to deceive you would say so', 'The dark elves don't want to make Vanaheim equal to Asgard, they want to make it more powerful'.*

Trembling, she forced herself to speak. "You are *the* Dark Elf, the one who wants to destroy Asgard."

The dragon huffed a gust of rotten egg smell, causing Ingrid to turn her face and fight her gag reflex, while her arms felt warm—like they were suffering a mild sunburn.

"So, you've spoken to one of my enemies. That's not how I hoped we could begin our relationship." The voice held a sharp edge of irritation.

Ingrid glanced toward the ash tree, and tried to calculate how fast she could run.

"You have been misinformed, as is to be expected from any fool that would oppose me. You will understand and agree with me once we have a chance to meet in person."

"What happens if I refuse? If I choose to follow my destiny alone?"

The dragon roared, shaking the ground and causing Ingrid to lose her balance. Using the motion as an opportunity, she sprinted toward the tree and flattened herself against its large trunk. Relief washed over her to have the barrier between herself and the dragon, even though she knew it was most likely a futile effort.

"Ingrid," the voice slammed against her mind, making her scream in pain. "Ingrid, my dear, I'm sorry to cause you pain. You need to understand that you must work with me—there is no other option. I have worked far too hard, for longer than your pitiful human existence can comprehend, just to have a small child stand in my way of achieving the greatest accomplishment the nine realms has ever seen. Success would be easier with you, but if you choose to defy me, it will not stop me. You will only make yourself expendable."

Exhausted, Ingrid stayed frozen to the rough tree bark. An odd sensation of confidence mixed with crippling fear flooded through her, coating her thoughts and pushing against her free will. Fighting against the invasion, she mentally created a barrier, and pushed against it, as if it were a door she could close and lock to keep herself safe and secure. A tightness squeezed her chest, and it took concentrated effort for Ingrid to stay standing and not double over into a ball, crying.

Gripping the bark of the tree, splinters forced their way into her palms and fingertips as she slowed her breathing, squared her shoulders, and inhaled deep, cleansing breaths. Keeping one hand on the tree, she stepped sideways and exposed herself to the dragon.

"I am not expendable. By Freya and Odin, I have the gifts of sight and healing to add the power of Midgard to the spell cast long ago and bind it for all the ages." Ingrid smiled and shook her head. "Thank you for your belief that I am the one you seek; now I believe it, too. I will not follow you, Prince Jarrick." Ingrid stood tall, the full acceptance and understanding of her destiny clear.

"That spell is a curse," Jarrick sneered. "It allows the Æsir to rule with their over-inflated egos, for their own purposes. They are liars who cheated to defeat Vanaheim. Justice must be served, and the rightful leaders must be restored for the sake of all the realms. Work with me, help me to accomplish what the others gave up on—peace and equality."

"I won't."

"Pity. Our accomplishments together would have no rivals, but . . ." Jarrick sighed, not with a heavy heart, but with acceptance. "If this is what you choose, so be it. I would have liked to know you better, Ingrid. Goodbye."

A flash of light bounced off the dragon's scales in a sparkling array of colors, and blinded Ingrid as she jumped behind the ash tree, pressing her body close to the trunk. Heat blasted at the tree and bushes around her, singeing the ends of her hair as it blew into the air.

I hope I have chosen right. Freya, if I am truly the one to bind the spell, please help me now.

When the flames stopped, the ash tree stood strong in front of Ingrid. Unblemished, it had protected her and she sagged against it in relief.

A gust of wind and a rumble through the ground announced the dragon's return to the skies. These were followed by a shriek that curdled the blood, then burnt wood and earth scented the air. When Ingrid looked around, all she could see was the charred bits of what remained of the lush growth.

In the air, the dragon, free from the influence of dark magic, became a predator once again, hunting for a prized possession, a toy rather than food. No longer taking lazy circles in a search grid, it concentrated its efforts toward the ash tree, this time shooting flames on Ingrid's right.

She slid around the trunk in time, and only her skirt caught on fire, which she patted out with ease.

Shooting past her like an arrow from new string, the dragon flew over Ingrid and turned to come at her from another angle. Flames scorched what remained of the living brush, leaving a desolate landscape.

Ingrid had to find cover; she knew she couldn't hide behind the ash any longer. Not more than twenty feet away, a pile of rocks hid the opening to a small hole.

A flash of light mixed with blistering heat shot out toward her. Diving to the side, she escaped the main blast, but screamed when her shoulder and upper arm bubbled and burned. Falling to her knees and grabbing at her arm, she cried out again.

Swooping down, the creature reached out its merciless talons, missing her body as it sailed over, but slicing into the forearm she'd raised to block her face. Before the dragon could turn around and try again, Ingrid darted as fast as her legs could go, diving headfirst between the rocks.

There was just enough space for her small shoulders to make it through, and then she was in cool darkness, surrounded by the scent of fresh, unburned dirt. Clumps of it fell on her when the dragon slammed back down onto the ground, and she scrambled deeper into the small burrow. She pulled herself through the earth until it opened into an abandoned den, and then she curled up, pressing herself against the back of the hole.

Shrieking and clawing, the massive animal raged in a fury, trying to find its lost prey. Ingrid could feel the vibrations through the trembling ground as the dragon walked to and fro, hunting for her.

Huddled in the dark, she made herself as small as possible. The burns on her arm screamed, but it was the slice through her flesh that worried her. Holding her hand over the wound, she didn't feel the usual warm tingle of healing.

Not once, but twice while Ingrid was tending to her injuries, the giant face leaned down, turning a blazing red eye into the cave, and then stomped away.

Remembering what Plintze had told her about the poor eyesight of the beast, she relaxed a little and prepared to stay in her hiding place as long as necessary. She thought of her home and family, vulnerable and at the mercy of Jarrick and his forces, and she felt like a sharp axe had been taken to her insides. If she could rest, get her gash to stop bleeding, and avoid the dragon, maybe she could still make it home before the others.

Why won't this close? I accept that I'm the healer—stop bleeding, already!

Spots danced at the edges of her vision. Dirt rained down on her as the dragon continued to stomp around outside, but she cared less and less about him. Keeping a vice-like grip on her arm, she leaned her head against the cool earth and closed her eyes.

Ingrid's eyelids and body felt heavy and immovable, but her mind fluttered awake, breaking free from the cocoon that held it captive. A spoon rattled against a pot, and the smell of warm stew and fresh bread woke her dormant stomach with a loud growl. A couple seconds later, a rough finger pushed against her eye, prying her lid open, and a shadowed face hovered inches from her own.

"Come on, finish this and wake up," a familiar voice growled.

I know that voice. Plintze!

The dwarf's hidden cottage, that's where she was.

As she struggled to bring herself out of the bonds that chained her to sleep, a moan slipped from her throat. Finally, she licked at her lips and cracked open her eyes. When she attempted to move her arms and push herself up, she realized that one of them was strapped across her middle. Fear sent an instant surge of strength through her, and she gasped for air as she bolted into a sitting position.

"Whoa, easy now," Plintze said as if she were a frightened horse.

Breathing hard and still confused, she looked around the room. It was the same as the last time she'd seen it, except now she slept atop a pallet of straw, with warm, heavy blankets over her.

"How?" Swallowing hard against her dry throat, she tried to follow the memories that swirled through her head: the dragon, the hole, the pain. Looking down at her strapped arm, it all flooded back to her.

"Here, eat this, and get some strength back." Plintze placed a bowl of stew in her lap and a spoon in her free hand.

"How did I get here?" she asked.

"I brought you. After that demon gave up and flew away," he said.

"I didn't think it would do that. I expected it to dig me out and . . ." Tears stung the back of her eyes.

"They aren't agile creatures on the ground; don't want to

dirty their pretty claws, either. Quicker than an arrow in the air, though."

"How did you find me and get me here?"

"Stop asking so many questions." Plintze played with something in his pocket, not looking at Ingrid. "I don't know why, but it felt like I had to search for you. Like something pulled me there. Eat!"

Ingrid hurried a spoonful to her mouth on reflex, then hunger hit with full force, and she continued to eat in earnest.

Plintze told her more of the story. "I came upon that beast circling the hole you'd crawled into, and stayed hidden until it left. Digging you out was no easy chore; carrying you over my shoulder like some ox didn't do me any good, either." Plintze took her empty bowl and filled it again, setting it gently back in her lap.

"Thank you. I expected to die." Staring into her stew, Ingrid saw an errant tear plop into the bowl.

"Humph."

Ingrid smiled through her watery vision. Despite the circumstances, her body relaxed, and she breathed easier.

"Why is my arm like this?" She didn't feel any pain, but her entire left arm was wrapped in linen and cradled in a sling strapped to her chest.

"You got a nasty burn and slice in that arm. The burns were already healing by the time I got to you, but there's venom in a dragon's claws. Helps them to subdue their prey. Your body couldn't heal that, I guess."

"It doesn't hurt. Did you fix it?"

"I had to get help, but you'll heal," he said.

"Help from who? I thought you stayed away from everyone."

"I do," he growled. "But you'd have died." The last part was said so low that Ingrid almost didn't hear it, as he turned his back to her and busied himself stirring the pot over the fire.

"Thank you," she said.

The cottage remained silent for several minutes. Finished with the stew and a slice of bread that Plintze had added to the second bowl, Ingrid's strength was returning. Rested and warm, she fiddled with the coverings over her legs.

"What's the matter?" Plintze looked at her over his shoulder.

"I need to go outside for a few minutes," she said.

Confused, he turned and stared at her until she cocked an eyebrow at him. "Oh," he opened his eyes wide with understanding. Opening the door, he helped her walk on her knees to get through the small dwelling and go outside. "Hurry."

Ingrid shook her head at the bossy tone, while letting her eyes adjust to the morning sunlight after the cottage's dark interior.

"Did you hear me? I said hurry," Plintze said when she hadn't moved.

"Back off, I'll go as fast as I can," she hissed.

Plintze stared at her and blinked without saying another word. Ingrid stretched her back, feeling the skin on her arm tingle as it rubbed against the linen wrap, and walked away from the cottage. She returned a few minutes later to find Plintze pacing in front of his door.

"Thought you might get it in your head to run off," he said. "Inside, quick."

Bending over, she walked through the door without help, and settled back onto the pallet. The fire was low, and the food was gone, but the room hugged her in warmth.

"How long have I been here, Plintze?"

The dwarf made some grumbles, and fidgeted with his sleeve before answering. "Three days."

"What?" Ingrid closed her eyes and let the instant tears slide through her lashes. *Three days. Too late, I'm too late.*

The elves would have made it to the village without a warning, which means Jorg and Selby had pulled Hagen into a disaster. Everyone she loved was most likely dead or dying, and she had done nothing to stop it. Sorrow turned to anger, deeper and darker than she had ever felt. It bubbled up from within, making her hands shake and her lip curl with the need for vengeance. Somewhere in the back of her mind, she felt a sensation, like a tapping of something trapped and trying to get her attention.

Ignoring the sensation, she looked at Plintze. "I have to go home. I need to know what happened."

"What's wrong? You don't seem like yourself," he asked.

"I'm fine, I just need to leave, that's all. Where's my pack? Did I lose it?"

"No, it's here. It was on the ground near where I found you."

Agitated, he stomped over to his bed and started throwing items onto the cover. Ingrid watched in confusion as he wrapped the cover into a bundle and shoved it into the pack she'd seen him wearing the first time they'd met.

Pulling her pack out from under his bed, he held it out to her. "No reason to dawdle. Let's go."

He threw open the door, jammed a wide-brimmed hat onto his head, and left.

Ingrid followed him. "Where are you going?"

"Close the door," he yelled.

Grabbing the handle and jerking the door closed, she ran to catch up to him. "Why are you coming with me?"

"You'll need to go slow, and I'll need to treat your arm again, so I have to come with you."

"You could give me the supplies; I'm capable of taking care of myself. You don't need to follow me."

She stopped walking and looked down at the ground, her eyes roaming back and forth as if searching for something.

"There, that's what I'm talking about," Plintze said. "You're acting snappish. It's not like you."

"I know, I heard it that time." Looking at him, her eyes went soft. The knocking in her brain was louder now, and she put a hand to her forehead, rubbing it to try and clear the noise.

"What happened out there? What haven't you told me?" Plintze asked.

Ingrid continued to rub her temples with her good hand, keeping her eyes closed. "Jarrick of Alfheim spoke to me through the dragon." She didn't open her eyes, but could hear Plintze's breathing quicken.

"What are you saying? How could he speak to you?"

"I don't know how. There was a flash of light, then his voice was in my head. It felt like tar."

"What did he say?"

"He wanted me to join him, to come to Alfheim. When I

refused, there was another flash of light and then the dragon attacked."

"We need to hurry. You are not safe out here."

"I feel like part of him is still inside my mind, sticky and dark. My head aches."

Plintze didn't say anything, and when Ingrid opened her eyes, he was staring at her. "He practices the dark arts. We need to get you to someone who can help you."

Ingrid nodded her head, as tears stung the back of her eyes and her lip started to tremble. So much had happened and the thought of dark magic influencing her was too much.

Plintze stepped away. "None of that, let's go."

Adjusting his hat, he strode off in the same direction she had walked days before.

19

Ingrid stood from refilling her flask with water from the bubbling creek she'd followed on her first trip through the valley. Stretching her back, she closed her eyes, trying to let the chirping birds and sunshine soothe her mind and spirit. The scent of mint floated through the air above the smells of moss and damp earth. Inhaling long and deep, she let the breath out slowly before opening her eyes and readying to continue the journey.

"Are you ready to go?" she asked Plintze, who was resting in the shade of some gorse bushes.

Without a word, he stood and turned toward the steep hillside, digging his walking stick into the earth as he began to climb.

"Where are you going? Shouldn't we keep following the creek?"

"This way is faster," he called back to her.

"Why didn't you tell me to come this way before?"

Ingrid grunted as she dug her feet into the incline and leaned forward to keep from falling. Her muscles were straining from staying in bed so long after the dragon attack, but she wouldn't admit it.

The little imp is probably trying to get me lost, anyway.

As soon as she had the thought, her head ached again, pressure squeezing her skull from the inside.

"Plintze," she called out to the dwarf, who was getting farther and farther away from her. "I don't think I can make it this way."

"You can. Keep moving."

Plintze didn't look back at her, and she snorted at his heartless lack of concern. Rubbing the back of her neck, she pinched her lips together and kept climbing. After what felt like hours, and with dirt stuck throughout the fibers of her gauntlet and smeared across her face, they reached the top.

Falling to the ground, Ingrid laid on her back in the grass, needing to catch her breath.

"Where's the wrap for your other hand?" Plintze asked.

"Why do you care? You're in too much of a hurry to get me home and leave me."

Plintze grumbled something Ingrid didn't understand, and took a few steps away.

When he returned to stand near her, he said, "I will not leave you. Do you still have the wrap or not?"

"It's right here. I had to take it off because it kept getting caught on the mountain I was forced to climb."

"Put it back on, and then we'll go. We can make it by nightfall if we hurry."

Ingrid rolled her eyes and huffed loudly while sitting up. Fumbling with the long strip of fabric, she struggled to wrap it in a secure way, taking it on and off several times with increasing mutterings and growls each time. Finally, she threw it onto the ground, and wrapped her arms around her knees.

"I don't need it, anyway."

Plintze sighed. "Yes, you do. Give it here, I'll wrap it."

"I'm sorry, Plintze, I don't feel right. Like everything is wrong, and it will never get better." Ingrid picked the wrapping up off the ground and handed it to the dwarf, who'd kneeled next to her.

"It's the dark elf. He used magic that's letting him manipulate you. He's riding around with us, inside your head."

"How do you know that? Why would he do that to me? How do I get him out?" Ingrid rushed out the questions without taking a breath.

Plintze looked up at her with a scowl. "Settle yourself, girl." He finished wrapping her hand and stood up. "I'll tell you while we walk. Let's go."

Ingrid stood up and followed as he headed off in the direction they needed to go. As they crested the hill, she stopped for a moment to take in the view.

Lush, green trees and white, yellow and pink blossoms dotted the ground in random patterns, lending their sweet scents to the air. A thick lump formed in her throat as a similar view came to mind, only it was blackened now and filled with evil. Plintze, either not realizing she'd stopped or not caring, continued down the slope into the forested cover.

Ingrid straightened herself, squared her shoulders, and hurried after him.

Under the thick canopy, the air grew cooler, and the light played games with the shadows. Several times, Ingrid felt as if someone watched her, flitting in and out of sight among the sunbeams.

"It's creepy in here," she said.

"It is. The faster we get through this part, the better."

Amazingly, Ingrid nearly had to jog to match Plintze's pace.

"I feel like I'm being watched. Is there someone out there?" she whispered, louder than she'd wanted to.

"Yes. The sprites live in this part of the forest. Never can tell how they'll behave; best to steer clear of them."

"The sprites? Have they always lived here, or are they newly returned as well?"

"They were here long before your kind."

"Hmm. Why haven't I ever seen one?"

"You don't want to."

"How do you know? You can't decide that for me." Ingrid felt the pressure in her brain again, telling her to focus on her frustration and anger. *I'm so tired of being told what I can and can't do. Now my own body has turned against me.*

"You want to meet a sprite, that's your business. I'd advise against it, that's all," Plintze growled, his patience growing thin with her attitude. "I don't want to be around when you do, though, so keep moving."

"Weren't you friends with one?"

"Yes."

"What happened?"

"I'm not talking about it here. Not all of them are bad, but they are all temperamental."

Ingrid scanned the trees and undergrowth, back and forth

and above her head, paying more attention to trying to glimpse a sprite than to her feet, and she almost tripped several times.

"Watch yourself!" Plintze yelled when she tumbled forward into him, not for the first time.

"How far away are we from the village? I don't recognize this area."

"Far enough. We should make it before dark, if you don't break one of us first."

"Humph." Giggling to herself, she ignored the retorted mutterings from Plintze at her use of his favorite word.

Not long after, the forest thinned, and more light pushed aside the shadows. Plintze allowed the pace to slow a slight degree, and they walked in silence. Without stopping, they pulled dried herring from their packs, staved off their hunger, and pressed on.

Starting its descent on the western horizon, the sun fired the skies in bright oranges and yellows by the time the pair finally stood at the top of the hillside above the village.

Ingrid's heart hammered in her chest, and her middle tied up in knots. They hadn't seen any smoky tendrils in the sky that would signal the buildings having been set to the torch, but the elves would have arrived days before, so it could just be that the smoke had time to clear.

When they looked down toward the bay, she sagged in relief at the sight of the boats bobbing without concern next to the docks. All looked the same as when she'd left, except that they were empty. No one moved about; no children running around, no men hauling in fishing nets, no hammers or conversations around the well. Silence hung like low clouds.

Plintze looked around, antsy and nervous. "It looks as though everyone might have left."

"They wouldn't all leave. Where would they go? The ships are all there, even the ones that went to Jorvik." *Except Papa's.* Ingrid felt a gagging sensation in her throat as she remembered tumbling through the rushing waters of the river.

"Only one way to find out what happened." He nodded to Ingrid, and they both set off down the hillside.

As they slowly made their way between the buildings and headed toward the well, it could have been any ordinary day—if there had been people, that is. Nothing looked broken or burned, and there was no sign that any fighting had taken place. Only the creaking of the wooden boats against the wooden docks suggested there might be life somewhere.

Evening frogs croaked along the shore, and birds twittered in the skies, but there weren't any chickens, goats, dogs, or any movement on the streets. Briny smelling fishing nets sat ready for the next day, buckets sat empty next to the well, and freshly dyed linen hung on a line. It was as if one moment, all had been normal, and the next, it wasn't.

They walked up to the longhouse doors and stood in front of them, listening. A scrape of wood against the floor, and a muffled cough finally gave a sign they were not alone. Taking a deep breath, Ingrid pushed open the heavy doors and stepped inside.

The hearth fire was cold, and not a single sconce was lit. Pitch-blackness filled the large space, but the smell of furs and warm bodies floated in the air. Something else hit Ingrid's senses, too: a metallic tingle of magic.

"Well, you finally made it. Everyone has been so anxious about you," a melodic but dangerous-sounding voice spoke from the dark, as a figure moved toward her.

The hairs on Ingrid's arms stood high, rubbing against her clothes. A heartbeat later, the hearth sprang to life, and a full fire rose above the charred and cold logs, spreading light throughout the building.

Standing before her was a tall, slender male wearing brown breeches and a deep green sleeveless tunic in the softest-looking fabric Ingrid had ever seen. It shimmered lighter or darker depending on how the light hit. Long, icy blonde hair hung straight over slim but muscled arms, framing alabaster skin so perfect it practically glowed. Light blue eyes stared at her from under white eyebrows and long, curling lashes. A straight nose sat in the middle of perfectly symmetrical, chiseled cheekbones, leading down to a somewhat sharp chin—but it was the ears that made her knees weak, and caused sweat to trickle down her spine. Elongated, pointed elf ears. Not like the soft beauty of Jorg's, but sharp and pronounced.

"You should come in as well, Plintze. I know you're out there," the elf said.

Ingrid didn't turn, but heard the door open and then Plintze stepped to her side.

Thanks for letting me stand here by myself, friend.

The elf laughed, "Friend? Naive girl, he's a dwarf. He'll do whatever brings the most profit, and that is rarely friendship."

Ingrid felt the thick tar creep within her mind, and smiled. "You are one of Jarrick's messengers, I suppose?"

"I am Dúngarr. It's nice to meet you." He crossed his fist over his heart and nodded his head, but the gesture was a patronizing act of insincerity.

"I can't offer you the same sentiment—I prefer honesty. Where is everyone? What have you done with my family?"

"They are here, unharmed. We've been waiting for you. Though, I must say, we expected you sooner. Did you run into some trouble?"

Ingrid looked to the floor and clenched her teeth together. The darkness in her mind battled against her heart. Her family was here, hidden in the dark at the rear of the room, and she wanted nothing more than to run to them. But the part of her that was stained and dripping with dark magic kept her still, standing ready for whatever this elven coward sent her way.

"Nothing we couldn't handle. Right, Plintze?"

"True. Don't let this dandelion-eater bother you. He has nothing valuable to say."

Ingrid tried to keep her face neutral, but Dúngarr's flaring nostrils caused her lips to twitch as she fought a smile. "What do you want? Why are you here, menacing my people? They are nothing to you—this is between you and me."

"They mean something to you. I'm not here to play games with a child and a misshapen termite. Your presence is required at the court of His Highness, Prince Jarrick, and I am to escort you."

Ingrid slid her hand in front of Plintze, as he'd tensed and leaned forward at the insult toward him.

"I have no intention of going with you. Jarrick and I came to an understanding when we spoke earlier."

Dúngarr stared, then sauntered toward her with an elegant

ease. Ingrid fought to keep her thoughts blank. There was no way she'd let this elf know she thought him impressive.

"That's far enough." A sound of shuffling feet and mumbled words from the back of the room caught her ear. "I want to see my friends and family. I have nothing more to discuss with you until I see they are unharmed."

Dúngarr stopped and drew in a long breath, releasing it slow and steady. Narrowing his eyes at Ingrid, he tugged the corner of his mouth into a menacing grin, and snapped his fingers.

The hearth fire lifted higher, and every sconce along the walls flared to life, lighting up the space. Cramped along the back wall were Ingrid's mother, father, and brother—along with Jorg, Selby, Helka, and several others from the village— though not all. Jorg was held on either side by elves who were dressed similarly to Dúngarr and equally impressive in their beauty, and several guards kept everyone wedged against the back wall.

The pressure in Ingrid's head increased, and the faraway pounding grew louder as she locked eyes with Jorg. His lips were tight and his muscles tense as he stared back at her.

Trust me. Ingrid sent the quick message, but dared nothing else. She knew it would not be a private conversation. She saw Jorg's jaw muscles twitch, and then he nodded so slightly it was almost unnoticeable.

Dúngarr looked at Jorg and smiled—an evil, twisted smile, like the kind worn by someone who enjoyed plucking the wings off butterflies. Turning back to Ingrid, he stepped closer until she was within reach. Lifting his hand, he slid his knuckles down the side of her cheek. "I suppose you could be seen as pretty, for a human." He then turned to Jorg, and projected his voice, loud and clear. "What do you think, Halfling? Am I correct that you ignore your elven side to blend in with *humans?*"

Ingrid closed her eyes and clenched her fists. Defending herself, she'd expected, but standing up to the leader of an elven group of barbarians would take more courage. The darkness filling her thoughts might be useful after all.

"Leave him alone."

"Are you going to let a little girl fight for you, Halfling? Not very noble, I must say," Dúngarr sneered.

Jorg tensed and stepped forward, but an arm snaked out and pressed against his chest. Klaus stood by Jorg's side, his muscles tensed and his chin high, keeping his eyes on Dúngarr.

"Don't engage with him, Jorg. He's just taunting you. It's not the right time." Klaus then lowered his voice. "Patience, son."

Startled by the support, Jorg pressed into his heels and stood still. He glanced over at Klaus, who gave a slight nod, and then Jorg relaxed his shoulders, ready for whatever might happen next.

"Interesting. You know what he is, don't you? Let's see those disgraceful ears of yours. That is why you keep them hidden, isn't it?" Dúngarr continued his enjoyment of exposing Jorg.

"I'm not afraid, and I'm not hiding," Jorg shot back.

"Then pull your hair back."

Jorg's lips were stretched into a tight, white line, and he

was staring daggers, but he raised his hands and pulled loose the leather string tying the half-knot atop his head, then swept all of his hair up and secured it in back. He kept his eyes on the smirking elf in front of him the entire time, not flinching when several gasps were heard from the crowd.

Ingrid's heart squeezed tight, feeling his pain—even if he didn't show it.

With a roar, Dúngarr laughed at Jorg's expense, and his companions joined him. "You have been worried to show those? Maybe when you are full grown, they will be more impressive."

Jorg sneered and made a low noise under his breath that sounded like a growl.

"I'm tiring of this. You are nothing—not human, not elf, and not worth my time."

"I thought your business here was with me," Ingrid reminded him.

"Ingrid, you need to leave. We can handle these beasts," Klaus called to her. "Go!"

"No, Papa. I'm not going anywhere. His idle threats don't bother me. He's not in charge; he's only doing the dirty work of a thrall, sent by his master."

Dúngarr turned toward her with a scowl. "You would have done better to keep my good humor. I am to escort you to Jarrick, that's true . . . but he didn't specify in what condition you need to arrive."

Ingrid took a step forward. Plintze grunted at her side and stepped with her.

A sound from outside made her stop, and drew the elves' attention.

Suddenly, Ingrid shoved all her body weight into Plintze, causing the two of them to tumble sideways to the ground as the front doors flew open, and fur-wrapped bodies streamed through with shrieks and raised weapons. They were faces Ingrid recognized, others from the village who must have gotten away and were now back to help.

Commotion erupted throughout the house, with the captives in the back rushing forward to trap the elves between the two groups of Norse warriors. Ingrid and Plintze scrambled to their feet and joined the fray.

The elves were outnumbered, but not outmatched. They slashed with their daggers and spun staffs that had looked like ordinary walking sticks before they were twirled and twisted with speed too fast for the human eye to follow. Backing themselves toward the side wall, the ten elves kept the fighters at bay in a semicircle, picking them off one by one as they rushed forward.

Plintze was holding his ground against two elves, keeping them away from the others. His skills matched theirs in speed and cunning.

Ingrid wanted to join in the fight, but rushed from body to body instead, healing the most severe wounds of her tribesmen as quickly as she could. So far, no one had shown signs of lethal injuries; she suspected that was on purpose.

The elves were toying with them. The smiles on their faces should have betrayed that, but the fighters were too focused on their own rage to notice.

"Stop!" Ingrid cried. "This will not end well, and it is only serving their purposes." Tired of healing as many wounds as she could while more and more surfaced, she wanted an end to the madness. "Dúngarr, I'm the one you want. I surrender."

"No, Ingrid, you can't!" Jorg was standing at the front, locked in single combat with an elf, but he twisted and pushed himself free as he yelled to her.

Rushing forward, she squeezed between the large bodies until she stood in front of Dúngarr. "I will go," she told him. "But on my terms. Stop this fighting, for one."

He gave her a satisfied grin. Closing his eyes, he raised one arm and chanted something in a language Ingrid had never heard.

All at once, the human combatants froze in place.

Ingrid looked around, stunned, her eyes wide and heart-beats pounding like waves in her ears. No one moved, bound in place, only above their shoulders left free.

"What have you done?" Klaus asked Dúngarr.

"Only as your daughter has requested, put an end to your dismal display of fighting skills. It was becoming a bore, anyway." Facing Ingrid, he asked, "What terms do you offer? Make no mistake, however. I'm under no obligation to enter into negotiations with you. Still, I want to hear what power you think you hold."

Plintze, unaffected by the elven spell, moved to Ingrid's side, and sneered at Dúngarr.

A movement on Ingrid's other side caused her to turn. Moving in measured steps, and with a trickle of sweat sliding down the side of his face, Jorg was walking toward her. Soft and grateful, her eyes spoke words she couldn't say. He smiled at her, then turned to face the other elves.

"I'm not surprised to see the pile of stones make a poor choice, but you must have more elven blood than I thought, Halfling."

"Enough, Dúngarr," Ingrid turned to face him. "You will leave and never return, letting my village live in peace. I will travel to Alfheim to see Jarrick on my own, after everyone here is safe, secure, and healed of the injuries you've caused."

Gently taking hold of Ingrid's arm, Jorg turned her to face him. "Please don't do this."

"Yes, Ingrid, we will find another way," Klaus agreed, still frozen in place by invisible bonds. "Listen to Jorg, and forget this nonsense."

Ingrid looked toward the sound of his voice, and saw her mother standing near.

She smiled at Ingrid. "I'm proud of you. Your path is clear. You must take it, whether others understand or not."

"You've known all along, haven't you?" Ingrid nearly whispered.

"Yes."

"Agnethe, don't," Klaus begged.

"We can't keep it hidden from her any longer. I would think our current situation proves that," Agnethe argued.

Ingrid turned back to Jorg, who still held her arm, but his eyes were closed. "Jorg, look at me," she said softly. "I know what I'm doing. Please trust me."

Opening his eyes, he stared at her unblinking. There was a flush to his cheeks. He leaned down and put his forehead against hers.

"I love you," he whispered.

Ingrid's breath caught in her throat, and she closed her eyes to capture the tears that instantly sprang into them. Her cheeks wobbled as she smiled, and she took a long, deep inhale of the sweet grass and pine smell surrounding her.

"I love you, too." Surprised by how easy it was to say the words, but not by the feeling. The truth had been in front of her for a long time and she wasn't going to deny it any longer.

"Isn't this precious," Dúngarr interrupted. "But it's a waste of time. I do not agree to your terms. Under no circumstances will I leave here without you. Look around! No one here can enforce your wishes."

"I can," Ingrid said. "You forget, I've already spoken with Jarrick—excuse me, *Prince* Jarrick." A half-grin curled her lip when she saw the elf bristle at her sarcastic tone toward his leader's title.

"He would not have agreed to let you come to him unescorted, I'm certain of that. Do better, little witch."

Growls erupted from either side of her, and she couldn't help but snort a quick laugh. Plintze and Jorg closed in tighter to her sides. She glanced to the ground with a smile before meeting Dúngarr's eyes and stepping forward, alone.

"Careful, you don't know how right you might be about that."

A sensation was building inside of her, like her blood was about to boil, and it made her skin itch all over. Opening and closing her fingers, she felt the energy pulsing through her, and the only thing stopping her from giving in to the stirrings was her worry for everyone else in the room. Whatever was going to happen was new, and she didn't know if she'd be able to control it. The darkness oozing through her mind pushed and rolled until she realized that it seemed excited.

Shaking her head, she smiled. "Do you think Jarrick would leave it to chance? What if you'd never found me, what would have happened then? He knows exactly where I am. Before he allowed his lizard to try to kill me, he gave me a gift." She glanced back at Plintze, who was smiling at Dúngarr.

Walking forward, she stopped within arm's reach of the Elf she understood to be Dúngarr's second-in-command. Smiling at him, she reached out and touched his arm. Pressure built within her, squeezing her lungs tight and making her want to scream—but she had no air.

Then, with a sudden gust, she felt the energy release through her fingertips, and the elf collapsed to the ground. Her chest heaved, and the tang of magic coated her tongue as she stared at the fallen warrior. She slowly lifted her gaze to watch the shock and fury take over Dúngarr's features.

"I will come when I'm ready. After you release everyone, go home and wait with your prince."

"Very nice," he praised, leaning toward her. "I didn't think you had the guts. Did you think I would leave before confirming Jarrick's essence had taken hold? You have until the second full moon to arrive. I'm assuming you found the village on your travels that held no value for us? Let that be your reminder of what will happen here if you don't make it on time."

Ingrid nodded, the memory of dead bodies and burning buildings flashing behind her eyes.

On his way to the door, Dúngarr stopped and turned to Jorg. "You'll come too, I hope." Laughing at Jorg's glower, he strode through the doors. The other elves followed, and two of them bolstered the collapsed elf between them. He was groggy, but reviving.

Some of the tension eased from Ingrid's shoulders when everyone else in the room was released from their invisible restraints.

20

Klaus, Agnethe, and Selby surrounded Ingrid within seconds of their freedom. Agnethe reached out and pulled her daughter into a tight hug, letting silent tears drop into Ingrid's hair. Sagging against her mother, Ingrid allowed the warm embrace to bring her a moment's peace.

Pulling back, Agnethe brushed the side of Ingrid's face and tucked an errant strand of hair behind her ear. "You've been through so much. Selby filled us in."

"How is Hagen?" With the threat removed, she could concentrate on everyone else. She also hoped it would deflect questions about what she'd done to the elf.

She brought a shaky hand to her forehead. Clamping her mouth shut, she closed her eyes and took a deep breath while she rolled her bottom lip between her teeth. When she opened her eyes, everyone was staring at her, but no one had told her how her brother fared.

"Is he okay? Someone say something."

"He's fine, no different from when you saw him last," Selby answered. "We were just giving you a minute."

"I'm sorry." Ingrid shook her head and looked away into empty space. "Something happened that kept me from getting here to warn everyone."

"Let's go in the back room, where we can talk in private," Klaus said.

Around the room, several people stood in small groups, trying to look like they *weren't* talking about Ingrid's powers or Jorg's ears.

"I want to help the wounded first," Ingrid said.

"I've been around the room. No one is so dire they can't wait for a while," Klaus assured her, putting his arm around her shoulders and steering her out of the room.

Agnethe glared at a couple in the corner that was staring after the family as they all walked toward the back of the longhouse.

Taking a seat in her parents' room, Ingrid started to tell her story until she realized someone was missing.

"Where's Plintze? He should be in here."

Jorg stood up. "I'll go get him."

Selby took the opportunity to fill Ingrid in on the rest of her journey to the village, which was uneventful except for the constant bickering with Jorg.

"Don't tell him, but . . ." She leaned back to peek out the door. "He was pretty good company, and it was actually kind of fun."

Ingrid smiled at her friend and felt a twinge of jealousy seep into her heart that she hadn't been there.

Outside the door, they could hear a whispered argument that wasn't so whispered.

"Plintze, come in here," Ingrid called. "I want you here while I tell everyone what happened. You need to explain the parts when I wasn't conscious."

A few grumbles and mutterings later, the dwarf peeked around the corner before taking a couple steps into the room. Jorg followed closely to be sure he didn't change his mind. Ingrid noticed that he had pulled the tie out of his hair, letting it fall over his ears again before he'd returned to the room.

Plintze nodded to the others, found a seat off to the side, and plopped down, folding his arms over his chest.

"Comfortable?" Ingrid asked.

"Humph," he said, and then looked up at her, trying not to smile at her giggle.

"I had to make sure you got it out before I start," she winked at him, and he turned away in feigned annoyance. "Without Plintze's help, I would not be here. I owe him my life."

Plintze fidgeted in his seat, uncomfortable with the attention and the praise. "Get on with it. They don't want to hear about me," he said.

"I would love to know more about you. Perhaps when Ingrid is finished with her tale, you can tell us yours," Klaus said.

"Nothing to tell, just listen to hers."

"Don't worry, he grows on you," Ingrid said with a small smile.

"What happened out there? What kept you?" Jorg stood

against the wall nearest to her; lines creased his forehead as he waited to hear her story.

She sat silent for a minute, gathering her thoughts. Lavender hung in small bundles around the room, giving off a sweet scent that helped to calm her nerves while she played with her fingers, which rested in her lap.

Not looking up at anyone, she told them about the dragon she encountered before meeting Plintze, and then again when she had to fight for her life. Briefly, she tried to describe her encounter with Jarrick, and who he was, but she still struggled with it herself.

She also didn't want to go into much detail about the vile darkness battling inside her head; her mother looked pale enough, when she snuck glances in her direction.

Finished with her story, they all sat in silence for a few minutes.

"You shouldn't have been alone. I shouldn't have let you be alone," Jorg said in a quiet voice.

"We both let her go off by herself," Selby said, her eyes glistening with unshed tears.

"Neither of you could have stopped me. I needed to go. I was supposed to make it here in time to warn everyone. No one would have gotten hurt if I'd have made it in time."

"Blah, blah, blah. It's no one's fault but the evil elf who's pulling all the strings," Plintze piped up. "He's not done, either, so don't waste too much time whining. We need to be figuring out what to do next."

The others looked stunned and a little offended, but Ingrid smiled. "Thank you, Plintze, for your keen wisdom. He's right, though. We need a plan to defeat Jarrick. If he manages to break Odin and Freya's spell before I figure out how to stop him, not only are we in danger, but so is every human in Midgard."

"One thing is certain—you are not going to meet him," Jorg said.

"I am. I gave my word, and I meant it."

"Ingrid, we can't let that happen. It's too dangerous," Klaus said. "There will be no more discussion about that."

"Papa, I understand why you say that, but I'm not a little girl anymore. If I don't go, it will be too dangerous for everyone, everywhere. Jarrick is not going to stop, he thinks he's doing the right thing. He talks as though he is repairing an old mistake, like we will all appreciate what he does. I didn't want to believe that I had anything to do with all this business about the spell and the healer, but I do. I *am* the healer, Papa. This is my destiny, for some reason only the gods know."

"Not only the gods; I know why as well. I had just hoped it wasn't true," Agnethe said. "I only wanted to keep you safe."

"What do you know? Who am I?"

"For generations in my family, there has been an unbroken line of women chosen to carry on a great secret responsibility. From mother to daughter, the information has traveled without fail—until the line got to me. I was to carry on the tradition, but before I could learn how, or the extent of the duty, my mother died. My grandmother had been dead for many years and no one else knew the story.

"As time went on, I forgot all about some old tradition told to me as a child. Until you were born, and I was visited by a strange woman." Agnethe stopped and rubbed her forehead in small circles with both hands. Klaus moved to her, taking a seat at her side.

Ingrid looked out the side of her eyes toward Jorg, hoping he would sit next to her that way. Her hands were trembling, and her stomach was in knots.

Selby jumped up from her spot and landed quickly next to Ingrid. "He can sit with you later. It's my turn right now," she whispered.

As usual, Selby's whispers traveled throughout the room. Ingrid grinned at Jorg's responding snort, and even Plintze gave an amused grunt.

"Who was the woman, Mama?" Ingrid had a suspicion she'd already met her, in the woods outside of Jorvik.

"Her name is Eir. She is a goddess as well as a norn and valkyrie. It is her job to train the chosen daughter of each generation so they are prepared in case they are the destined one. You know how I have feelings about future events, sometimes?"

Ingrid nodded to her mother.

"Because of that, Eir believed that the prophesied daughter of our heritage was closer than ever to appearing. I couldn't imagine my sweet little baby carrying that big of a burden. So I forbade her to train you." Agnethe leaned closer to Klaus as pain lined her face.

"Why us? How is our family lineage connected?" Ingrid asked.

Freya has two daughters. One left Asgard, fell in love, and married a human man. She hid herself among the mortal realm, and lived a happy life as a wife and mother. Hoping to draw her back to Asgard, Freya bound the spell to her daughter's bloodline. It didn't work though because Gersemi never went back. She's lived here among the humans she loves so much, waiting for the promised descendant to be born."

"Gersemi. I thought you might say her name was Hnossa," Ingrid said. Selby squeezed her hand when she felt Ingrid's breathing quicken.

"No, but Hnossa is her sister," Agnethe said. "Why would you think that?"

"I've been to Asgard."

"You have? When?" Selby looked at her with a little flash of anger. Jorg pulled away from the wall and looked at her with the same expression.

"I felt like I was going crazy and didn't want to believe what was happening, so I didn't tell you. I was also warned not to. But remember the night that I went for a walk after Hagen got hurt, and I didn't make it back until morning?"

"How could I forget, that's when I saw the elves by myself while lover boy went to find you."

Ingrid blushed as she glanced quickly at Jorg and saw his grin at the memory. "I was pulled into Asgard through a shining doorway, and met on the other side by Hnossa. She took me to her home and explained the story of the spell, but her version was a little different. It was all so confusing. I was overwhelmed with the beauty—everything sparkled from gold and jewels and smelled like flowers and sweets. There were the most delicious treats, called cookies," Ingrid sighed. "I accepted everything she told me. She warned me not to tell anyone."

"She used a portal because she didn't want Heimdall to know," Plintze said. Ingrid saw her mother flinch at his gravelly voice, forgetting that he sat in the corner. "I'd bet every piece of dwarf gold that she is working with Jarrick."

"I think so, too. She told me that the elves needed to restore the balance of magic between Asgard and Vanaheim. That's what Jarrick is trying to do. Both of them told me they were trying to find me before anyone could taint my understanding."

"Another reason you should not go offering yourself up to the Dark Elf himself," Jorg said.

Ignoring him, Ingrid turned toward her mother. "You said you met Eir before, that she came to you when I was born."

Agnethe nodded. "As you grew, you were such a happy child, sweet and loving toward everyone. And so small and fragile. I grew to believe she was just some crazy völva who'd made a mistake." Agnethe stopped and swallowed hard; a single tear rolled down her cheek.

"Until I tried to save my sister," Ingrid whispered.

Both Klaus and Agnethe snapped their eyes toward Ingrid and stared. "I didn't think you remembered that," her father said.

"I didn't until I healed that boy on the docks before we left for Jorvik. I had a vision of her and how I didn't help her. Just like how I couldn't help Hagen."

"Her injuries were so severe, and you were only a child. The way you tried though . . . I knew that what Eir had told me was true. I convinced your father to help me keep it from you. When your sister, Merin, died, you were so distraught that you blocked the memories, and we did our best to help them stay hidden. I'm sorry, Ingrid. Maybe if we'd been honest with you, if we hadn't tried to hide who you are, you'd be more prepared for all of this now." Agnethe covered her face with both hands, tears falling freely into her lap. Klaus kneeled down and cradled his wife in his arms while Ingrid watched the anguish they shared.

They deserve to feel bad. Closing her eyes tight, she pushed against the intrusive anger. *I will not let you win, Jarrick.* Frustrated and tense, she jumped when a hand touched her shoulder.

Jorg crouched down in front of her and took her hands between his. He held her gaze. "We will fight him together."

Biting her lip, she nodded, relishing in his touch. "Will I ever be able to hear you?"

He raised his eyebrows and smiled. "I think it's better that you can't."

She shook her head and looked down at their hands. Jorg pulled one to his lips and kissed her knuckles. A throat cleared across the room, but they ignored it.

"Alright, already," Selby said, still sitting next to Ingrid.

Without looking at Selby, Jorg said, "You'll get used to it."

Selby groaned and shook her head.

"Maybe she will, but for now I'd like to deal with the issue at hand. We can talk later, Jorg," Klaus said with a raised brow, a smirk pulling at his lips. Ingrid felt a small surge of heat in her cheeks.

Jorg winked at her then stood and turned to Klaus. "I look forward to it."

Ingrid stood and walked across the room to her parents. "I don't know if I could have ever been prepared enough for all of this. I wish I'd have known, but it's okay; I know now. Let's focus on what happens next, and not worry about anything else."

Agnethe stood and pulled Ingrid close to her. "I love you."

"I love you too, Mama." Ingrid squeezed her mother and then pulled away to hug her father. "Before we do or say anything more, I'd like to see Hagen."

Ingrid followed her parents to another room, where they found Helka sitting on the edge of Hagen's bed, holding his hand and talking quietly to him. Selby hesitated at the door, but she walked in and leaned against the wall. Standing next to Helka, Ingrid watched as Hagen's chest moved up and down with slow, methodical predictability. The rest of his body lay motionless.

Anger boiled up again within Ingrid at the sight of her brother, and she did her best to force it out of her voice as she spoke. "May I stand closer, please, Helka?"

Helka moved out of her way without a word.

Aware of all the hopeful eyes staring at her, Ingrid closed her eyes and tried to settle her nerves. *I can do this.*

Opening her eyes, she saw only Hagen, letting all other sights and sounds fade away. Unwrapping the annoying linen strip from her left arm, exposing her jagged scar, then pulling the tattered gauntlet from her right, she let each slip to the floor. Slowing her breathing to match the rhythm of Hagen's, she felt a small tingle bloom in her chest. Warmth spread from her middle outward through her body, into her arms and down into her hands. Rolling her lip between her teeth, she hovered her hands over his chest, bringing them down slowly until she touched him.

Heat flowed through her arms, into her hands, and she held steady, closing her eyes to concentrate. A feeling of weightlessness came over her, and she could see a string of light flowing into Hagen's chest, seeking out his pain. Ingrid watched as it moved like hair underwater, floating along in a graceful ribbon until it reached his mind. Images flashed one after the other; some she recognized, most she didn't. Being in water, a man sitting next to a tree, walking through the moors and a flash of light. At the same time, a jolt shot through Ingrid's hands so strong she winced, but she held firm against his chest until the sensation was gone.

Opening her eyes again, she felt dizzy and a little disoriented. The room went black for a several seconds and she leaned on her brother until she revived and focused on his face.

Hagen didn't look any different.

Disappointed, confused, and frustrated, she pulled her hands off his chest, and clenched them in fists at her sides. As she was about to turn away, his fingers twitched.

Snatching his hand in hers, she held her breath. Under his eyelids, she could see his eyes moving back and forth.

"Hagen, can you hear me? Wake up now. Open your eyes," she commanded.

His throat bobbed as he swallowed, then he made a noise.

Squeezing his fingers, Ingrid leaned in and put her other hand on his forehead.

Fluttering, his eyes worked their way open, and Ingrid started to laugh and cry at the same time.

"Hi," he croaked. His voice sounded raspy from disuse but it was as music to her ears.

She leaned down and put her head on his chest, letting her tears wet his shirt. She could hear the others crying. A heavy, clumsy hand slid onto her head, and she turned her face to see Hagen trying to smile at her.

Shifting Hagen's hand to her cheek, she leaned into it and breathed in the sweet smell of dirt and sweat before placing a kiss on his palm.

"Thank you," she whispered. He smiled.

Aware of the others watching, she rose and moved out of the way. Exhaling long and slow, she turned and saw Selby wrapped in Jorg's arms. Irrational anger flooded through her, replacing all her joy in less than a heartbeat.

Jorg raised his hand in an attempt to reassure her, but she pressed her lips together and glared at him. *Stop touching her.*

Tapping Selby on the shoulder to get her attention, he moved her away from him and stepped closer to Ingrid. Ingrid, for her part, was staring at the floor, trying to steady herself; her eyes roved over the surface without seeing anything.

"Ingrid." Jorg said her name quiet and gentle while lifting her chin to look up at him. "What is it?"

Her chin wobbled against his fingers. "I get so angry so fast. I have to get him out of my head." Tears slipped through her lashes and Jorg pulled her in tight.

Slipping her arms around his waist, she held onto him as she fought to regain control of her emotions. After several minutes, neither of them had made any attempts to pull away, but she knew they should.

Without releasing her grip, she craned her neck to look up at him, smiling when he stroked her hair.

"Better?"

"Yes. I'm sorry."

"Don't be. It's not your fault—although I don't mind this part at all." His eyes traveled to her mouth and back to her eyes with a lazy grin on his face.

Smiling at him, she raised an eyebrow, daring him to finish his thought, but he looked over her head and tensed. Ingrid squished her eyes shut and lowered her face into Jorg's chest.

"I think it's a good time for us to have that talk," her father said behind her.

Unwrapping her arms from his waist and placing her hands at her sides, Jorg then moved his hands to her arms and rubbed them as he gently pushed further away from her. Following her father out of the room, he turned and smiled at her before walking through the door.

A thousand butterflies spilled out of her heart, and she covered her mouth with her fingers trying to hide the broad grin making her cheeks ache. Startled, she jumped when her mother wrapped an arm around her shoulders and kissed the top of her head.

"I'd tell you to guard your heart, but I'm too late, I see."

Ingrid could only nod.

Out of the corner of her eye, she saw Helka back at Hagen's side, while Selby stood at the foot of the bed. Stepping away from her mother, she moved next to Selby, slipping her hand into her friend's.

"How are you feeling?" she asked Hagen.

"Good," he whispered, then put a hand to his throat.

"You haven't talked in a while. It's been nice," she teased, and wiggled his foot.

Smiling, he closed his eyes and shook his head. "Just wait." He paused to catch his breath. "Tomorrow."

"Of course, I'm sure you'll have lots to say."

"Come on girls, let's give these two some time alone," Agnethe said as she turned Ingrid and Selby toward the door.

Ingrid squeezed Selby's hand as they walked out of the room.

When they entered the main room, Jorg was gripped in a handshake with Klaus, who slapped him on the shoulder before walking away. Ingrid met his smile and started to walk toward him, but noticed his mother heading in his direction, so she hung back to give them some time.

Jorg turned his attention to his mother with softness in his eyes. As her hand reached out to touch his arm, a rough voice barked her name. From across the room, Jorg's father approached the two, disgust curling his lip as he looked at his son. Ingrid ambled closer, trying to stay discreet yet feeling the need to be close for support.

"Step back, woman," Jorg's father said to his wife.

Bending her head, she stepped aside. Jorg's body stiffened, and he set his shoulders as if waiting for an attack.

"I've done the best I could for you, boy. Tried to ignore what you are and believe you could be my son. You've proven you can handle yourself as a man now, so there's nothing more you need from me. Do whatever you need to, but don't come home. We've uprooted ourselves enough for your sake." He spat the last of his hateful speech and turned to leave, nodding to his wife to follow.

"Petr, before you leave . . ." Klaus called out to him.

Ingrid turned to her father, but Jorg kept his eyes on his mother. Klaus now stood in front of Jorg's father.

"I think you should reconsider what you said."

"My family is my business, Klaus. I don't answer to you or anyone else about that."

"That's true, and I won't interfere with your family. But, the good of the village is *my* concern, and I'd like you to reconsider your opinion of your son."

"I will not. In fact, I question your ability to lead this village if you plan to allow his sort to spend time with your daughter."

Ingrid sneered at him and clenched her fists as she saw Jorg do the same.

"You question *me*? Well, let me answer that for you. We don't need your '*sort*' spreading your plague to the rest of us. Jorg has a home here—you don't. Pack your things, and be gone by morning."

"You are bringing death to everyone. I'll be glad to leave this place." Striding to the front of the hall, Petr left, motioning again for Jorg's mother to follow.

At the door, she hesitated, holding onto the frame without walking through.

Ingrid heard Jorg suck in a small breath, and she held her own as they waited, biting the inside of her lip to keep herself from shouting out.

Don't do this to him. Please turn around.

Then, the woman who had saved Jorg, loved him as her son, and protected him, slumped her shoulders and left without a glance.

Ingrid looked at Jorg, and watched his eyes grow hard and his jaw muscles pulse. Before she could go to him, though, her mother caught her hand and stopped her.

"Give him some time. Go to him later, when there are not so many eyes to watch."

"Are you saying that because you don't want me to be seen with him?" Ingrid hissed in a whisper.

"Of course not, and don't ever insult me like that again. I say it for the sake of his pride. You will make it worse for him if you go over there now."

In her head, Ingrid knew she was right, but her heart ached to take away his pain.

Selby tugged on Ingrid's sleeve. "Let's go back and check on Hagen."

"Why do you want to do that to yourself?"

"Nothing better to do." Selby grinned and looped her hand through Ingrid's arm, once again bringing lightness to a difficult situation.

"Isn't Helka still in there? Won't you feel awkward?"

"An hour hasn't gone by without her sitting by his side from the moment we dragged his heavy arse back here; might as well get used to it. Besides, he's awake now, and I want to know if he remembers anything."

"You want to know if you've been caught." Ingrid grinned and nudged against Selby.

"True. You know me too well."

As they approached Hagen's room, Selby coughed and cleared her throat while shuffling her feet extra loud.

"What?" she asked when Ingrid turned her head to stifle a giggle.

"Nothing. I don't want to walk in on anything, either. It's good to know you have limits."

Shelby shrugged and smiled as she lifted the door curtain and peeked inside. "Everyone decent in here?"

"Selby! Come in and keep out the draft." Helka acted angry, but there was a blush to her cheeks.

"How is our favorite patient?"

"Why are you worried about a draft? Is there something wrong?" Ingrid drew her eyebrows together as she hurried to the bedside. The room smelled like mint and saffron from a small bundle of purple crocus sitting in a bowl.

"I'm fine, feeling better every minute. She's being a mothering hen, that's all," Hagen answered.

"You look good. There's color in your cheeks again."

Hagen reached across his body to take Ingrid's hand, not disturbing the one entangled with Helka's.

"Thank you. Helka has been filling me in on what happened while I was knocked out. Who knew that my dancing, singing little sister held the power of life and death in her fingertips?"

It feels like forever ago that I was that girl. Ingrid gave a half-hearted smile. "Don't you forget it. You should think twice before you pick on me again." She poked his shoulder and broadened her grin.

Lifting his hand from hers, he held it in the air. "No more teasing, I wouldn't dare. Promise," he said with a smile, but his eyes were serious.

"Oh please, don't get all soft on us, we won't know it's really you," Selby snorted from the end of the bed.

Hagen looked at her for a moment before a mischievous

glint shone out of his eyes. "Thank you, Selby. I know it wasn't easy, pulling me all the way home, and having to spend all that time bickering with Jorg." He leaned forward a little and whispered, "And telling me all your secrets when he wouldn't talk to you anymore."

Every shade, from pink to bright red, crossed over Selby's cheeks as she stood motionless, gaping at Hagen.

Ingrid slapped him playfully. "You're horrible." Walking over to Selby, she took her hand. "He's teasing you."

"Am I?" He tilted his head and smirked.

"Yes," she said firmly. Then she looked back at her friend. "Ignore it, I've been on the receiving end of that look too many times. It's just not hard to imagine you talking the whole way home." Ingrid tried to stifle a giggle.

Selby huffed. "I have a lot to say, that's true."

"A lot of words flow out of your mouth; that's not the same as a lot to say," Jorg pointed out as he walked into the room. "I don't know how you put up with it," he teased Ingrid, smiling. Everyone chuckled, including Selby.

It felt good to have a moment of lightheartedness surrounded by those she loved. Ingrid closed her eyes and let it wrap around her like sunshine on a warm day.

After more banter and teasing between Jorg and Selby over who pulled Hagen the most, and who dealt with the most annoyance from the other, the room settled into a companionable silence.

Hagen interrupted it. Looking up at Helka, he asked, "Shall we tell them?"

"I've been dying to say something." A smile lit up Helka's face as she stared back at Hagen.

Ingrid moved closer to Selby, and a rock settled in her stomach. They'd both known it was coming, and she wanted to be happy for her brother, but her heart wrenched for her best friend.

Selby stood tall, her face schooled into a pleasant smile. Ingrid saw Jorg glance up at the ceiling and shift on his feet.

Helka looked over to all of them. "We are getting married in the fall," she announced.

"Congratulations," Ingrid said and hugged both of them.

Selby followed Ingrid, and held her sister tight. Jorg leaned over and clasped Hagen's hand, and Ingrid saw her brother flash his eyes toward her as he stared at Jorg.

Turning away quickly, her knees wobbled, and she wanted to run from the room.

Thankfully, she heard Jorg whisper, "One thing at a time."

Focusing her attention on Selby and ignoring the tremble in her hands, she was grateful that Jorg avoided looking in her direction.

Minutes later, while Helka was excitedly talking about her plans for the wedding, blissfully unaware of her sister's discomfort, all of their parents walked into the room.

"There's quite a party in here," Klaus said, slapping the back of Selby's dad's shoulder and shaking his hand.

The two moms hugged, and joined Helka to chatter over the happy news. Selby shifted toward the far wall, using the crowded room as an excuse to distance herself.

Ingrid followed and pulled her into a hug. "You should come with me," she whispered into Selby's ear.

"Where?" she asked, but she looked like she'd go anywhere as long as it was out of that room.

Glancing over her shoulder to make sure everyone was still preoccupied, she kept her voice low. "I have to find Eir. I need her to train me so I can get this intruder out of my head." She stiffened as she felt hands on her shoulders.

"Are you ever going to listen to reason and stay put?" Jorg had leaned down to speak low next to her ear.

Ingrid shuddered as his breath tickled her cheek, and she shook her head.

Selby tried to keep from smiling, but she didn't succeed. "You knew she wouldn't. I guess we'll all have to go."

"Go where?" Agnethe asked from across the room.

Ingrid rolled her eyes at Selby. "You really need to work on your quiet voice."

Stepping around Jorg, she faced her parents in the suddenly quiet room. "I need to find Eir, Mama," she said walking toward Agnethe.

"I know you do, and you should. Even though I will worry every second you are gone." Placing her hand on the side of Ingrid's cheek, she let her eyes rove over every part of Ingrid's face. "Although, you can change your mind . . . stay and train as a shieldmaiden."

Ingrid met her smile with a chuckle of her own.

Several days later, life was returning to normal.

After the morning meal had been cleared, Ingrid found Plintze sitting in her favorite corner, sipping a cup of tea.

"I'm glad you stayed. I was worried you would head back

home once everything settled down," she admitted, plopping down next to him.

"Thought about it, but didn't think it would hurt anything to stick around for a few days."

Ingrid smiled while she rubbed her hand over the fur they sat on. "I need to leave. I would like it if you came with me."

"Humph."

"See, how could I go anywhere without such great advice and conversation?" After a moment's hesitation, she asked again. "Will you come with me? I need you."

"You really think I've stayed here for the noise and smells? When do we leave?"

She broke into a grin. "Today. I can't take any more sitting around, and I can't risk Dúngarr coming back for me."

"Good, it's about time."

"Then I'll go tell the others, and we'll get ready."

"What others? Well, that half-Elf, I suppose, but who else?"

Ingrid saw the way he narrowed his eyes, and suspected that he was already preparing himself for the answer. "You will learn to love Selby. She's like you—grows on you like a fungus." Patting his arm, she hurried away before he could say anything else.

Jorg was standing near the center of the room, talking with Klaus and Hagen, who was up and walking around like nothing had ever happened.

"I'm going to find Selby, and then we're getting ready to leave," Ingrid told Jorg. "I can't wait any longer." All three men stared at her without saying a word. "Okay, then. I'll meet you back here within the hour."

As she walked off, she heard her father say something about being unsure who to worry for, and she smiled to herself as she headed toward the back wall where Selby stood near their mothers.

"Mama, I'm leaving today. It's time." Ingrid's words were strong, but lines creased her forehead as she waited for her mother's response.

"I know it is. I've been thankful for the last few days, but I understand."

Turning to face Selby's mother, she said, "I know there's a lot to do for Helka's wedding—"

"Stop there," Selby's mother interrupted. "I wouldn't dare keep Selby from going with you. Just try to keep each other safe as much as possible."

Throwing her arms around her mother, Selby hugged her tight. "Thanks, Mother."

"Both of you follow me. I have something for you," Agnethe said as she walked in the direction of the bedrooms.

Selby let go of her mother and kissed her cheek, then rushed off with Ingrid.

A short while later, Ingrid stood with her mother's hands on her shoulders, being held at arm's length and appraised from head to toe.

"Now you look ready to leave," her mother declared as she pulled her in for one last tight hug.

Ingrid inhaled the scent of wildflowers and linen while she held onto her mother. This was the woman she'd always thought of as soft and over-cautious, who protected her too much, held her back, and loved her more than she ever knew. Her heart strained at its edges as she realized how fierce and brave her mother truly was. It was a feeling she'd need to remember as strongly as the embrace that held her.

The two girls emerged from the back room to find Jorg and Plintze ready to go, and talking with Klaus, Hagen, and several others while they waited.

Jorg noticed Ingrid, and stopped talking to stare at her.

No longer wearing their maiden dresses, the girls were prepared for anything they might face. Kohl surrounded each girl's eyes, and braids pulled their hair back from their faces into a ponytail. They were both dressed in black linen trousers, with tunics belted at the waist. Selby wore a deep blue, while Ingrid wore burgundy. Dark leather gauntlets covered her hands and forearms.

Though she didn't wear her hangerok apron anymore, Ingrid still secured her beads to her tunic, hoping that the amber one would help lead them to Eir.

"I hope that's the reaction you wanted, because I don't think he's breathing," Selby whispered to Ingrid in her discreet way, which made everyone around them snicker.

Ingrid smiled and walked straight to Jorg, saying nothing.

"That's a new look," he said.

"Mmhmm."

"It suits you." He smiled despite trying to act casual.

"Meyla, you look like your mother," Klaus said pushing Jorg aside to give his daughter a hug.

"She said this would help us move easier, wherever we needed to go."

"I have something else you'll need," Klaus said, and pulled Ingrid's shield out from behind a barrel. Handing it to her, he pointed to the new paint it displayed. "I had Einar add runes for you: some for healing, some for success, and some for persistence."

"How is this possible? I thought it was lost with the boat." Ingrid held the shield in front of her as she scanned the runes and smiled.

"We found it." Klaus hesitated and cleared his throat, "When we were searching for you."

Ingrid looked up at her father, her eyes beaming with love and a hint of pain for how he must have felt. "Thank you," she said, and wrapped her free arm tight around his waist.

Hagen shook hands with Jorg. "Good luck," he said, nodding toward the girls and laughing.

As they made their way around the room, saying goodbye to everyone, Plintze grew more and more agitated. He was pacing near the doors, groaning and muttering to himself.

Finally, Selby spoke up. "Okay, enough admiring how great we look, let's get going. That dwarf is making himself crazy, and we have a norn to find."

"Humph," Plintze muttered and pushed through the doors.

Ingrid laced her fingers through Jorg's and they followed Selby outside.

Undercutting Ingrid's happiness, the sticky mental intruder pressed against the inside of her temples.

Don't worry Jarrick. I'll find you, too.

GLOSSARY OF TERMS

Asgard — *(ahs-gahrd) Realm of the ruling gods of Norse Mythology*

Midgard — *(mid-gahrd) Realm of humans*

Alfheim — *(alv-heym) Realm of the elves and where many vanir resettled*

Vanaheim — *(vah-n-a-heym) Realm of the original gods who lost a war with Asgard*

Svartalfheim — *(sv-aht-alv-heym) Realm of the dwarves*

Jotunheim — *(yoo-too-n-heym) Realm of the giants*

Muspelheim — *(moo-spel-heym) Realm of fire*

Niflheim — *(nee-th-la-heym) Realm of ice and mist*

Helheim — *(hel-heym) Realm of the dead that die of outside of battle*

Æsir — *(ey-seer) The gods of Asgard*

Dúngarr — *(Doo-n-garr) Royal palace guard member and enforcer for Jarrick*

Eir - *(Ay-eer) Goddess of Asgard, handmaiden of Odin's wife Frigg, a lesser norn and a valkyrie*

Hnossa — *(Nah-sah) Freya's youngest daughter*

Jarrick — *(Jair-ik) Prince of Alfheim proficient in the dark arts*

Jorg — *(Yor-g) Half elf/half human love interest of Ingrid*

Jorvik — *(yor-vik) The capital of the Danelaw (known as York, England today)*

Norn — *(nor-n) Three women of fate who live at the base of the Yggdrasil tree*

norn — *(nor-n) Many women who helped the Norns throughout the realms*

Seidr — *(say-thr) Norse magic concerned with
discerning the course of fate*

Skause — *(scow-ss) Stew*

Valkyrie — *(Val-keer-ah) Maidens who collect the
heroic dead for Valhalla and Odin*

Vanir — *(vah-neer) The gods of Vanaheim*

Völva — *(vol-vuh) woman who uses seidr*

Yggdrasil — *(ig-drah-seal) The tree of life that
connects all the realms*

ACKNOWLEDGMENTS

This book would not have come together without the help of so many others. I am eternally grateful for the opportunity and privilege it has been to have the freedom to find within myself the strength to put my heart on a page.

First, I'd like to thank my Grandma. I believe it is her creativity that has been passed down to me. Every birthday, Christmas, Easter, or random Tuesday, she had a poem for everyone. An entire notebook exists of the music and lyrics she wrote. Not until late in her life was she able to perform and enjoy the love she had for song. I hope that she enjoys this journey with me as she watches from Heaven.

Craig, I could not have done any of this without you. I threw you a curve ball early in our lives together and you accepted who I've needed to be every day since. You have given me the time and space to not only find my passions, but to pursue them. I love you more and more every day. Sydney and Audrey, you are my heart, my biggest accomplishments.

I'm so proud of you both and the dreams you have followed. You are the inspiration that spurs me forward every day. To my other two love-bugs, Libby and Bear, I also believe you give me the strength to get up every day and put another foot forward. I will tell your story one day, Bear, after all yours is the one that started all of this! To all of my family and friends, I appreciate your love and support more than you know. I am blessed to know that I can count on you to encourage me and believe in me; it means the world.

To my editor Jen—Thank you! You swept away all the dirt and helped me create a final professional product. You helped bring my work to a whole new level and I am forever grateful!

Finding my Indie Author Mastermind group has been a lifeline. You were the push I needed to cross the finish line and make sure my business would succeed. Our coffee shop meetings are invaluable and I'm so grateful to each and every one of you.

My book would not have come together without the tremendous help from my critique partners and beta readers. I have the best out there, and I mean that! Your input challenged me to bring out the best in my book and myself. Ashley, especially, thank you for your advice, putting up with all of my questions and my technology-challenged breakdowns!

Alfred Obare, I cannot express my thanks enough for your talent and the beautiful cover art you created for me. I can't wait to work together again many more times.

I don't know if I can express in words how grateful I am to you, my readers, for taking a chance on a new author and reading my story. My heart physically squeezes inside my chest when I think of you and what you mean to me. I look forward to building a long, lasting future together.

Finally to my Lord, without whom I have nothing, but with You I have everything!

ALSO BY KELLY N JANE

The Viking Maiden Series

Ingrid, The Viking Maiden - Book 1

Amber Magic - Book 2 (Sept. 2018)

Realm of Destiny - Book 3 (2019)

Reviews are the lifeblood of an indie author and essential in the ocean of books on the market today. I would be beyond thankful if you could take a moment and leave a review on Amazon or Goodreads

Let's stay in touch!

www.kellynjane.com

@kellynjanebooks on Instagram, Twitter and Facebook

Made in the USA
Monee, IL
10 September 2022

13730433R10184